KILL LIST

A NICK LAWRENCE NOVEL

BRIAN SHEA

SEVERN RIVER PUBLISHING

Severn River Publishing
www.SevernRiverBooks.com

ISBN: 978-1-64875-373-2 (Paperback)

ALSO BY BRIAN SHEA

To find out more, visit

severnriverbooks.com/authors/brian-shea

This book is dedicated to my father. I'm sorry that I didn't complete this while you were around to enjoy it. I have envisioned you reading this, feet up in your favorite recliner numerous times during this writing process. Thank you for believing in me.

PROLOGUE

The smell of stale cigarettes and body odor permeated the car. A dank reminder of the sea of informants who had graced the worn leather interior since the department began using the seized Acura as a soft car. The city was a different beast at night. Inhabited by a special breed that occupied the investigative efforts of Declan and his narcotics unit.

Surveillance was a big part of Declan's current assignment. He'd acquired the requisite skills to do it better than most. People rarely recognized him as a police officer. His long unkempt hair, matted beard, and tattered clothes added to his urban camouflage. A cigarette hung precariously from his lips. The embers cast an eerie glow across his rugged face.

This evening's target was a low-level heroin dealer. Most citizens saw the war on drugs as a large-scale battle that could never be won. But Declan saw its impact at the local level. The heroin epidemic had taken the northeastern United States by storm. Its effect was catastrophic. Not only were the numbers of overdose deaths out of control but so was the accompanying criminal activity. Most burglaries and larcenies were deeply rooted in the drug trade. Junkies desperate to support their habit often sought quick money. Anything to stave off the sickness, ever-present in their system.

The unit shifted its approach toward drug investigations. They now targeted the dealers responsible for, or linked to, any overdose-related deaths. Declan's assignment tonight was in response to a recent fatal OD. Marisol Torres, mother of three.

He sat in the faded gray Acura at the corner of Silver Street and Broad. Waiting. Several hours had passed since Declan backed into the long, cracked driveway of a neighboring multi-family house. His bladder was relentlessly pleading for relief. Slumped in the driver's seat, he waited with his Nikon. A telephoto lens attached gave him an increased range. Declan waited patiently. The last three hours ticked slowly by. *All this effort for a photograph of a dealer.* All he had was a street name. Lemon.

Declan's informant was reliable. As snitches go. Lemon was an unknown. *Maybe he was new to the area. An up-and-comer. Or more likely his informant was protecting him.* Declan only had a limited description. Skinny with yellow hair. Thus, the nickname. So far, none of the foot traffic in front of the target address matched. Declan was on drug-dealer time. No schedule to account for. Patience was integral. But tonight, it seemed his bladder would not cooperate. He eyed the empty Gatorade bottle longingly. It lay an arms reach away on the passenger side floorboard. Declan seriously debated turning it into a makeshift urinal.

The radio tucked under his seat crackled to life, "Unit 37, Unit 34, and Unit 30." The dispatcher paused, allowing for the named units to respond. Never a good sign when more than two units were called. Declan perked up. The units acknowledged receipt. The dispatcher's burst of information followed, "Start heading to the intersection of Broad Street and Grove on a male with a gun." A hint of anxiety evident in the dispatcher's transmission.

Gun calls trumped drug investigations. Declan threw his car into drive. Only two blocks away. He made fast work of the short distance.

Dispatch gave the gunman's description. "Black male red hooded sweatshirt and jeans. He's standing at the corner waving a gun." Declan accelerated, pushing the Acura's limits. He swerved onto Broad Street. Officers chimed in, updating their location. A useless waste of valuable radio time. *Get there quickly and assess the situation.* The others were a distance out. He'd be the first on scene. Declan was used to that. He was a shit magnet, often finding himself at the epicenter of disaster.

One block away. The male stood at the corner frantically pacing. Declan gave a quick radio transmission, "Enright on scene." Declan announced his arrival. He didn't want to catch a round from a pumped-up rookie. Under duress, responding units may not immediately recognize him as a cop.

Declan slammed to a stop. He exited the Acura twenty-five feet from the deranged man. Screams filled the air as his door opened. Declan made a quick, low-profile approach. He used parked cars for cover. His badge swung freely from the chain around his neck. Better visibility at center mass. Critical in high-stress situations.

The distance closed. Declan assessed the threat. The screaming man didn't notice his arrival. The guy looked stoned out of his mind. His eyes jerked like wipers on a dry windshield. Cottonmouth crusted lips. Rabid. Sweat drained from his pores. *God, how many times have I been in this position? Too many to count.* The squared muzzle of a handgun pressed hard against his temple. All bad signs.

Declan had no vest. A misstep tonight. A parked car his only semblance of protection. He rose slowly. The movement undetected. His department-issued Glock 22 pressed outward. His body squared to the target. "Police! Drop the gun!" Declan boomed, going into autopilot. Experience his guide.

"Kill me! You have to! Only way out! Do it! Do it now!" Visceral anguish in the pleas. Frothy spit flew from his mouth. He was a cornered dog. Frightened and desperate.

"What's your name, bro? I'm Declan." Trying to humanize himself. Harder to kill someone when you know their name. Not impossible. Just harder.

"Jamal. My name's Jamal." His bloodshot eyes widened. His pupils a metronome. Panic saturated his voice.

"Jamal, let me help. I don't want to hurt you. And I don't want you to hurt yourself either, bro." Declan yelled. He needed to be heard. His voice was steady. Jamal's erratic movements slowed. His attention shifted to Declan.

"I don't give a fuck about you! Or what you want! I need to die. Just kill me! Please shoot me!" *Suicide by cop. It's a worst-case scenario. Too scared to do it himself. He wants me to finish it for him. A shitty position to put me in.*

Jamal began screaming unintelligibly. The rantings of a madman. Tough to negotiate with insanity. Declan's pulse quickened.

Sirens in the distance. The sound announced the imminent arrival of other officers. The surrounding buildings echoed their call. The noise and additional units could rapidly escalate things. Declan bore the weight of this increased stress. His face stoic. The epitome of calm.

A surge of urgency filled Declan. Jamal's head on a swivel. Desperate. Declan tried to keep Jamal's focus on him.

"Stay with me man. No one wants to hurt you. Put the gun down so we can figure this out." Declan projected. His voice washed out. The background noise amplified. Exacerbated further by the incoherent rantings of Jamal.

"Jamal, drop the gun!" Declan commanded. Nothing. Jamal gave no indication of dropping it. Declan took the slack out of his Glock. He held fast at the break point.

"Take your finger off the trigger!" Declan shouted over his new acquaintance's repetitive death wish. Jamal's right index finger slid off and came to rest on the rectangular frame of the semi-automatic pistol.

A small gesture. But it demonstrated a level of compliance. A willingness to listen. The first sign of a potential resolution. Without violence. It also gave Declan the advantage. Action versus reaction. Jamal couldn't win the draw now. Declan made a mental checklist. He established the point of no return. If Jamal put his finger back on the trigger, moved the gun from his head or advanced on any of the responding officers or civilians, then Declan would take the shot. He hoped it wouldn't come to that. Anticipate the worst and hope for the best. The fast-paced negotiation continued. Life hung in the balance. *Please don't force my hand.*

"Jamal, tell me what's eating at you? I'm no shrink, but I'll listen." Declan did his best to convey compassion.

"My baby! He's going to kill him! I've got to. Just kill me! Do it! My baby! If you don't..." Jamal screamed. His breathing ragged. He babbled incoherently. More to himself now. It sounded like he was saying "Me or him." But impossible to be sure. The whisper a sharp contrast. Then Jamal went silent. Silence is bad. Lost to himself. No longer focused on Declan.

Jamal's sudden despondency a concern. Declan continued to try to reach him. To bring him back. "Your baby? What are you talking about? Is there something wrong with your child? How can I help you if you won't talk to me?" He hoped to stall. Slow things down. "Help me understand."

Three officers arrived on scene. Positioned at various angles to the unhinged gunman. A rookie, Adams, stopped his cruiser behind Jamal. Declan made a subtle adjustment. He needed a clear backdrop if this broke bad. The move exposed Declan. The parked car no longer provided cover.

The backup officers added to the pandemonium. The patrolmen began yelling at Jamal. Each command different. Drop the gun! Get on the ground! Don't move! A barrage of inconsistency. Jamal was overwhelmed. The pendulum of control swung away from Declan. A recipe for disaster. Any early gains made by Declan's initial negotiation were quickly dissipating.

Jamal turned his gaze on Adams. An animalistic scream erupted from him. His eyes shifting their focus. *Shit. Adam's has a taser out. Rookie mistake. Jamal's got the drop on him.* The gun no longer pressed against his temple. It was now sweeping outward. In the direction of Adams.

Jamal's finger back on the trigger. Conviction in his eyes. The point of no return reached. The unnatural human dilemma. Take a life to save a life. A zero-win scenario.

"Jamal don't!" A last-ditch verbal command. The words not received. Jamal was committed.

Declan's Glock kicked rhythmically. The tang slapped against his firm grip. The sound muted by focus. Tunnel vision created this auditory exclusion. Three controlled rounds left the Glock. Jamal crumpled to the ground. Declan exhaled. He surveyed the deadly result. Jamal down. Not moving. The blood quickly darkening the sidewalk. A testament to Declan's split-second decision. He knew that Jamal was dead before he hit the ground.

The patrolmen were momentarily frozen. Their brains played mental catch-up. Cautiously they approached Jamal. Guns at the ready. The unresponsive Jamal was handcuffed. Lifesaving efforts were made. Pressure to the wounds. CPR considered, but the hole in Jamal's forehead and two in the chest told the tale.

He left me no choice. It was him or Adams. Bile in his throat. The byproduct of his body's confliction.

Declan kept his distance as the other officers evaluated the scene. The whispered conversations and quick glances in his direction. He saw it on their faces. The transparency of their judgment. *They didn't shoot. So why did I? Didn't they see the threat? I saved Adams for god's sake.* A flash of anger quickly gave way to fear. *Was I justified? Righteous?*

Declan saw the on-scene supervisor, Sergeant Glenn Macalister, approach. He placed his hand on Declan's shoulder. He quietly asked, "Are you okay?" Not leaving room for comment he continued, "Good job. You did the right thing. The guy forced your hand." Pausing momentarily to take stock of Declan. "I'm not going to talk about the details. And I don't want you to talk to anyone else until the union rep arrives." Macalister, a lean man in his late fifties, had garnered a reputation for being fair and firm, looked around awkwardly and then leaned in, "I need to take your weapon. You know the drill."

Declan handed over his service pistol. Macalister then did something unexpected. He filled the void in Declan's empty holster with his own duty weapon. "No cop should be without. Especially after what you just went through." Declan, shocked by the gesture, only managed a nod of appreciation.

"I'll get that back from you later." He watched as Macalister secured Declan's pistol, minus three rounds, in the trunk of his supervisor SUV.

Emptiness filled him. An uneasy wariness washed over him. *There's always a choice. Did I make the right one?*

Declan stood twenty-five feet from Jamal's dead body. Amid all the commotion of officers and medical personnel, he had never felt more alone.

1

ONE YEAR LATER

He was submerged again. Trapped. The dark water relentless. Its tight grip unbreakable. Each wave pounded him deeper. His body twisted. Disoriented from the churn, he no longer knew which way was up. Vertigo had set in. He fought for air. The blood, no longer oxygenated, burned inside his muscles. His body would not cooperate. It resisted his will. Overwhelmed, he gave way to the ocean's pull. The end near. Blackness crept in as his lungs filled.

Declan roared. His body launched upright. He tore off the sheets of his bed and allowed a moment for his eyes to adjust as daylight penetrated the blinds. Sweat soaked and disoriented, he took in his surroundings. It had been years since he had that nightmare, but he understood its return. He was drowning again. This time, out of water. But drowning none the less.

Nothing like waking up exhausted. Declan shook off the feeling and got up. He walked to the only bathroom in their small house and guzzled a cup full of lukewarm tap water. He heard the commotion in the kitchen below and looked at his watch. It was already eight-thirty. He hadn't slept past six in a long time. Stress had messed with his system.

Declan kept secrets, a hallmark of his past. Big ones. Little ones. But never from Val. Until now. He'd held back to protect her. To ease her mind. She knew it was bad but didn't comprehend its gravity. He shouldered its unbearable weight, telling himself that it would all work out. He knew better. Money had been tight before. This was different. A game changer. He needed time to find a way out of this mess. The hourglass almost empty.

He'd always been the cornerstone of his family's security. The provider. A perpetual optimist. As of late, that was not the case. He was depleted. Most days he could barely muster the energy to fake a smile. His girls saw through his façade, but they tried not to let it show. That hurt him most. His burden displaced on those tiny shoulders.

There had been easier times. Contented and carefree. Those memories satiated and balanced him, propelling him forward.

Today was his last chance. It all hinged on the meeting with the bank.

Declan entered the kitchen. The whirl of movement was a stark contrast to his slow gait. His girls readied for school. Val in full speed. She looked up for a moment and eyed his ragged appearance, "Wow, you look like a rock star this morning." A wink of mock approval followed.

"Thanks babe. I love you too." Declan smiled.

Lunch boxes stuffed into backpacks and shoes on, the girls shot by their dad in a blur as they raced to the door. Each gave a hug and poorly aimed kiss. All but Laney. The door opened, and the train of bobble-headed chaos marched out to the minivan. Val shook her head in mock defeat as she hurried after them. Those last few minutes before school was madness personified.

Silence filled the room in their absence. Declan poured a cup of coffee and embraced the calm. He'd learned to appreciate these small moments. A rare commodity when raising three strong-willed little girls.

He grabbed the rubber mat from the corner and unrolled it on top of the ornate Turkish rug that covered the hardwood floor of the living room. The rug, acquired on one of his many deployments, was something Declan treasured. A piece of his past. Over the years his girls had contributed greatly to its current condition. They had added their personal stamp in the form of spilled juice and the like.

Declan's toes gripped at the soft neoprene surface. He took three long, controlled breaths and hit play on his iPod. The rhythmic sound of Enya filled his ears. His feet pressed down and connected to the ground. Rooted in Mountain Pose. Breathing controlled. He stepped back with his right foot. His stance solid and his back gently arched as he stabilized into Warrior One. He held the position until the muscle fibers in his quadriceps pulsed in defiance.

Declan transitioned seamlessly through the routine. Val exposed him to yoga at his low point. He'd resisted at first. A total departure from the physicality of his previous fitness programs. She told him that he needed it. A way to reset after his termination. Val turned him into a believer. *If his buddies saw him now.* He never missed a day, even though he still feigned resistance to his wife. The routines centered him. Physically and mentally. He would need that today.

It wasn't long before sweat emptied from his pores. His body quaked from the exertion. Invigorated. He'd heard Val return with Laney midway through, but she hadn't disturbed him. She allowed him time to complete his sequence. Finished, he called out, "Hey babe, I'm going to rinse off."

"Good idea. You don't want to smell like an old gym sock during the meeting this afternoon."

Declan had time. His meeting wasn't until late afternoon. The shower revitalized him. He got dressed and went downstairs to find Laney. She had therapy after lunch. That left him a couple hours with his daughter.

"Hi my love."

Nothing. She sat with a Where's Waldo book. Her eyes flickered across the page. Her finger drifted along in a steady pattern that shifted from side to side and dropped marginally lower with each pass. Then her finger stopped. Her eyes shot back to the image of the Waldo she was tasked to find. She held steady on one of the characters in the sea of red and white distraction. Declan peered over her shoulder. She isolated Waldo from the crowd. The page turned. She began the same search pattern. Never deviating.

"You're so good at this. I'm proud of you."

Nothing. The only sound was that of her finger as it moved across the oversized glossy page.

Declan was used to this treatment. Not offended by her silence. He held out hope that his presence was perceived by Laney. That she embraced his words, even though she had never spoken her own. Hours were spent by her side each day. He wondered if he reached her. The doctors and therapists said that her speech would most likely be delayed. They warned that it may never fully develop if at all. A hard thing for any parent to hear. The only form of verbal output that Laney had provided in her three years of life came in the form of tormented screams. Those times challenged the mental reserve of both Declan and his wife.

Declan sat close to his daughter. He avoided contact. She did not respond well to physical touch. It was difficult to love someone so much, but never be able to hold them. Laney reacted to a hug like someone touching a hot stove. Occasionally he would be lucky enough to lay a kiss upon her head. He wanted her to know how much he loved her. Declan told her at every opportunity but feared that the words never reached her.

He watched his littlest child. Lost in a world of Waldo impostors. He couldn't imagine the impact on his family if today's meeting didn't go in his favor. The impact on Laney. Her routine was so regimented. And was so by design. It comforted his little one. She did not do well in new surroundings. She needed this house. She would be as lost as Waldo without it.

Declan sat in the waiting area of his local bank, the Clover Leaf Bank. His muscles still quivered from the hour of mat time. A subtle reminder.

But nothing quelled his nerves. Declan caught himself holding his breath. The involuntary action of desperate people. He prided himself on control, angry at his lack of it now. He'd experienced things that shook the toughest of soldiers and had walked away unscathed. His mind Teflon. Yet, here he was. In the bank's climate-controlled environment. Terrified. He saw his reflection in the glass partition that separated the lobby from the bank's management division. He looked weak. A shadow of himself. How far he'd fallen.

Anticipation was worse than death. Declan knew this was his last chance to salvage their financial downturn. He dreaded the potential outcome.

Months passed without a paycheck. Their bank account, already tight, was nearly empty. He'd always landed on his feet in the past and told himself that this would be no different. A lie. *Everything happens for a reason.* Val's mantra. She used it on the good days, the bad days, and pretty much everything in between. Declan disagreed with the logic. He made his own luck. He cut through adversity, though this time he'd come up short.

Their mortgage had been refinanced a year ago while he was still employed. Still a cop. Even then the financial squeeze of Connecticut gripped them tightly. The refinance saved a couple hundred a month but extended the years owed on the house. A short-term trade-off to alleviate the monthly burden. Even with all the cutbacks and budgeting, the bills continued to stack up.

Val had been prepared to return to work as a school psychologist. But then Laney was diagnosed with Autism. It rocked their world. A dynamic change of plans. They held a family meeting and decided that Val would not return to work. A tough choice. Their girls, Abigail and Ripley, had reached school age. They needed the second income, but Laney required so much attention. Val's expertise would be more beneficial at home.

Declan never took Val for granted. He was lucky to have found her when he did. He was adrift. The Navy's inconsistent moves and assignments his only constant. The teammates he served with were his family. Then he met her and it all changed. At the time, she was completing her master's degree in psychology at Old Dominion University. She'd received approval from the Navy to study the effects of long-term exposure to combat stress on elite soldiers. Declan had been selected by his commander to participate. Against his wishes, he agreed. It turned out to be the best order he'd ever received.

Val challenged him during their sessions. He liked that. Most women fell head over heels for Declan. Yet, his charm and mystique had no effect on her. She made him work for her attention. The more he worked, the more he fell in love. Once that happened, he was done for. *To hell and back for her.*

He realized that there was no way the relationship would survive the strain of his training workups and deployment rotations. He'd seen too many fail. Good marriages shredded by the grind. So, he made the choice to walk away. Thirteen years of service and he called it quits. His commanding officer tried to convince him otherwise. Declan was not a man that could be influenced easily. He separated from the Navy and never looked back.

Val completed her master's degree and planned to return to her home state of Connecticut. Closer to family. Something Declan was unaccustomed to. A welcomed change. Over time the decision to leave the service and follow Val was reaffirmed with the birth of each of his three girls.

He'd never given much thought to civilian life. But law enforcement seemed a good fit. From one uniform to another. The rules of engagement different. But Declan adjusted. The children followed shortly after. Val stayed home. It was important to her and to Declan. Things had been tight on one income. Declan picked up extra shifts when possible. A constant juggling act between work and family. Many couldn't find that balance. He had managed to.

And then it all fell apart. Betrayed. Left to hang. He'd been placed on administrative leave after the Jamal Anderson shooting. A normal procedure. In the interim months, Declan had battled the demons of that night. He replayed those final seconds. Scrutinized every aspect of his decision. The outcome undesirable. But justified. A righteous shooting by his account. His actions saved the life of a fellow cop.

The department initially showed support. The administrative leave only a formality. Time passed. Rumors flew. The investigation shifted course. The decision, termination. He had been blindsided by the outcome. No criminal charges were filed against him. A violation of policy at the root. The union said that they would fight the verdict. He was told not to worry. They'd get his job back. But then union leadership changed hands during his appeal process and with it, so did their support. Without the union's backing, Declan was forced to hire an outside attorney, on his own dime, to help get his job back. It didn't work. The lawyer was only able to reach an agreement that prevented decertification. That meant he could be a cop somewhere else if any agency would be willing to hire him.

Declan applied to numerous local departments in the wake of his dismissal. He was told his recent termination would have no bearing on the process. Rejected at every turn, Declan read the writing on the wall. Blacklisted. His police career tanked. After that nobody would hire him. He'd even been turned down by several local construction companies. He'd seen ex-cons get a better shake. He went from the military's elite to a decorated police officer to unemployed. A hard pill to swallow.

Laney's medical costs were stifling. Therapy sessions were initially covered by the city's insurance. One of the fallouts of his unemployment was that the deductible cost them thousands in out-of-pocket expenses. Money they didn't have. Declan applied for state aid. He was wait-listed, told that the process could take several weeks. That was three months ago. Delinquency notices stacked up.

Declan tried to stay afloat. The bills had mounted, and the credit cards had found their limits. Everything they'd built together was falling apart like an asteroid fragmenting upon entering Earth's atmosphere.

Val looked at job opportunities, but she was such an integral part of Laney's routine. The change would be devastating.

Friends and family passed the hat. His pride shattered. They'd become a charity case. Declan had forgone his mortgage payments for a few months in the hopes that limiting his output would enable him to cover other bills. Keep the basics at status quo. Food on the table. Temporary amnesty from shutoff and collection notifications. The mortgage company began foreclosure on the house. Pressure mounted. Declan needed to secure a loan to cover the spread. Buy a little time. Stall until something broke in their favor.

That desperation brought him to the red faux-leather seats of the Clover Leaf Bank's waiting area. Other people went about their business. They took no notice of him. Normally he welcomed anonymity. Today it left him feeling odd. Declan sat at his breaking point. An all-time low. The patrons around him laughed and carried on. A steep contrast to his fog. He didn't fault them. Jealous he'd guessed. An emotion he wasn't familiar with.

His patience waned. He'd been waiting for nearly forty minutes beyond the scheduled meeting time. He'd always lived by the saying *early was on time and on time was late*. The manager must not have learned that lesson.

A thin Hispanic man with a dark button-up shirt and white fedora sat down across from him. Although well-dressed, Declan observed the calloused hands of a worker. Eager. Fidgety. He looked at Declan and nodded. "Been waiting long?"

"Too long." Declan not feeling the small talk.

"This is a big day for me. I'm here to see if I qualify for my first house. You?"

"I'm here trying to save the house I have."

The quick, jaded response shut the man down. Not much to say after that. The man broke eye contact and Declan returned to his thoughts. Normally he would have enjoyed this conversation. Declan enjoyed drawing out information from strangers. But today he had no energy for such games.

A heavyset woman approached. Her body tested the limits of the blue pantsuit. A gaudy floral brooch accented the ensemble.

"Mr. Enright?"

He nodded.

"Good afternoon. Please follow me back to my desk so we can discuss how I can help you today."

She led him to a cubicle containing a desk and a couple cheaply made chairs.

"I'm Janet Morgan, the Assistant Account Manager for the bank. Hopefully, I will be able to help you with your banking needs," She said warmly.

Declan nodded again.

"I hope you don't mind, but I took the liberty of pulling your accounts prior to our meeting. I wanted to have a better understanding of your financial situation." Janet's tone hinted at concern. The depleted account balance would be worrisome to any banker. She continued, "So, let's begin by discussing what you need and maybe I can figure out a solution that will work for you."

Her stubby fingers banged at the keyboard. Declan's financial history populated the screen. He had joined the bank at Val's request seven years ago. *That had to account for something.* Customer loyalty. Companies needed that in today's ever-changing economy. *Right?*

"We're desperate Ms. Morgan. I really need this loan to help keep my family afloat until I can find employment. We've been through a lot since I lost my job. I'm not a man prone to begging, but I'm out of options." Declan was not comfortable with desperation, but he felt it now and knew that it was evident in his expression. He added, "Please, I know that there must be some loophole that will allow the bank to assist me."

In an instant, he knew that Janet would be denying his request. Declan had been told by many fellow servicemen and cops that he had a gift for reading people, but he knew differently. It wasn't a gift. It was time. Painstaking hours spent observing and interrogating others. He picked up on the subtle physiological clues a person gave off. He could watch people in conversation and understand what was said, without hearing a word.

Janet had yet to answer his plea. A person with lesser skill wouldn't have recognized the clues. Declan noticed. A slight dip in her shoulder. A minuscule interruption in her breathing pattern. That was all it took, and he knew she was going to deny his loan request. He waited patiently for her to speak. To nervously fumble with the words. He wanted her to work for this rejection.

"I wish there was something that I could do, but your debt-to-income ratio is so high that I can't approve a loan that would meet your needs." Janet Morgan seemed truly regretful at her inability to help. Regardless, Declan's face warmed. Her attempt at softening the blow only fueled the flames of his deep-set frustration.

She continued in a soft voice that only managed to irritate Declan further, "Twenty thousand dollars would not be a feasible loan without any source of discernible income to back it. You've already taken collateral on your Toyota and the refinance of your home left you without any equity to borrow against."

Janet deflected ownership in the decision, claiming that banking protocols would not allow for the loan's approval. Declan half listened and then interjected, "I'm willing to take a higher interest rate. Extend the repayment deadline. Anything to help us keep our house." He knew the odds of a favorable outcome were unlikely based on several other recent attempts he'd made online.

Declan had calculated that he needed twenty thousand dollars to get him over the hump of the next few months. Without it, he and his family would be sunk. The local bank was his last hope. His best chance was in this face-to-face meeting. A sudden sense of failure swept over him. A foreign sensation that sickened him.

Declan laid out his case in plain language. "Without the loan, I'm going to lose our home and displace my family."

Janet Morgan wouldn't budge. "Mr. Enright, your application for the loan has been reviewed and our bank is unable to meet your needs at this time. I'm truly sorry that there isn't more that I could do to assist you." Janet's tone indicated that she'd given this speech many times before. It sounded rehearsed.

"I've been with this bank for several years and my wife years before that. We've been good customers. I'm just looking for some flexibility in your bank's decision-making process," Declan pleaded. A last-ditch effort.

Janet was kind, uncomfortable with conflict. Her thick cheeks flushed. Her denial of the loan request was based on a computer program's algorithm that crunched the numbers and determined the outcome. An inhumanely cold existence this world had become. Declan held out a modicum of hope that she could break free and see the human being sitting before her. Wishful, but futile.

Janet Morgan was rigid in her decision. The meeting concluded. Declan pushed upward from his uncomfortable seat. He knew that he had mumbled some parting words but couldn't recall them as soon as they left his mouth. He was numb.

Declan had been in bad places during bad times before, as many of his brood had been, but the failure at the bank rocked him to his core. An emotional flash bang of fear and confusion. He stumbled toward the exit in a haze and bumped into another patron, as he walked out to the sidewalk.

The crisp New England air crossed his face. An early taste of fall in the breeze. The sensation normally revitalized him, but now it left him drained. A reminder of what he might lose.

In his stupor, he slumped against the hood of his Toyota. Desperate for a moment's reprieve from the imminent discussion with Val.

Everything slowed, time no longer held significance.

Deep in thought, frantic for the solution, his mind raced. *How would he tell Val about this failure? Where do we go from here?* She would be strong for him. The thought of losing their house would now be a reality. There'd be no way to hide this from her. Val would see the disappointment on his face as soon as he came home.

There are always options. He'd been trained by the best to win at all costs. He needed to find the answer. In his old life, Declan mastered the art of the impossible. His teammates remarked that he always had an ace up his sleeve. Thus, his nickname was born. Declan "Ace" Enright. The calm in the storm.

Now he was failing to save his house and take care of his family. He'd played by the rules and that didn't work. Rules could be bent, broken, or obliterated if the mission called for it.

Declan ran his fingers over the hood of his beat-up Corolla. The red paint faded. Its lacquer long ago had yielded to the harsh winters and warm summers of New England. He glowered at the bank that had just screwed his last chance of salvation. Declan found himself facing the drive-thru of the bank's Automatic Teller Machine. And then he saw it. The solution.

Declan watched as an armored car leisurely pulled through the bank's parking lot. It stopped at the ATM located in the drive-thru banking attachment. He observed as a male exited the passenger door and ambled toward the teller machine. Declan guessed that he was in his mid-thirties. He looked average. His physical condition diminished through the years, most likely due to long days and limited personal drive. He wore the guard uniform with as much pride as a pizza delivery driver. His pasty skin indicated to Declan that he rarely spent time outdoors. Declan named him Casper, accordingly. Always good to assign nicknames to targets. It improved recall.

Casper paid no attention to Declan while he carried out his responsibilities. As a matter of fact, he seemed completely oblivious. He stumbled as he stepped up on the curbing near the ATM. Casper reddened at his misstep. Embarrassed. He waved to the bank teller visible in the window and gave an obligatory smile. She dismissed him with a wave of her hand and hurriedly returned to her business.

Casper gave an exasperated shout toward the armored truck's driver. Declan strained to hear her name but was out of earshot.

The driver looked younger than Casper. Her dark red hair pulled back into a loose ponytail that exposed a tattoo on her neck, located just beneath her right ear. She was too far away for him to make out its details. From where he stood it looked more like a Rorschach inkblot than a tattoo.

She carried an air of arrogance. Maybe she felt that she deserved a better life. Maybe she did. She wore large hoop earrings, which Declan assumed must be against the uniform regulation. She didn't look like a person that would care about such things. He named her Hoops.

Hoops handed Casper a clipboard. A brief conversation accompanied the exchange. Declan interpreted the interaction between the two guards. He deemed that Hoops and Casper were friendly toward each other but were not friends.

Declan didn't know anything about the armored truck business, but he'd run enough security during protection details to understand the basic principles. Experience told him that these two had no prior military training. And if they did, it wasn't in a combat unit. Hoops should have never left the vehicle. The driver's door should have remained closed and locked until Casper returned. But she failed to do either.

Hoops stood there, outside of the truck, pulled out her cellphone, and started scrolling through the touchscreen. Probably checking her Facebook feed. Declan used his cellphone sparingly, if at all. He could never wrap his mind around this ever-growing need for digital connection. People moved through their daily lives with faces buried in the tiny screens, oblivious to the world around them. Hoops was apparently no different.

Casper moved to the rear of the truck. He unlocked one side of the double doors and removed a beige rectangular canister. Casper's face showed the strain of its weight. He put the container down so that he could close and lock the rear door.

Declan realized that the guards must be replenishing the ATM. He looked at his watch. It was 5:06. Thursdays the bank remained open until six o'clock. The one day that the Clover Leaf Bank stayed open past the normal four o'clock closing time.

Casper had to put the canister down a second time to access his keychain that was attached to a lanyard on his belt. He then unlocked the front panel door to the ATM. And after fumbling with the interior, Casper withdrew a similar looking canister from the machine. Both metallic boxes rested side by side on the curbing. *How much was in those containers?*

Casper then placed the new one inside and secured the ATM. He waddled back to the rear of the truck and proceeded to lock up the used container. He noted something on the clipboard, returned to the passenger side, and entered the vehicle. Hoops became aware of his return and climbed back in. The two adjusted themselves in the vehicle prior to pulling forward. They drove north toward the city of Hartford.

Declan had been around money before and was never tempted. Several of his military targets were men of extreme wealth. He'd seen tables covered in gold and rare jewels, but the thought of taking any of it never crossed his mind. As an undercover narcotics detective, he'd raided several houses. The dealers, even at the street level, had large sums of cash on hand. Temptation never presented itself. That was before. The rules were different now. Declan faced a different enemy. And it was a fight he couldn't afford to lose. *Bend, break, or obliterate the rules. Pays to be a winner.*

The persona of Ace resurfaced. He needed to be that guy again. This time in service to his family.

He needed Val's support on this. *"The good, the bad, and everything in between."* As he drove home from the bank he replayed the vow that they had said, in unison, on the night of their wedding. It was time to test the strength and veracity of those words.

Declan arrived at their small gray colonial. He saw, through the weathered window panes of the side door, that Val and the girls were seated in the dining area around their small kitchen table. He paused before turning the knob. Everything that mattered to him was on the other side of this door. His world visible through those small pieces of glass. Seeing their smiles only intensified the pain of his failure at the bank. Normally, he loved watching them when they didn't know he was there, but today it had a crippling effect.

He entered. The loose knob jingled and announced his arrival. Val gave him a worried glance. She must have realized that he was later than expected. Her attention was quickly diverted back to the girls who were in an intense debate. They paused from their discussion about which Little Pony they liked best to yell their greeting. In unison, they shouted, "Hi dad!"

Laney sat in her chair with headphones on. She was somewhere else. Some days she would react to his entrance by simply looking up, but other days she was completely disconnected. Declan learned not to take these moments of isolation personally. He smiled and went from head to head, kissing each one. Laney allowed the kiss, but he felt her head pull back slightly. An involuntary reaction, like magnets of opposite polarity.

Val didn't ask about the bank. Not in front of the children. But she took his hand and gave him a slight squeeze. A subtle gesture of support given in a fraction of a second, but a much-needed one. Declan let out an audible sigh. He pursed his lips and gave a single shake of his head. Val registered this. Her head drooped a fraction lower. Deflated.

Declan gazed into his wife's eyes. The Little Pony discourse continued in the background as he silently mouthed, "It'll be okay. I have a plan."

There would be time to discuss things later. Right now, he needed to enjoy the reason he would take such a risk: his family.

2

The lack of warmth provided by the late August sun was a far departure from his homeland. He donned a light windbreaker to counter the slight chill in the air as temperatures dipped far below the average for this time of year. *I have been in this country too long. I'm getting soft* he thought to himself. But, time no longer held any meaning to him. Not since that day eight years ago. From that moment forward, his life existed to serve only one purpose: to right that wrong.

His skills sharpened in an unforgiving climate. It was no surprise to him that the average American was so weak. They were not born into adversity. He had seen their definition of challenge. Self-worth defined by trivial purchases or the latest trends. They didn't understand what it meant to fight for basic needs. True survival. That's why Khaled knew that he was destined to succeed.

Khaled's justice would not be swift. It would be calculated and deliberate. His plan born from a pain so deep that it had divided his life into two distinct time periods. "Alnaeim", or Bliss. And "Al Harq", the Burn.

Alnaeim

Sonia was his everything. She gave his life purpose. His wife had died shortly after giving birth to her. He was left to father his little girl alone. A role that men in his country did not typically assume. Khaled never blamed his daughter, as some of the villagers had suggested he should. In fact, the opposite had happened. He looked at Sonia as his wife's final gift to him. A blessing.

As Sonia grew, Khaled grew with her. He re-experienced life through her eyes. Every day on the way home from school they would pass by the market. Sonia would make him stop for a shaved ice. Khaled would throw up his hands in mock protest. Sonia would look up at him with that toothy smile. She could bend his will with a tilt of her head. *What he would give to see that smile one more time.*

Every beautiful memory brought with it an agony that was indescribable. That same pain now drove him forward against all reason. The goal of filling the void in his heart was the only incentive that held him to this world. *What would he do when he carried out his plan?* A ponderous thought. Maybe there would be a sense of peace, but life had taught him many lessons and through those, came the hard answer. He knew that would not be the case. Regardless, he would finish what they had started eight long years ago.

She would have been sixteen now. He speculated what she would have been like as a young woman. Every father wonders how his children will shape the world, but the answer had been stolen from him.

Thinking back to those years with Sonia, he recalled how simple their life had been. Khaled taught school in the village. In the ever-changing landscape of Iraq, he was a respected man. Education was revered. Khaled had been one of the few to leave, receive an education at an American university, and return home to share that gift. He completed his education at Northeastern University in Boston. He had intended a much different path for the utilization of his mechanical engineering degree, but the death of his wife had forced him to simplify his priorities so that he could raise his Sonia.

He had enjoyed his experience in the United States while residing in Boston on his student visa. At the time, he had held no ill will toward its people. That came much later.

Beyond his role as a teacher, Khaled also served as an advisor to the village elders. When the war came, and the Americans fought in the hills of his country, the elders sought to understand their village's role. Khaled served as a translator. He interpreted for the council when military units came through. The actual fighting always seemed to take place in other villages. For many years his people had avoided the violence associated with the war.

Khaled was open-minded enough to see the reason why the U.S. military had originally entered his country, but he also believed that the overall goal of the mission was flawed. The war had dragged on. Khaled was convinced that the Iraqi people were destined to live under military occupation without end.

As a devoted father, he hated seeing helicopters flying overhead or the distant sound of gunfire and explosions. His daughter would ask, *"Why did they come to our home? Why don't they go back to theirs?"* The answer always came out sounding contrived. But Khaled tried his best to explain it to his inquisitive little girl, *"They think that they are protecting the world against evil-doers. Even with honorable intentions, the outcome is many times unpredictable."*

Over time, Khaled became comfortable in his role. The translated conversations with military troops happened with increased regularity. Most of the men he spoke to were special forces operators. Some spoke his language, but poorly, and he found it easier to use English when communicating with them. When they found out that Khaled had studied in Boston they relaxed a little more.

The Americans were always on a hunt for wanted men. Resistance leaders, people who opposed their occupation. Sometimes the information they received would bring them to the village. Each time they came, no person of interest was found. The village became labeled as friendly, or at the least neutral. A fragile trust had been established.

Khaled was a keen observer and began noting the details about these military units, specifically its people. He learned their terminology for the equipment they carried, the uniforms they wore, and the meaning behind the patches on their sleeves. Softly he probed the soldiers in a friendly, inquisitive manner that never raised suspicion. Khaled eventually was able to identify all of the rank structure. From there he moved on and studied their name tags. Khaled felt it was important to keep a journal of these things. He told the Council of Elders about his book, but they did not seem concerned nor were they interested in his hobby.

Khaled excelled at facial recognition. It was made easier because, as time passed, many of the same units came through his village. Some of the servicemen recognized him as well. The greetings were friendly, but not overly so, because all alliances in his part of the world hung in a delicate balance.

The Council did not seem to mind the visitors, and at times were genuinely interested in the exchange of information. But more important were the resources the Americans provided the village. The military men almost always brought food with them, an age-old gesture of appreciation.

Sonia loved when they brought chocolate. Khaled pictured his daughter. Her small hand as she pulled on his sleeve. The tugging would cause his head to slowly dip, aligning with hers. Beautiful little Sonia would cup her hands gently around his ear and whisper, *"Please Papa, one chocolate."* Her breath tickled his ear as she spoke. He would give anything to have one more moment with his daughter. *Alnaeim.*

Time passed. Attitude toward the Americans shifted within the Council. As with any political agenda, there was always someone jockeying for position. In their small corner of the world, it was the Council Elder's son, Aziz. He did not see the American presence as noble and quietly argued his ideas away from his father. Khaled had overheard the subversive plot on several occasions, and Aziz's opinion gained momentum with others.

Aziz was concerned about when the Americans would depart. Something that was bound to happen sooner or later. The village would be retaliated against for providing safe harbor. The results would be devastating. Khaled had worried about this too but felt that it would be far worse to become an enemy of the U.S. military.

Aziz pushed his ideas on the villagers over the course of several months. With support established, the Council had begun to listen. Khaled, as the translator, earned a front row seat during the tense negotiation with the American soldiers. It was his words that carried the message of the Elders. At the time, that had made him very worried, but he had taken solace in the fact that their little village had survived for centuries on the wisdom of the

Council. He ultimately relied on their judgment to make the right decision that most benefited their people.

Khaled remembered the day that he was called into the Council Chamber. The space was a large dusty room with an elaborate rug of red and gold stitching that covered the dirt floor. Several tattered pillows were set in a circle, designed to provide a modicum of comfort to the members as they sat and discussed their agenda. Khaled recalled that on this particular day the air was colder than normal. The wind whipped the outside walls making an erie low whistle, like that of a tea kettle on the verge of boil.

The Elder spoke in his native tongue and greeted the foreigners gathered in the room. Khaled translated into English. Several of the Navy special operations men were present. Khaled had long ago noted that the patch above the breast pocket represented their affiliation. The Budweiser, as they called it, was the SEAL team emblem. These were hard men, who had done hard things. Khaled respected them.

All the men in the room that day had been in the village many times before. Their names already logged in his book. Only two of these men sat, Commander Banks and Lieutenant Richards. Khaled knew them to be the officers that oversaw this unit. Khaled did not know Banks well, but he had seen him on one previous occasion.

Khaled and Richards had early on established a fast friendship. It grew out of sidebar conversations after these council meetings. The two found common ground in the fact that both had attended universities in Boston around the same time. The Charles River split the difference between Northeastern and Richard's alma mater of MIT. *Strange how life intersected.*

The additional two Navy men present stood and kept watch during the meeting, one by the door and the other near the window. Even though Khaled's village was considered friendly toward the U.S., these Navy men never completely relaxed their sense of worry. Trust is a fickle friend in war. Khaled assumed that was a necessary mindset to have if your goal was to stay alive in a hostile country.

The Elder spoke, and Khaled translated. "Gentlemen, thank you for coming to meet with us at our request." A simple statement with a tone aimed at easing the tension. The sound of Khaled's voice aroused the group. He noted that the men seated before him adjusted their position on the pillows.

Khaled continued, "I am afraid that we have some important matters to discuss. We hope that after this conversation you will see our point of view." Khaled's voice was steady when he spoke, but tension percolated.

Pleasantries had passed, and the discussion shifted to the real matter at hand. "Your kindness and generosity shown to my people over the past year have been greatly appreciated." He paused, listening to the Elder who spoke rapidly in Arabic. Khaled heard the context and was concerned at how the next statement would be received by the Americans. "It has been decided that we can no longer provide shelter and support to your military efforts."

The Navy Commander, Banks, flinched at this statement. His eyes darted to the two standing SEALs. His right hand slowly drifted toward the sidearm strapped to his thigh. A barely perceivable movement, but Khaled saw it.

"Council Elder, help me to understand your change in position. Did we do something to offend you? Is there anything we can do to regain your trust?" Banks spoke calmly, a man obviously accustomed to such dealings.

The Elder waited patiently for Khaled to share his translation and then paused for a long moment as if to contemplate the implications.

The Navy men stirred. Khaled immediately could sense that this topic of discussion did not sit well with them. The man at the door whose name tag read "Morales" took a slight step back and subtly adjusted his equipment. His eyes scanned the room. The man named "Enright" appeared to become more still, if that was even possible.

Khaled realized what had happened. The impact of the Elder's words. He immediately attempted to diffuse the situation. The Americans must have thought it was a trap. Like any cornered animal they would soon bare their teeth. Khaled quickly explained his perception to the Elder and requested permission to speak freely so that he could ease the tension.

The words were simple. He directed them more toward his friend, Richards, rather than to Banks. Khaled spoke softly, "This is not a trap. We are not the enemy. The Council's decision is not based on some new alliance but is merely about the long-term survival of our people." This brief but clear statement by Khaled seemed to ease the strain. Some visible slack released from Banks's erect posture. Banks and Richards refocused their attention back to the discussion with the Council.

The Elder spoke again after Khaled had relayed to him the content of his last message. "As Khaled has just advised, we do not want to be your enemy. We have come to the realization that the longer we give you safe passage, the more we are perceived as the enemy by our own people. Our village will stand long after you leave, and we will be forced to deal with those consequences without your assistance. Please understand that this decision is one made for the benefit of my people. I hope that it is one that you will understand and respect." Khaled's delivery of the Elder's wishes conveyed its conviction.

"Although we are disappointed in your decision, we will respect it. On behalf of the United States, we thank you for your months of generosity and wish you prosperity in the years to come." Banks's tone was serious but compassionate.

By Khaled's assessment, the meeting appeared to have gone as well as could be expected. The American Navy men seemed to accept the terms set forth. The Council would no longer offer the village as a safe harbor for the U.S. military. Their rationale explained, the Council, in an attempt to maintain relations, told the Americans that no member of the village would take up arms against them.

In the months that followed after the last meeting with the Americans, things in the village remained relatively unchanged. Minus the perks of those visits.

Sonia would occasionally ask, *"Papa, where are the Golden Men?"* She had affectionately named them "Golden Men" because of their tan skin and light hair. Khaled had explained that they had to leave to keep the village safe. She would whine slightly and say, *"But Papa, who will bring me my chocolate?"* Khaled remembered laughing out loud at this. The simple, yet beautiful mind of his child.

Winter came, and things began to change. The village, set in the foothills of the Cheekha Dar Mountains, provided a strategic outpost because of its proximity to Iran. With the Americans gone, a new group had begun to fill their void. Khaled knew who these men were and what they represented. They called themselves *Maharib Lilhuriya* "freedom fighters", but they were more commonly known as the *Muqawama* "resistance." Khaled knew that these men were targets of the American military. Aziz had bent the will of the Elder Council and had convinced them to give refuge to these men. A dangerous deal.

As days and weeks passed, more of these men arrived. They brought large crates of equipment. Khaled had assumed the boxes were filled with weapons. Unlike the Americans, they were not kind to the villagers. And to Sonia's disappointment, they did not share chocolate with the children.

The Muqawama used the small schoolhouse as their headquarters. They took over the big room in the back of the building where books and materials were kept. The cramped space tightened. The children were forced to use the smaller two rooms located toward the front.

Khaled remembered that he could feel the uneasy tension build among his fellow villagers. The smiles were scarce. People stayed off the streets as the Muqawama began making their presence more visible. Khaled was respected because of his status within the village, but the new visitors were guarded around him. He figured that it was most likely due to the fact that he spoke English and had lived abroad during his years of advanced education.

And then it happened. Everything in Khaled's life changed.

Al Harq

The crack of the first shot sounded far in the distance. Khaled looked out toward the direction it came from, but the open space made it impossible to pinpoint the exact location. However, the gap in time between the snap of the rifle and its final destination was long, an indication of the distance traveled. Seconds later, the zip of a high-velocity round sailed past Khaled, hitting a Muqawama soldier standing only a few feet away. A plume of fine red mist burst into the air from the man's chest. Khaled couldn't look away from the soldier, still standing, a face frozen in confusion and terror until his knees buckled, and his body crumpled to the ground. Disoriented and unable to move, Khaled found himself in the middle of the battle.

Looking back on this day, he remembered the overwhelming panic that rushed over him, the shortness of breath. His initial thought was self-preservation, just the instinct to survive. Then, in a sudden moment of clarity, his mind flashed to Sonia and he made a mad dash for the school. He remembered running, pushing through his physical limits, but not moving fast enough. His legs felt sluggish like he was running in mud and everything seemed to move in slow motion.

It's funny what you recall when your senses are heightened. He could still smell the spiced lamb of the small meat shop when he rounded the corner. He could still see the old man with a wide smile, seated in the dirt holding a chicken calmly in his lap.

When the school became visible, he watched in horror as the Muqawama soldiers pointed their machine guns out from multiple windows of the school front. The aim of their sporadically fired shots seemed random. He looked up and noticed one of the two black-robed men on top of the building hoist a long cylindrical tube onto his shoulder.

He remembered hearing the drumming sound of a helicopter approaching in the distance. It was the Americans. Then a loud burst of noise, like a burp through a megaphone, erupted from a big gun mounted inside of the helicopter.

The front of the building exploded in a cloud of dust and dirt as the rounds struck the stucco walls. The destructive impacts crept quickly up toward the men on the roof. The Muqawama man holding the rocket launcher stumbled forward. The rocket shot out as he fell. But, instead of heading toward the intended American target, it propelled down through the roof of the school.

Khaled ran faster than he had ever run before, his mouth filled with the metallic taste from his lungs' exertion. The thumping of the helicopter's rotor blades and deafening gunfire only fueled his rage-induced pace.

Nothing he did next would matter. The rocket penetrated the poorly constructed roof and entered the interior of the building. The lower floor burst into an explosion of dirt and fire. As random debris hit Khaled's face, blood dripped into his eyes, blurring his vision as he scrambled forward.

Even though he remembered screaming, "Sonia!", he heard nothing but the ringing in his ears. Still choking on dust, the intense heat projected from the burning school reached Khaled all the way into the alley. Adrenaline allowed him to continue even though it felt like walking straight into a furnace. For her, for Sonia, Khaled would walk through the fires of hell.

Muffled screams from dying men filled the air while bewildered children staggered out into the streets. Khaled desperately pawed at each of them, spinning them around searching for her face. No Sonia.

Khaled tore off a portion of his sleeve and wrapped the cloth over his nose and mouth to make a makeshift respirator. As he entered the fiery rubble of the village school, the heat became unbearable. His eyes watered as the smoke encircled his head. The torn shirt did little to improve his breathing as he toppled over the wreckage.

The acrid black smoke swallowed the light. Darkness and muted flames surrounded him as he moved wildly through the jagged concrete and rebar on hands and knees. A flicker of light caught his attention. Sonia's bracelet! The bright blue stones glimmered between two mangled cinder blocks, calling to him like a lighthouse beacon. He'd given it to her when she turned six and she never took it off. He felt his heart drop when his vision cleared enough to reveal the bracelet was hanging from her blackened arm.

Then, a scream. A sound that was more animal than man. He was surprised to realize that it came from his own mouth. Khaled clawed relentlessly at the rocks that covered his beautiful Sonia. His fingernails tore as he pulled and dug at the endless pile.

"Sonia! Please, no! Sonia, don't leave me! I'm here, my beautiful! You are safe now, Daddy's here!"

With his last reserve of strength, he dragged her free. The smell of her burnt flesh made him sick. This smell would haunt his dreams until his last breath. He slumped against the rubble and hoisted her lifeless body onto his lap. She was so small in his arms. He held her gently, like cradling a baby. He looked down at her face, barely recognizable. He let his tears fall freely now, causing the smoke in his eyes to burn even more.

Khaled held his daughter's lifeless body and waited to die, willing the fire or smoke to take him. Without Sonia, he had nothing. Without Sonia, he was nothing. He allowed himself to slip slowly into the darkness, content to let the remains of the collapsed school be the tomb they would share together.

To his disappointment, Khaled did not get to escape a life spent living without his Sonia. He began to hear muffled sounds, followed by a tug on his shoulder. He drifted in and out of consciousness like the flicker of a bulb just before it burns out while feeling that strange sensation of floating. *Where is my Sonia?* It was his last thought before he drifted away.

The sounds slowly amplified. Hushed words. English. Khaled struggled to understand. *Great paradise is run by Americans too.* As quickly as the thought had entered his mind, he realized that he wasn't dead. His unresponsive body was sprawled on a cot in a medical tent. The smell of the sterilization chemicals mixed unnaturally with the ever-present dust in the air.

"I know this guy. I can vouch for him." A deep raspy voice said. "He's one of the villagers. A local. He helped translate for their Council."

"How do we know he's not with them?" The other voice quieter and nasal, agitated. "I think we should send him for debriefing as soon as he's well."

"I'm telling you that I know him. He was holding his dead daughter when we found him, for God's sake!" The raspy voice familiar, but in Khaled's haze, he could not place it. "Let him rest and I'll talk to him when he wakes. Tell Banks that this is the guy from Boston, the translator. He'll know who I am talking about. Spend your energy on someone else!"

"It's on you if you're wrong," the quiet man said.

The room returned to silence, minus the beeping and rhythmic whooshing sounds that poured from the various medical machines. Everything blurred. Blackness again.

Khaled was later told by an American military doctor that he had been in and out of consciousness for three days. He took stock of his injuries. His hands were heavily bandaged and his head was wrapped in gauze, discolored from a mix of dried blood and iodine. The doctor explained that that laceration to his forehead had required several stitches. The burns on his hands were being evaluated for a skin graft. The visible wounds of that day paled in comparison to the gash that tore his soul apart. The scars became a lasting reminder of his failed effort to save his daughter.

"Sonia?" Khaled knew the answer but asked anyway. The doctor shook his head solemnly. He pointed at a small paper bag on the nearby chair. Khaled reached for it. The movement carried with it a pain so intense that he nearly passed out again. The doctor placed the bag on Khaled's lap. Inside was her bracelet. A cold numbness washed over his body. "Why couldn't you just let me die?" He screamed. A coughing fit followed, as his lungs, damaged from smoke inhalation, protested the exertion.

"You've taken everything from me!" Khaled had always been a man of control, but he was trembling and filled with an insatiable rage.

His sweet little Sonia was taken away from him. All for what? Because the Americans came to his country. They attacked the Muqawama soldiers. They had killed Sonia.

Khaled centered himself. He quickly regained his composure and then spoke in a calm voice, "Thank you for all that you have done for me, doctor. I am sorry that I snapped at you. I am just trying to process my daughter's death."

The doctor put a gentle hand on his shoulder, "I totally understand. There is nothing to apologize for. Your daughter's death was a tragedy. I have children of my own and can't imagine how I would feel if I were in your shoes. Please rest and I will check back with you later."

Khaled made the apology to the doctor because he didn't want the angry man with the quiet voice to suspect him as a threat, an enemy of the U.S. Word of his outburst could mean that he would be subjected to interrogation. He needed to remain "the Boston guy" so that he would stay under their radar.

The doctor's comment spawned an idea. *I have children of my own,* he'd said. Why do these men get to enjoy their families when the only piece left of his Sonia was wrapped in a paper bag? Khaled made a pact with himself on that day. The Americans responsible would pay for what they had done. They would know his pain because they would feel it firsthand.

The anguish of Sonia's death fueled his vengeance. It pushed back against his sadness and divided him. Like the phoenix, he was born again from the ashes.

3

Nicholas Lawrence stared at the image on the computer screen, lost in thought. Always amazed that in a business inherently filled with the potential risk of robbery, banking executives did not spend the extra money to get quality surveillance systems. Typically, more was spent on tile flooring or decorative marble pillars than on a security camera that could record a clear and usable image. And due to this shortsightedness, he had spent the last few hours tweaking the pixelated still shot of the masked man at the teller's window. He adjusted the settings on the monitor and fiddled with the replay options. All in the hope of getting a discernible image of the robber's face.

These cases didn't satisfy him. The work lacked a sense of purpose. Very rarely were there injuries and the banks were all heavily insured. No real victims. Not like his previous assignment with Violent Crimes Against Children (VCAC). The victims in those cases epitomized the true sense of the word.

He'd joined the Bureau after completing four years of service as an Army officer. Seemed like a good idea at the time. During his service, he'd made some friends employed by many of the three-letter agencies. They'd convinced him to make the jump into federal law enforcement.

The FBI's hiring process was rigorous. Even more challenging because

Nick did not fall into one of their preferred categories, lawyer or accountant. He had learned Arabic during his time overseas, but nothing that would rate him as proficient. So, he had applied under the Diversified track. It qualified him on the combination of his education and military experience.

He was warned by the recruiter that the entrance exam weeded out a large number of applicants and not to get his hopes up. Nick found the test easy. Actually, he thought it was fun. He moved through the rest of the application process quickly that included four days of intensive interview, psychological testing, and polygraph examination. Nick excelled at each stage. At the completion of a thorough background check, he found himself standing on the legendary training grounds of the FBI Training Academy at Quantico, several months later.

He'd always envisioned that he would work violent crimes or counterterrorism. Those units seemed to be paths that suited his aptitudes. He had been a decorated infantry officer. A Ranger. And prematurely, he believed that the Bureau would utilize that experience. Nick quickly learned about the agency's bureaucracy.

His first assignment was in Texas, tasked to a unit that handled crimes against children. Texas was not on his wish list. His wife, Kerry, did not like the idea either. But the choice was not his to make.

Nick, originally assigned to the San Antonio Field Office, was rerouted shortly after his arrival. He was sent to the satellite office in Austin, referred to as a resident agency. Austin's climate and atmosphere appealed more to him than San Antonio had. It eased the adjustment to the Fed life. Kerry was an elementary teacher and found work in a neighboring city.

Nick soon found that the work called to him. He became passionate about his cases. The work ultimately consumed him. Nick and Kerry had no children of their own. The children in his investigations filled that void. He felt a responsibility to save them, an innate fatherly instinct to protect these victims. To right their wrongs.

Looking back, he realized that the balance between the work and his personal life had been lost. He worked late most nights. And when he did come home it was often with a case file tucked under his arm. Kerry, desperate for attention that he no longer provided, filed for divorce after two years.

The two genuinely cared for each other, but Nick's attempts at reprioritizing his devotion from his casework back into their relationship failed. The damage had been done. Further exacerbated by the death of Nick's father. The strain on his dissolving marriage with Kerry hit an all-time high. His mother, living in Connecticut, had started to show the early onset of dementia. He tried to keep her affairs in order as best he could. It was a tedious and seemingly endless task, worsened by the geographic separation. Nicholas needed to be near his mother. Her rapid decline necessitated the move. Kerry had resisted the idea.

Nick saw an opportunity for reassignment to the New Haven Field Office in Connecticut. He knew that his marriage was tanking. He applied for the transfer. He had told Kerry about it after his selection. He could still picture the look of sadness on her face. She'd come to love the Austin area and her job. Kerry stayed behind. Their marriage over.

They lied to each other. They said that they would continue to work to reconcile, but they both knew that it was finished. The divorce had been relatively painless. With no children, they had parted ways as friends.

Nick had moments of self-pity. The thought of his life now and the turn of events that brought him here weighed heavily. He now lived with his mentally ill mother in the small home of his childhood. He loved his parents but had never planned on returning to Connecticut.

The grainy image of a bank robber gazed back at him. Nick snapped out of his self-absorbed disappointment. He took a second look at the image in front of him and attempted to discern any distinguishing features.

Nick did not typically make excuses for his current circumstance. He was angry at himself for allowing his mind to drift. It contradicted the mantra of his mentor, Sgt. Dave Paulson. *Excuses are the bricks that built the house of failure.* Paulson was a legend in the Ranger community. He was Nick's primary instructor, a black hat, at the elite training grounds of Ranger School, and later the two served together in Afghanistan. The wisdom bestowed by Paulson had helped Nick prevail in times of adversity. It would assist him now.

4

The nighttime routine consisting of bath, snack time, and bedtime stories was completed. With the girls tucked into bed, Declan and Val finally had an opportunity to talk. They sank into their tattered couch, each with a glass of wine poured from their favorite boxed brand. Declan took a deep breath. *Why was he so nervous?* Maybe he was in shock at the desperation of his plan. *Would she judge him for it?*

"I'm not sure how to begin." Declan's voice was soft. Almost delicate. He sipped slowly at the Merlot.

"You can tell me anything. We're in this thing together."

"I can get us the money we need."

"That's great babe!" A smile shot across her face. "I knew that you would. You're like a cat that always lands on his feet."

"It's the how that I need to talk to you about."

Val's smile receded. She nodded for him to continue and pulled hard from her wine glass.

When he finished explaining his proposal, Val was silent for what felt like an eternity. Declan prided himself on being able to read people, but he found himself at a loss when it came to his wife. Val was deep in thought. Her brow furrowed.

Val finally spoke, and her voice broke the profound silence. The sound startled Declan.

"I'm in. Whatever you need me to do, I'll be there." Her voice steady and eyes sharp. Sincerity present in every word she spoke as she continued, "I love you and I know that you love us. If you tell me that this will work, then I am telling you that I trust in you completely."

The faith she had in his ability to provide always surprised him. If at any moment he wavered, he knew that Val would be there to push him forward, encouraging ever so slightly. A smile crossed Declan's face and the two embraced. He didn't want to let go.

They set aside the task ahead and turned on the television. Val curled up in the crux of his arm. Tonight, he would use this time to clear his mind. Tomorrow, the real work would begin.

Surveillance was a skill he had honed over his thirteen years in the Teams. He was better than most. Declan hid in plain sight. To be invisible in the open was the goal. It's not like the movies where operatives wore thousand-dollar suits and fancy sunglasses as they moved through a crowd. Declan dressed for whatever the environment dictated. Today, a subdued gray T-shirt and faded blue jeans sufficed. Nothing that would draw attention. The clothes carried no brand logos or recognizable graphic designs. A layperson might notice these things. And therefore, remember him. The more generic the better. Be forgettable.

Declan located several vantage points from which to observe the bank. The building was on a main road with two lanes of traffic in each direction. Its only entrance was south of a congested four-way intersection controlled by a traffic light. Adjacent to the bank was a gas station with a three-foot decorative white-picket fence that separated the two parking lots. Across the street was a small strip mall filled with a smattering of low-budget businesses. The traffic was constant. A steady flow of cars in and out.

He needed to map out the ATM delivery schedule. He wanted to confirm his assumption. Over the next two Thursday afternoons, Declan sat patiently within visual range of the bank's drive-thru. A bus stop bench across the street, near the strip mall's entrance, provided an excellent observation post. The volume of foot traffic on this side of the road made it easy for Declan to blend in.

Declan sat, his face idle. He removed his cell phone from his front pocket. A swipe of his finger activated the screen. He scrolled through his apps. With Candy Crush open he would look like any other bored citizen passing time while he waited for the bus. In today's world if you didn't have a phone in your hand then you were more likely to stand out. It was probable that no one would take notice of him anyway. Most people had their faces buried in phones of their own.

Declan deployed another trick of the trade. He lit a cigarette. Like a cloak of invisibility, smoking reduced suspicion. It was common for smokers to stand in isolation while they took their nicotine break. He'd used this ploy numerous times during his stint in the narcotics unit. Even though he did not regularly smoke he had conditioned himself so that he did not cough, although the first few pulls burned. A subtle reminder of the long gap since he'd used this guise.

The armored car delivery happened around the same time on both Thursdays. 5:07 p.m. and 5:13 p.m. respectively. Declan concluded that these transfers were scheduled for 5:00 p.m. The variance in time was most likely due to traffic or possibly a lack of discipline by the driver. Declan knew that he would have to account for the possibility of an early arrival in his planning. A necessary precaution if Murphy's Law took hold and they happened to be on schedule on the execution day.

On every bank run, Hoops drove, and Casper reloaded the ATM. During these runs, Declan noted that Hoops had only exited the vehicle on one occasion. But every delivery, she had opened the door to chat with her partner. Casper was consistently slow and distracted, sometimes on his phone or talking to a random passerby. Declan witnessed that during each visit Casper would attempt to get the attention of the teller with a smile and a wave. He was rejected without fail. But like a loyal dog, Casper never faltered. Declan pitied him.

Casper never visually scanned his surroundings. Too many deliveries without incident had apparently lowered his guard. Declan had seen the same thing happen to guys overseas. Lulled into a false sense of security after long gaps between conflicts, usually with disastrous consequences. He'd lost friends to complacency. And had therefore forbidden its lure.

On the third day of surveillance, Declan had noticed a man of Middle Eastern descent standing in the shade of a tree. The man looked like he was taking notes. Initially concerning, but Declan deemed that this man had no interest in him. His interest appeared to be solely focused on the arrival of the bus. Watching this man scribbling into the notebook, Declan thought he recognized him. A sense of Déjà vu. It was a fleeting thought. Declan had refocused on his task and when he looked back toward the maple, the foreigner was gone.

The timeline had been established. Weaknesses of the guards exposed. The operational planning was underway.

Rehearsal. The cornerstone of his former unit's success. Drill it until the movements become so natural that they could be carried out with the same simplicity as pouring a cup of coffee. And Declan drilled his op. As he had done in the Teams. The difference this time was that he would be alone. Success rested squarely on him.

He measured his planned start position to the armored car to be roughly twenty-one feet. Equal to the maximum distance that a person could close before a holstered gun could be drawn and fired. Based on the observed skills of the two guards, he determined that this would not be a factor. Declan knew that he would be able to cross a minimum of seven of those feet before Casper or Hoops would even register his presence. By that time, it would be too late for them.

Declan used the fenced-in backyard of his home to practice in relative seclusion. His daughter's plastic red and yellow cab car was used as a reference point for the armored truck. Two five-gallon water jugs bought from a local Army surplus store replicated the relative bulk of the money containers.

He clocked each pass with a stopwatch. Speed would be critical to the success. He prepared for several days and the rehearsals went late into the evening. His girls had joined in when they arrived home from school. They followed their dad as he ran the gauntlet, giggling and cheering as they gave chase. Abby took on the role of drill sergeant, pushing her dad to best his time on each run. A natural leader.

During most of these days of rehearsal, Laney stood by and watched. Close but far away. Her eyes tracked the movement. Her face placid, no effect.

"Daddy, why do we play Fetch the Water every day?" Ripley asked, coining the drill's name.

"I love this game. Imagine that we must bring these water jugs to a village of thirsty people. Lives depend on us." He was saddened by his response. The words couldn't be truer.

5

THURSDAY, 4:30 P.M.

Declan arrived early but not so much so that it would draw any suspicion. Approaching the bank's parking lot, he observed that the parking space that he'd selected for the assault and escape was occupied. Using this as an opportunity to conduct one final reconnaissance, he looped the block to scout for any cops who might be parked nearby. All clear. *Luck favors the prepared.* He returned to the bank. The space was now vacant, and he backed his Corolla into it. A focused intensity surged inside him.

Pulling out his cell phone, Declan pretended to make a call. It was not out of the ordinary for people to be parked in front of a business while carrying on an in-depth conversation. No one would give him a second thought. He knew that the bank's external cameras would pick up his vehicle as he entered the lot and Declan used this to his advantage.

Earlier in the week, he had walked the parking lot of a rental car agency in Hartford. He located a Toyota Corolla of the same make, model, and approximate year as his. He snapped a quick photo of the New Jersey license plate attached. Later, using the image, Declan created two replicas using his computer and some do-it-yourself laminate. The simple process had effectively disguised the registration of his car. Double-sided tape affixed the mock plates to the front and rear of his Corolla.

Declan had also picked up a couple of cheesy bumper stickers. He strategically placed them on the rear bumper using clear packing tape so that he could quickly remove them without leaving any residue. The surveillance cameras would record these plates and identifying stickers. The effect was designed to add a layer of misdirection to any subsequent investigation.

Declan was unrecognizable. He had picked up some non-prescription contacts, changing his blue eyes to brown. Val was employed to assist. She showed him the proper way to insert the lenses without poking his eye. It took several attempts before he was comfortable with the thin plastic film overlays. He bought a cheap afro wig. Using scissors, he trimmed it down to give him an unkempt, nappy look. A heavy bronzer cream darkened his complexion. He could be mistaken for a dark-skinned Hispanic or light-skinned African American. Misdirection was a critical element in surviving the fallout.

Declan was grateful that fall had arrived early. The dip in temperature gave him a slight reprieve from the heat produced by the layers of his disguise. The New England air was crisp for late August. The warm days were not yet completely gone, but today's high teetered at fifty-three degrees, ensuring that the black skull cap secured atop his head would not be out of place. The long-sleeved shirt he wore meant that he only needed to bronze his hands and a small portion of his forearms, reducing the time he would need later to remove evidence of the disguise.

Val had come up with a brilliant addition to his masquerade, finding some temporary tattoos at the Dollar Store. Declan had adhered a black scorpion on the outside area of his right wrist and an eight-ball on his neck, giving him the look of an ex-convict or gangbanger.

In position, Declan inhaled deeply, preparing for the next phase.

Declan had long ago learned that anyone who claims that they don't get nervous before an op has either never been in a real-world combat situation or is completely full of shit. He had heard all the macho bravado before, but he had also done things that the average person couldn't fathom. Each time before battle, he felt those nerves. Each time he suppressed them. Declan wasn't good because he was fearless. He was good because of his ability to acknowledge the fear and take total control of it.

· · ·

4:55 p.m.

Declan sat in his Toyota with his air conditioning on full blast, ensuring that sweat did not damage any of the makeup covering his exposed skin. He looked down at the four prepaid cellphones resting on the passenger seat, mentally pregaming the upcoming sequence of events. The fifth burner phone was with his wife. He flipped open the first cell phone and punched the numbers. Declan knew that based on the geolocation of his call that he would be automatically directed to the Wethersfield Police Department.

"911. What's your emergency?"

"I'm at the intersection of Prospect Street near Back Lane and I just saw a car accident." Declan covered his left nostril as he spoke, giving him a nasally tone.

"Do you have a vehicle description? Is anyone hurt?"

Declan responded, "I don't know. I kept driving. I'm late to pick up my kids. I've got to go." He hung up and threw the phone on the passenger side floorboard. One call down. It had begun. No turning back now.

Declan was selective when he picked the intersection of the imaginary car accident. It was several miles from the bank. He knew from his time as a police officer that smaller departments typically operated with four patrol officers and a supervisor on a shift. There might be one or two detectives working. Lower numbers meant limited ability to respond. The intersection of Prospect Street and Back Lane was picked because it was located on the boundary of Wethersfield. The jurisdiction abutted the Town of Newington, creating the potential for a multi-agency response. And more confusion for the officers.

It wasn't long before sirens rang out in the distance. Declan placed call number two.

"911. What's your emergency?"

"I'm stuck at an accident on Prospect Street!" Declan used a high-pitched voice, bordering on being shrill to portray himself as an important person with important things to do. He delivered his act as a man agitated by the inconvenience of delayed traffic.

"Sir, we have already received a call on this and officers are on the way." The dispatcher relayed this with a hint of annoyance.

"There's smoke coming out of the front of one of the vehicles!" Alarm present in his voice.

The dispatcher's voice sounding less annoyed as she registered this new information. "Do you see any fire?"

"I don't kn—" Declan ended the call mid-sentence and tossed burner number two on the floorboard. The fire department would be dispatched to the scene. Firetrucks were a cop's worst nightmare on the simplest of accidents. They were loud, blocked roads, and caused supervisors to show up.

Declan waited until he heard the distinctive sound of firetrucks sirens as they cleared a nearby intersection. The calls had begun to work their magic. He had engineered an event that was now forcing at least two police officers, a firetruck, and most likely a supervisor in the direction of Prospect Street and Back Lane. The dispatcher had probably already contacted the neighboring jurisdiction to let them know it might be their accident. The game of "whose crash investigation is this" had begun.

5:00 p.m.

Call number three.

"911. Go with your emergency." The dispatcher said hastily. Declan heard the apprehension in her voice. Frustration had set in. A dispatcher's stress transmitted over the radio commonly increased the anxiety and tension of the responding officers.

"I'm stuck in this damn accident. The road is blocked," Declan projected in a deep, angry voice.

"Sir. We already have units responding—"

"Well tell them to hurry the hell up! The guys are fighting in the street!" boomed Declan, staying in character as he interrupted her explanation. This loud, irritated version of Declan commanded the dispatcher's attention.

"I have an officer close by. Do you have a description of any of these people?"

"Shit! Hurry!" Declan pretended not to hear the dispatcher as he hung up. Burner number three done and on the floor.

. . .

5:03 p.m.

Call number four.

"911."

Declan covered the phone with a handkerchief and gently rubbed it over the mouthpiece, giving the effect of movement, simulating a butt dial.

He never spoke directly to the dispatcher, but began yelling, "Stop! What the fuck is your problem? Get back in your car you son of a bitch!" Declan then rubbed the phone harder, giving the impression to the listener that a scuffle was actively occurring.

"Can you hear me?" The dispatcher spoke with obvious notes of stress in her speech.

Nothing.

"Drop it!" Declan yelled through the cloth, creating a muffled effect before he disconnected the call. Burner four down.

Declan paused. He took several deep breaths. He was aware of the importance of oxygenating the brain prior to combat. The initial stage was underway.

The fifth call would come from Val using the last burner phone. Declan knew that she would be calling them at exactly 5:05. They had rehearsed it numerous times throughout the week. Val would place the call to the 911 operator. She would scream that the people involved in the accident were now actively fighting. Once dispatch began their barrage of questions, Val would interrupt. Her script called for her to yell "He's got a gun!" After a few seconds of unintelligible screaming Val would hang up. Declan knew that this last ruse would push any remaining officers and detectives out toward the chaos.

All responding police and fire units would be forced to navigate rush hour traffic to get to the location of the made-up crash. Even with the lights and sirens, traffic created its own issues. Once on scene, the true pandemonium would ensue. Police from two neighboring jurisdictions would be jockeying for ownership of the call and with the introduction of fire department personnel, lots of people would be battling to assume command.

Declan was confident that the difficulty in finding the non-existent crash would stall the officers. Once in the area of Prospect Street and Back Lane, officers would be three and a half miles from the bank.

Declan had timed the route without traffic. It had taken eleven minutes. He estimated that the high speeds of the police cruisers would cut the time to approximately six minutes, but rush hour would add an additional minute or two to the commute. Declan calculated eight minutes of time.

Supervisors and officers would race around the neighboring streets looking for an accident that had quickly escalated into a disturbance involving a firearm. Protocols would dictate their inability to break off from a service call of this magnitude until they determined that the area had been thoroughly searched. A minimum investigative standard needed to be met before a supervisor would begin releasing officers back to their regular duties. And that would take time.

5:08 p.m.

Declan could see the front of the armored truck approaching from a block away, stopped at a red light. The two occupants appeared to be engrossed in an animated discussion, totally unaware of what was about to happen. Declan found a contentedness in this moment of calm, like being in the eye of a hurricane.

The armored truck entered the parking lot, passing Declan's car. They paid him no mind, lost in their conversation. The truck disappeared behind the bank and then reappeared in the ATM lane a moment later.

Casper and Hoops pulled to a stop facing him. Declan inhaled slowly. He began the last of his pre-battle preparations, tensing and releasing his muscles to allow for the adrenaline to disperse throughout his body. A technique that had been learned from his hand-to-hand combat instructor. It had served him well in times past when a steady hand was needed.

His Toyota idled quietly. The loud rumble of the armored truck provided him with additional stealth and would drown out the sound of his approach. Declan opened the door slightly. He watched as Casper began the routine, lazily sauntering around the front of the truck. His back to Declan, he waved at the teller. *Routine created complacency.*

Hoops had opened the driver door, sitting half in and half out. She continued her heated discussion with Casper. Declan heard her voice for the first time and noted the slight rasp of a chain-smoker as he heard her say "...you know that she loved him from the start. He was just acting like he didn't care." Declan had surmised that they did not seem like readers. He deciphered their conversation must have been about some reality television show they watched.

Casper had opened the front of the Automated Teller Machine, turning his attention to Hoops. "You always talk about that love crap. Who cares? She obviously was using him. Why would he want to be with her cheating ass anyway?" Casper threw his hands up and mumbled something under his breath. He walked toward the rear door of the armored truck.

Casper began lumbering back toward the ATM in the same manner that Declan had observed him do repeatedly over the past several weeks of surveillance. He put the box down and turned toward Hoops who was now completely out of the truck.

Declan was already moving. They didn't see him approaching on foot. *Slow is smooth and smooth is fast.* Declan never moved faster than he could shoot or act. The weeks of preparation showed in his ability to close the distance quickly. As he moved he pictured Abby holding the stopwatch and cheering him on.

Ten feet away from the two guards, and they remained unaware of his presence. He pulled on the skull cap, rolling down the black dry-fit ski mask over his bronzed skin. The mask, by design, only covered his face, ensuring that his eight-ball tattoo was exposed on his neck. The black latex gloves were size medium, a tight fit for Declan's large hands. This caused the rubbery material to stop at the wrist, intentionally exposing the fake scorpion tattoo.

In one swift, fluid movement Declan pulled a silver starter pistol from his waistband. His left hand simultaneously slid a blackjack from his pocket.

Canting the gun sideways, giving him the appearance of a street hood, Declan roared, "Don't do anything stupid! It's not your money!"

To Declan, everything was in slow motion, but he knew from personal experience the speed at which he was now moving. Scientists called this flow. Legendary athletes had been studied because of claims that everything slowed down when shooting a basket or swinging a bat, making it almost impossible to miss. Declan Enright had achieved this as an operator

in the military and was subconsciously applying it now. He was the
Michael Jordan of special ops.

Casper's hand began moving toward the holster on his hip. "What the
fu—" His words cut short as the loud bang of the starter pistol erupted next
to his left ear. Simultaneously Declan struck the right side of Casper's head
with the blackjack. Declan banked on the brain's inability to comprehend
multiple stress events. He knew the gun would consume their attention.
Casper went limp and crumpled to the ground.

The effect on Hoops was immediate. The only thing moving was her
eyes. This happened sometimes. Most people were aware that the mind
responded to stress in one of two ways: fight or flight. Declan knew that
there was a third and less common reaction, freeze. In the face of extreme
danger, some people lost the ability to physically react. Hoops stood in
front of him completely frozen.

Declan yelled at Hoops to snap her back, "Get on the ground! On your
face!" Her body initially resisted the movement, but slowly she took up the
prone position as requested.

"Look away from me and close your eyes!"

"P-p-p-p-lease don't shoot me. I have children. I don't want to die. Take
the money! I didn't see your face." Hoops pleaded to Declan in a whispered
voice.

Declan continued to play his role, "Bitch, you don't move, you don't get
shot!" He quickly bent down and grabbed the gun from the worn leather
pistol belt wrapped around Casper's urine-soaked waist. He tossed it on the
front seat of the armored truck. Hoops followed his orders and continued
to lay motionless on the ground.

"Start counting to 100!" Declan spoke these words through clenched
teeth. Hoops began the slow rhythmic count as he released the holster's
retention safety and tugged her sidearm free from her hip. Declan pitched
it in the truck and slammed the door. He created a barrier between the
guards and their weapons. He didn't want them to try some act of heroism.
Although he had already surmised that would be unlikely.

"9. 10. 11..." Hoops droned on. Her cadence slow and flat. Declan had
already started moving back toward his car. Both containers swung
awkwardly from their hinged handles. The unbalanced weight caused

Declan to strain as he attempted to stabilize. He was glad that he had trained with the water jugs. Carrying the sloshing water in training paid off now.

5:12 p.m.

Declan got in the car and pulled out of the parking lot. He intentionally lifted the ski mask up, exposing his darkened skin. He threw the containers on the floorboard of the back seat and covered them with a blanket. The Toyota sped out onto the road, heading north into Hartford.

Khaled sat on the bench of the bus stop across the street from the Clover Leaf Bank, watching as the red car pulled into the lot. He recognized this car, but not the man sitting in the driver's seat. It was not the "Golden Man." It was not Enright.

Golden Man. The thought of her brought him back to Alnaeim, and for a brief moment, he could hear Sonia's voice resonating in his ears. It never seemed to lose its hold over him. A whirlwind of memories, like fireflies trapped in a jar. This disorientation only lasted for a moment before he saw what was taking place across the street in the bank's parking lot.

He pocketed his notepad and stared in disbelief at what he was seeing. The dark-skinned man in Enright's car had parked and waited in the vehicle. An armored truck rounded the building and stopped in front of the ATM. The dark-skinned man exited the red car and moved across the parking lot. His movements were quick and purposeful as he crossed the asphalt toward the two uniformed truck personnel.

With the precision of a trained soldier, the dark-skinned man was able to neutralize the male guard and render the female useless in a matter of seconds. The gunshot was loud, but Khaled did not see the red mist he'd become so accustomed to after a headshot. But the male guard collapsed to the ground. Khaled recognized the absolute skill to take on two armed guards during daylight hours. He was now convinced that this man was in fact Enright. *The Golden Man* had gone to great effort to conceal his identity, but Khaled had long studied this man and now saw clearly through his deception.

An interesting turn of events. The Golden Man had sat on this very bench two weeks ago while Khaled was doing his own reconnaissance. *What were the chances that two men acquainted in the desert of Iraq eight years ago would run into each other in a small town in Connecticut?* Khaled laughed to himself. He knew that chance had nothing to do with it.

6

"Nick, come in here when you get a chance," Jake Nelson called out from his corner office.

Nick stood with his desk phone pressed against his ear and gave a silent thumb's up, acknowledging his boss's request before returning to his conversation. He sat back down in his chair and pulled the phone's receiver close so that others around could not hear the exchange taking place.

"No Mom, Patrick is not playing hide and seek. He's not home." Nick struggled to mask his frustration as he spoke.

The voice on the other end was silent for a moment and then a small laugh broke the tension. "I know that sweetie, I was just testing you," his mother said in a sheepish tone.

"I have to go now, Mom. Push the red button on the controller." Nick heard the television come to life in the background. His mother hung up without saying another word.

Nick had sadly become accustomed to this routine. The genesis rooted in his brother's death a few years earlier. Patrick had survived some intense combat while overseas, but the residual impact had greatly affected him. Nick had also lived through similar experiences as a U.S. Army Ranger. The chest full of medals bore testament to this. Nick left the military psychologically intact, but Patrick was forever changed. Everybody processed traumatic events differently.

Pat slipped into a deep depression that drained the light from his boyish grin. He made the decision to end his life without much warning. At the time, it had caught the family completely off guard, but in retrospect, the signs were all there. Hindsight gave clarity to those red flags, bringing with it the burden of failure that only an older brother can know. Nick was supposed to look out for his younger sibling. To shield and protect him. Time had not lessened that guilt, and it was his alone to shoulder.

As his mother's mental health began to deteriorate, she began to ask for Patrick with more frequency. She spoke as if she had just seen him. Initially, Nick tried to explain to his mother that Patrick was dead. That had disastrous results and had sent her into an inconsolable screaming fit. Nick had started placating his mother, telling her simple things like "Pat went out for milk" or "He's over at a friend's house." As time passed Nick had learned to listen carefully to his mother's comments because they would tell him what age Patrick was, in her mind. Nick would ensure that his responses were appropriate to that time.

It was a tedious task, and it drained Nicholas more than he cared to admit. The only solace he took was that his mother was spending time with Patrick, even if it was only an illusion. He knew that this was not an optimal plan for handling his mother's declining mental health, but it was a band-aid until a more permanent solution prevailed.

"What's up boss?" Nick said as he walked into Nelson's office. Nelson prided himself on being an approachable guy. And he was, for the most part, although he and Nick had butted heads on more than one occasion. Their relationship remained professional but guarded.

"The locals are working an armored truck robbery that occurred yesterday around 5 p.m." Nelson said this in the excited tone that supervisors got when assigning a new case. Nicholas knew that this excitement quickly died down as people higher in the food chain found something else to focus on. Law enforcement supervisors were the ficklest of creatures and Nick had learned patience in dealing with them.

"Okay, so what do you have so far?" Nick felt like this kind of information should not need to be solicited. Nelson enjoyed knowing more than others even if it was only short lived.

"A shot was fired and one of the guards was injured. I don't have all the details yet, but the lieutenant that I spoke with said they have good video footage from multiple angles. It should be pretty simple," Nelson said. He handed Nicholas a sheet of paper covered with his chicken scratch notes, containing the address and some contact numbers for the local police department in Wethersfield.

"I'm going to grab Martinez to assist." Nicholas found that it was always better to tell a supervisor what you were doing rather than ask permission.

Nelson nodded. Nick went over to the cubicle of Isabella Martinez. He leaned against the poorly constructed partition and looked down at Izzy who was busy scrolling through some bad guy's Facebook profile. She looked up and smiled. "What steaming bag of shit did El Jefe give you?" Nick loved how she always cut to the chase.

"Armored car job. It may be fun. Do you want to come play?" Nick trusted very few people, but Izzy had made the short list of those he did. He knew she would always have his back. She had proved that early on.

Isabella was attractive. Her shoulder length black hair fell straight and framed the delicate features of her face. She could have been a model, but she was called to law enforcement, following in the legendary footsteps of her father. Nicholas saw her as a good cop and nothing more. It was rare in this profession that a female could transcend gender, but she had done it and was considered one of the guys. Albeit a better-looking version.

"Anything for you." She mockingly gave an exaggerated wink. "To be honest, I need to get the hell out of this office for a bit. I feel like I'm losing my mind staring at this damn computer."

Movies made it seem like FBI agents were always out on some crime scene wearing their blue windbreakers with bright yellow lettering. That couldn't be further from the truth. Most of the grunt work took place in the sterile environment of an office cubicle. The slow grind.

"Coffee?" Nick never showed up to a scene without a cup in his hand. It was probably his most important investigative tool, aside from his mind. He was considered by most to be a gifted agent whose skill was only matched by his tenacity.

"Do you really need to ask?" Izzy said. She grabbed her notepad and stood.

Nick stopped at his cubicle and removed the gun from his desk drawer. He hated wearing it while seated in the office. It always felt odd to type all day with a gun strapped to his hip. There were periods of time that he had gone several weeks without taking it out at all.

Izzy drove so that Nick could make the call to the local PD. He dialed the number on the sheet of paper that Nelson had given him. The note said, Point of Contact: Lieutenant Patterson - Wethersfield Police Department.

" Lieutenant we're on our way and should be there in the next thirty to forty-five minutes. It's not our intention to step on any toes. I was just assigned the case this morning and I'm behind the power curve. I'm going to piggyback off anything your patrol or detectives have done up to now. I promise that I'm transparent and will work with your people, keeping them in the loop throughout."

"We are looking forward to your assistance on this one. I'll meet you in the lobby and bring you to our detective bureau where we can get you up to speed," Patterson said in a welcoming manner.

Nick noted that Patterson gave off a professional demeanor during the brief conversation. He'd learned that agents were typically considered outsiders. Every local agency reacted differently to the FBI's presence. This would be the first time that he had any experience with the Wethersfield guys, but his initial impression was that they were receptive to the federal assistance.

Coffee in hand, Izzy and Nick walked into the main lobby of the Wethersfield Police Department. For a small PD, the facility was well designed. Some decent money had been dumped into its construction, an indication of a good tax base and supportive population.

Patterson entered the lobby from a secured door and approached the agents with a broad smile. His friendly face matched the personality conveyed over the telephone. He shook their hands and exchanged pleas-antries.

Patterson took them in through the secure door, up to the second floor of the building and into the detective bureau. The office space contained six cubicles of modest design. Not much different from the one that Nick and Izzy used. The Lieutenant approached a heavyset male seated in his swivel chair.

"Darryl, this is Agent Lawrence and Agent Martinez," Patterson said, sweeping his arm back in the direction of the guests.

Darryl Reynolds stood. He was a short stocky man. A light glisten of sweat shone on his brow just beneath his unkempt, matted hair. He wiped the palms of his thick hands against his khaki pants before he shook with both agents. "Welcome to the shitshow."

Nicholas could see the stress lining Darryl's face and felt it in his moist handshake. "I'm Nick and this is Isabella."

"Call me Izzy," her voice gently interjected. Rank and titles got in the way of police work. It had its place in the military, but in policing it was more of a hindrance than a benefit to the investigative process.

"I'm not sure what you've been told so far, but the robbery was a success as far as bank jobs go. Still waiting for the bank's official loss. They gave me an initial estimate and as it stands now they're looking at $60,000 plus on the hit," Darryl said. The tension present in his voice exposed the likelihood that he had not handled a robbery of this magnitude before.

"Jesus. That's a big number," Patterson interrupted, pausing only for a second before he made his exit. He added, "I'm going to leave you guys to it. Let me know if you need anything." He said this and then demonstrated the classic technique of an administrator who realized the potential workload. He left it to the worker bees.

"My boss said that you had some good video of the perp?" Nick asked.

"Yes. Looks like our doer is a banger. The guy wasn't thinking. He didn't pull the mask over his face until he was only a few feet from the guards. The cameras picked up his face. The car he used was also visible on camera. It shouldn't be too challenging to find this guy." Darryl spoke, looking for the validation of his assessment from the FBI agents.

"Izzy is going to be reviewing the video footage. She is our resident techie. Do you have the recordings or is it still on the bank's server?" Nick's brain was on autopilot, rapidly moving through his mental checklist.

"I've got a digital copy of all the cameras from that day. I can give you a quick tutorial on how to use the program so that you can manipulate the settings and replay functions," Darryl said, showing no resistance to working with Izzy. A sign of a professional investigator. He was able to put the case before pride and was on board with the Bureau support. Things always moved quicker when inter-agency friction was minimized.

"Sounds good. Show me what you got," Izzy chimed in.

"I am going to need the list of witnesses. Have you conducted a thorough interview of the guards?" Nick asked in a non-confrontational tone.

"The officers on scene took a statement from them. I can get you copies. They were not brought in for questioning, if that's what you're getting at. It was pretty much their version of the circumstance. No real interrogation was done." Darryl said this with a hint of defensiveness in his voice. His response indicated that he had already ruled out the guards' potential involvement.

"I'm going to need to bring them in for a formal interview." Nick shot a quick glance over at Izzy. She knew exactly what he was getting at. The guards needed to be interrogated to determine if they had any knowledge of the crime. An interview like that could not be done on the side of the road, amid the chaos of a crime scene.

Darryl began banging away on the keyboard with his thick stubby fingers. The printer behind Nick came alive, spitting out several pages.

"That's the initial case report that includes the witness information. Pretty much everything we've done up to this point." Darryl seemed nervous. Nick understood why. Nobody liked to have their work judged by someone else. Especially the FBI.

Nick picked up the stack of papers, still warm from the printer, and began moving toward the hallway. He nodded at Izzy. She smiled back. It was her way of giving him the green light to go.

"Thanks, Darryl. Izzy has my number if you need to reach me. I'm going to head out for a bit. Are you guys good?" This last question was said aloud but was directed at Izzy. She winked in response.

Nicholas Lawrence stood outside of the front doors of the police department. He looked down at the GPS on his phone and punched the address of the bank into his maps app. He stared down at the phone in disbelief. He assumed it was an error. Nick looked up. He squinted his eyes against the mid-morning sun and realized that he could see the façade of the bank on the opposite side of the street, about an eighth of a mile down the road. *This guy had some serious balls to pull off a robbery this close to a police department.*

Nick walked past his government vehicle and continued on foot in the direction of the bank. Time to find out if this robbery was as open and shut as Darryl thought.

7

Declan sat on the faded blue plastic Adirondack chair in his fenced-in backyard and slowly sipped a glass of wine. His girls danced around him in a manner that resembled a tribal ritual. *His tribe.* He put a smile on his face, but his mind was still reeling from the robbery. One day had passed since his crossover into the criminal world. But to Declan, it felt like an eternity. That invisible line of right and wrong disintegrated.

He wondered what his children would think of him if they ever learned what he had done. Would they understand and see that it was all for them? He hoped the time would never come where he had to find out.

There was no going back. Only forward. *The Only Easy Day Was Yesterday.* The words hung from a weathered sign in the courtyard where his SEAL physical training took place, affectionately known as The Grinder. The poured concrete surface left scars on its users. Both physically and mentally. That slogan had been drilled into his brain. That ethos etched into the core of his makeup.

He replayed the op's execution in his mind. An after-action review. This had been done after every operation and live-fire drill. Critical assessment of the good and the bad was a necessity. In the Teams, errors made were drilled until corrected. The body never forgot those lessons. Declan had learned long ago that there was no such thing as perfect. *Find the flaw. Train the mistake. Learn the lesson.*

He was lost in thought. The noise from his children was distant. He melded into the formed plastic of the cheap lawn chair.

"Daddy, look at me! I'm a cheetah," Abigail, his seven-year-old, chanted as she circled him on all fours. Her words broke his trance. Abby's hands slapped the ground and her feet sprung her forward, like the hunter-cat she now portrayed. Declan smiled. He shouldered an imaginary hunting rifle.

"You better run. Wild Jack, the great and fearless hunter, is on the prowl!" Declan said in a horribly overacted Australian accent. He lurched forward and slowly began to stalk his prey.

Abigail giggled with delight, running in the direction of her weather-beaten playscape. She spun and called to her five-year-old sister, Ripley. "Run! The hunter is coming!"

The two girls screamed and darted around the yard in mock attempts to dodge the hunter's aim. This game had been played out many times before and Declan knew his role. In the world of daddy-daughter theater, he would've received an Oscar.

He put aside his mission review. He chose to embrace this moment with his daughters. He knew there would be time later to assess the success of his first armed robbery.

Declan continued his backyard theatrics with his oldest two girls. He caught a glimpse of Laney. She sat on the swing with her feet dangling. The light breeze blew her long curls and gently rocked her. He couldn't tell if she registered the things happening around her, but he held out hope that she was aware, even though she did not join in the play. Declan had comforted himself by believing that she derived some joy from being around it.

Laney had not yet spoken a single word. To Declan and Val, her silence was louder than any screaming the other two girls could muster. And it took its toll on all of them in different ways.

. . .

Later that evening, after the girls were bathed and stories had been read, Declan retreated to the living room to resume the process of evaluating his op and finding his mistakes. Every operation had them. He needed to know if his were big enough for anyone else to notice.

He wrote nothing down. The details were tucked in his memory. He inhaled deeply as he began the process.

The trick to any successful review was a true-to-fact, pull-no-punch kind of honesty. Egos and false bravado got in the way of many operators' ability to improve. Declan had shed those roadblocks, leaving himself humbled to the premise that *even the best could be better.*

After considerable contemplation, Declan had dissected the details of the armored truck operation. He had found three mistakes. The first occurred when he looped the block before entering the lot. That could have drawn suspicion, but after careful consideration, he felt this mistake was likely to have a minimal impact.

Mistake number two. He threw the guards' weapons in the truck. His goal was to eliminate any reason to seriously injure the guards. He had worried that if he didn't secure the guns then one of them might try some type of stupid hero crap as he was walking away. Bullet holes in his car would make for some tough explaining later. Securing them in the truck came to him on the fly, but with the driver's door open it seemed like a smart move. Plus, he had shut the door and knew that would have slowed down any attempt to follow. Kill two birds with one stone.

He had thought it was a good idea, but looking back on it there was a downside. His "character" was supposed to be a street thug. *What gang banger would pick up two guns and not take them?*

He wondered if the investigator would catch this anomaly when the video was reviewed. Declan decided that this mistake was not likely to connect him to the crime. The cops might even think the robber was a "good dude" because he showed restraint by not killing the guards or taking their guns.

The third error in his operation came when Declan drove into Hartford. He had not gone far, driving only a quarter mile before he looped back to Wethersfield on a back road. He had pulled under a bridge. Selected because he'd found no visible surveillance camera system. The residential section did not begin their line of closely built houses until further down the road. Declan had timed it during his rehearsals and that it took twenty-seven seconds to park, exit and remove the fake license plates and decoy bumper stickers. In real time, it turned out to be less than twenty-one.

After completing the quick task of removing the exterior camouflage from the Toyota he got back in the car. He removed the gray hooded sweatshirt and began the process of wiping off the bronzer. Declan used his wife's make-up remover which returned his face, neck, and wrists to their regular complexion. The adhesive tattoos on his neck and wrist also came off with relative ease. During this brief time, a car drove by as he was cleaning off his neck. The driver, an older female with wire-rimmed glasses, looked at him a split second longer than he was comfortable with. Maybe she had just been lost in thought. Or worse, she might be the neighborhood busy-body, noting anything suspicious. Part of a citizen watch group. *What did she see? A man cleaning his face. Would that draw her interest?* The news would release a vehicle and suspect description, but he was unsure whether this woman would be able to put the two together. These unanswered questions left lots of potential for increased risk.

Three mistakes. Declan closed his eyes and replayed the op again. *Did he miss anything else?*

8

"Okay. What's the damage?" Nick asked with the bored resignation of someone who had seen how petty the yield on most of these robberies typically turned out to be, unlike the movie's portrayal.

"The total loss was $87,140. The reload canister was full at $60,000 and the rest came from the residual cash left in the machine's container." Janet, the bank manager, said this with a subtle panic in her voice. This reaction was indicative that this was probably her first robbery and although trained in proper protocol, she lacked the experience to be comfortable in her role under the circumstances.

"That's a bigger haul than most. I'll need to set up times to meet with you and every one of your employees. That means all the bank employees, to include even ones that were not working on that day. I will need a list of workers that have been fired, transferred, or voluntarily resigned within the last year." Nicholas knew what he needed, cutting right to the chase. His best bet was to get the manager working for him and to keep her busy enough so that she did not become overly nosy in his investigation.

"I can do that. I will have it for you within the hour. Is there anything else you need right now?" Janet asked, seeming eager to help. Nick realized that this desire to assist the investigation stemmed from a sense of guilt. The pressure from senior bank managers asking questions of Janet's protocols would feel like an accusation into a lack of foresight on her part. That somehow, she had left the bank unprepared for the robbery. This blame game was normal but completely misguided.

"I'm good for right now. I will let you know if something comes to mind. I'm going to walk the bank's exterior and take some pictures. I shouldn't be too much of an interruption to your daily routine here at the bank," Nick said, knowing that it was important to let people know what you were doing on a scene. It lowered anxiety.

Nick stepped out of the bank's sterile atmosphere into the brisk air. For as much as he missed his life in Texas, he definitely loved fall in New England. It was actually one of the only times that his coworkers didn't have to listen to him complain about Connecticut.

He moved about the parking lot stepping to different corners, looking at the bank from various angles. He always tried getting an idea of the potential witness's points of view. Nick also needed to stand in the suspect's exact spot to see things from his perspective. That was the challenge with law enforcement. Too much time spent thinking like a criminal and that line between right and wrong could become skewed. Nick knew the pitfalls but also understood its value as a necessary investigative tool.

Nicholas Lawrence stood in the spot where the suspect had parked his vehicle. He looked out toward the ATM. *This guy had a plan and this spot had a specific purpose. What was it?* Nick noted that the parking space created the most direct approach to the armored car. A key factor in closing the distance to the guards quickly. It also provided an excellent angle to exit the parking lot during the getaway. *This guy was smart.*

While Nick stood in the parking space used by the robber, he heard the chirp of a police siren, directing his attention back to the headquarters located a quarter mile down the road. *This guy was really smart.* From his current vantage point, Nick saw that he had a visual of the police station. The robber would have been able to simultaneously monitor both the armored truck and the police response. He was impressed but equally concerned. Either this bad guy had some amazing luck, or it was meticulously planned. Nick didn't believe in luck. Especially because recent life events had left him feeling as though all of his had run out.

"Anything?" Nick had called Izzy, looking for an update.

"It's like watching a Jon Woo movie. This guy moves like a ninja." Izzy sounded impressed. Nick aware that this was not easily accomplished.

"You sound starstruck Izzy. I've never heard you so giddy," Nick said, chiding her.

"Well, I haven't seen someone move like this except in the movies. At first, I thought something was wrong with the replay function. Like it was stuck on fast forward. When I realized that it was set to the normal play speed I was shocked," Izzy said, trying to conceal the level of her enthusiasm.

"When we catch him, I will get him to autograph his booking photo for you. Hell, maybe I can set up a conjugal visit." Nick shook his head as he spoke, realizing that he sounded like a jealous boyfriend.

"Beyond his amazing superhero-like moves, was there anything else that stood out to you?" Nick's mind was back on task.

"It took me a few times to catch it, but the bad guy, who I have nick-named Flash." Izzy paused. She giggled like a school girl and then continued, "I noticed that he pulled something from his left pocket as he was pulling the gun. Flash fired the gun next to the guard's head. He managed to strike him on the opposite side of his head with the object while the gun went off. This blow to the temple seems to be what dropped the guard."

"The initial police report stated that the gun went off when the suspect had pistol-whipped the guard. So, I'm assuming that the video was not reviewed by police at the time the report was written?" Nick asked, seeking clarification.

"That's what I have been trying to tell you. They had reviewed the video. Flash moved so damn quickly that even I didn't catch his left hand's movement. Not until I had slowed the footage down and watched it several times." Izzy was starting to show a trace of excitement again.

"Good stuff Izzy. I will be back in a bit. I've got the bank manager gathering up the usual employee files. Any luck in getting a good image of the license plate?"

"Actually yes. It's a New Jersey plate and I ran it through the system. Comes back to a rental company out of Middletown. Same make and model. Looks like Flash screwed up. I already have a call into the business to get the renter's information. I'll let you know when I hear back," Izzy said, her confidence evident, developed over her many years of investigations.

"Keep me posted."

Nick clicked the phone off and began photographing the scene using his small Fujifilm X100F. He knew that the Bureau would send their crime scene techs out if Nick requested, but at this stage of the investigation, he did not feel this was needed.

Nick knew that initial crime scene photos had been taken. It was noted in the police report that Darryl had given him. He was sure that the photos would be adequate by investigative standards, but he was equally sure that these images would be relatively useless to his investigation. Nick had found it extremely important to take pictures or video from the perspective of the suspect. Nick liked having his own photos to support whatever theory he developed. He found it always better to do it himself. And this is what he did.

Nick began taking the series of photographs from the exit point of the suspect's car. He took three photos from that spot. The overlap of the pictures would give him a 180-degree visual range. Nick progressed forward, snapping three more pictures every four steps that he took. He continued this methodical process until he stood at the point where the two guards were subdued. Then Nick repeated the process as he walked back toward the suspect's parking space.

Nick was good at what he did, yielding arrests in cases deemed by other investigators to be unsolvable. Hopefully this time it would be good enough, because after his conversation with Izzy he got a feeling that he was dealing with a pro. Even pros made mistakes. It was his job to find and exploit them.

9

So, the FBI has come to Wethersfield? They would have come in a few days anyway, Khaled thought, as he sat on the bus bench across from the Clover Leaf Bank. A newspaper folded on his lap and coffee in hand. He watched the agent inside the bank as he took a sip of the hot liquid. American coffee was weak compared to what his taste buds were accustomed to, but he made do. Diluted coffee was a minor price to pay for this opportunity.

Khaled observed as the agent canvassed the parking lot. He was methodical. His movements were slow and deliberate. He appeared to be very perceptive. Khaled continued to watch as the FBI agent began taking pictures. The agent caught Khaled off guard. He pointed the camera out toward the street, taking photographs in arcing fashion. Khaled was delayed in his reaction. The telephoto lens swung in his direction. He tried to raise the newspaper to shield himself from the camera. In the process he spilled the hot coffee on his lap, causing him to jump up and yelp in pain. What American coffee lacked in taste it made up for in temperature.

Khaled attempted to regain his composure. He looked down at his pants. His face no longer exposed. He held out hope that he had not drawn the agent's attention. Or worse, been photographed. He remained head down and patted at the wet coffee with the newspaper in a futile effort to blot the stain.

After he'd taken a reasonable amount of time to attend to his spill he looked up. He caught the agent as his gaze shifted back to the bank. He had been looking in his direction. *Did he see me?* Khaled could not answer that question and that bothered him greatly. Plaguing him further was the thought that this agent may have photographed him sitting across the street from the bank. It would mean nothing to them now, but in three days it would matter. He contemplated trying to get the camera from the agent, but Khaled quickly dismissed the thought. It was not worth the possible exposure. Too risky.

The phone in his pocket began to vibrate. Only a select few had his number. Khaled answered it on the second ring.

"Hello, my friend. How are you?" Khaled spoke in a manner that would sound genuine to anyone eavesdropping in the area. He also chose to speak English during these conversations because it lessened suspicion in the post-9/11 world.

"Status?" The voice on the other end was cold and direct.

"I can pick you up. No problem. Yes, of course, Monday will work for me. How does 3:15 sound?" Khaled sounded elated. And part of him was truly excited. His long journey finally had brought him to this point.

The cold voice said nothing. Khaled heard the click, indicating that the phone call was over.

The bus arrived. It slowed to a stop a few feet beyond where he stood. Khaled smelled the all-to-familiar odor of diesel fuel as the mechanical hiss of the hydraulics lowered the bus and the doors swung open. He entered and walked to the rear. He took his seat as it lurched forward. Northbound into Hartford.

J's Pizza was a take-out and delivery-only style restaurant. It sat near the corner of Russ and Lawrence Street in an area of Hartford known as Frog Hollow. It was a predominantly Hispanic section of the capital city. Most of its residents hailed directly from Puerto Rico. Khaled's "friends" had bought the establishment several years ago and had selected this neighborhood because they could blend in. Their olive skin and dark hair gave them the appearance of possibly being of Hispanic descent and working in Frog Hollow had almost guaranteed that people would assume it. Khaled's "friends" kept to themselves and spoke very little to the few customers that entered their store.

The pizza was nothing more than a generic frozen brand. The kitchen area was not visible to customers. It consisted of two very cheap ovens. The sign on the door read: "Cash Only." This simple marketing scheme kept away most customers in this age of debit and credit cards. Nobody carried paper money anymore.

It didn't matter what the store sold in pizza. It always generated roughly $45,000 annually. That number, by design, was $14,000 less than the national average. Khaled's "friends" had these businesses all over the United States and the money rarely came from customers. Khaled did not get too involved in the financial matters of his benefactors. He knew that it was better not to ask questions.

He entered J's. The chime of the door opening alerted anyone in the back of his arrival. He walked past the counter and through the heavy red sheet that hung nailed to the doorframe. This makeshift door covered the kitchen area from view.

There was a back room adjacent to the freezer. Khaled knocked. He heard the creak of a chair and could see the shadow cast under the door as he was examined through the peephole. Several locks slid out of their secured position, an indication that his identity had been verified. The door opened. Silence enveloped the hushed conversations that were taking place in the room prior to his arrival.

The air was heavy with cigarette smoke. It looked as if low hanging storm clouds had settled into the small poorly lit room. Two men sat at the table. Both nodded weakly to Khaled as he entered. The man who had opened the door returned to his seat without saying a word. Khaled sat. This was a serious time and the four men at this table all knew what lay ahead.

"Is everything ready?" Khaled asked in a confident manner.

"It is. We received the items made by the Technician. I believe that he still has eight of his ten fingers," the heavier of the men said with a slight chuckle in his voice. The joke was a feeble attempt. And further wasted on Khaled because he knew that the fat man had never actually met the Technician. Khaled was the only one to have ever had a face-to-face encounter.

Khaled did not acknowledge the fat man's joke and continued with the business at hand. "I will need the money and car now. As soon as this is done I will be leaving for my next location." Khaled had not always displayed this level of confidence, but in the years since Sonia's death, he had created a new persona. He had earned a mythical status among the Muqawama. He had become known as the Dust Devil.

"Where will you go?" Asked the heavyset man.

"I thought that it was explained to you. I only speak to the One. You are but a small part of my support network. You are a pawn. A piece to be used and discarded. That is all." Khaled's eyes hardened as he spoke. All the men in the room suddenly looked uneasy. It was not wise to upset the Dust Devil. Everyone in their circle was aware of the consequences.

"Your car is out back. The Technician's package, as well as the additional items that you requested, are in the trunk's spare tire compartment area. The money is set under the rear passenger seat in a green backpack. I did not count it. I was told that you would know how much?" The fat man's fear was evident. He swallowed hard after he spoke. A bead of sweat formed above his thick eyebrows. Khaled took pride in noting this.

Without another word, Khaled stood. He eyed each man in the room. The eye contact held long enough to convey the unspoken message. The fat man slid the car keys across the table. "Good luck," he said. The fat man breathed a barely perceptible sigh of relief as Khaled picked up the keys and made for the door.

Luck has nothing to do with it, Khaled thought to himself as he exited the building.

He sat in the older model blue Honda Accord and took a moment to acclimate to the car. This vehicle was selected for its commonality and therefore it would be unrecognizable. He drove off into the night. Khaled, the Dust Devil, had much to do before Monday came.

10

Declan finished counting the cash in the partially finished basement of his small house. He used the laundry area so that the children didn't see. No need to have the unwanted conversation of trying to explain a big pile of money to his little ones. It took almost an hour to count by hand.

The partially carpeted floor of the laundry room was covered with stacks of money. Each stack was labeled with a sticky note denoting the different sums. He placed the money into three vacuum bags. Declan used his wife's food sealer to remove the pockets of air. A Sharpie marker was used to label the plastic exterior with the amount of cash contained inside each one.

Done. He sat on the floor and stared at the total. Relieved, but sickened at the same time. He was conflicted but took solace in the fact that no one was killed in the process.

Val was sitting on the floor of the living room playing a sensory activity game with Laney. His littlest organized the colored shapes into patterns. Declan stood quietly and watched the two. It gave him peace to take in moments like these. It reminded him of why he had taken such a huge risk with the armored truck.

He decided not to interrupt. Instead, he walked outside to the fenced-in backyard of his house and surveyed his property. He looked at the homemade pirate flag atop the playscape. *I'm a modern-day pirate,* Declan thought. And with that, an idea popped into his head.

Declan grabbed a shovel from the shed and proceeded to dig in his wife's flower bed. He uprooted her flowers and created a space, roughly four square feet. The dirt was removed and set aside. The hole was hollowed out one foot deep. Declan placed the sealed packages of money into his makeshift safe. $60,000 dollars in twenty-dollar bills did not look as grand when sealed in plastic. He kept the remaining $27,000 accessible in the house. He returned the displaced dirt and scattered the leftover earth along the fence line. He stood back, evaluating the quality of his work. *Buried treasure. The sign of a true pirate.*

He added a finishing touch by giving the entire flower bed a light watering. *A good spot.* During his time in the Narcotics Enforcement Team, Declan never dug up a yard on a search warrant. The money would be safe. *Maybe I should mark it with a big X?* He laughed at the thought, as he stood dirt covered and with shovel in hand.

The remaining cash was needed for some immediate finances. He had to get his mortgage current to stave off the foreclosure. Declan's t-shirt, purchased at Goodwill, was stamped with a construction emblem. He wiped some more dirt and dust on the shirt, the sweat from the dig adding to the effect. He looked the part of a day laborer. Declan had always been gifted at blending in. Hook, one of his spec ops buddies, had jokingly called him the Chameleon because of this ability.

Declan took enough cash for the four months of missed mortgage payments plus penalties, totaling $6,140. He held the money in his hand for a moment before putting it into a manila envelope. He scribbled his first initial and last name on the front, adding some mathematical calculations accompanied by dates and amounts, the calculations totaling $7,000. Declan figured that this would be typical of under-the-table work and should not draw suspicion from anyone at the bank during his transaction.

Declan drove his wife's minivan to a bank on the other side of town. He decided that it was a good idea to let his Corolla sit for a few days before taking it out in public. Declan arrived at the bank and purchased a money order listing his mortgage company as the payee. He called his lender as he walked out of the bank, telling them that the check was on its way for the full amount of missed payments. The customer service representative was very cheerful as if the money was going straight to her pocket. She told Declan that the payment promise had been noted on his account and that when the money was received the account would be out of delinquency.

He hung up the phone and leaned against the side of the dark blue minivan. A weight lifted from his shoulders and for the first time in many months, he felt like things were going to be okay.

11

Nick leaned over Izzy's shoulder in Darryl's cramped cubicle. They'd been watching and re-watching the surveillance footage. The video camera that provided the best overall angle for capturing the incident in its entirety was positioned on a light pole between the bank and the neighboring gas station. It looked down into the parking lot at a forty-five-degree angle. The camera did not have much in the way of a zoom, but the quality was clearer than most.

The first time Nick watched the robbery in the normal playback mode, he too was amazed at the speed that the suspect had moved. Izzy was right to nickname him Flash. Beyond the speed was Flash's precision. Slowing the replay mode enabled Nick to see that Flash had a total economy of movement, expending no unnecessary energy in the attack.

Nick had been considered a good operator during his time as a Ranger, but he knew that he had nothing on the skill set of Flash. He was mesmerized watching him move on the computer screen in front of him. He'd seen skills like this before in some of the Delta guys that he crossed paths with overseas, but the thing that stood out most to Nick was that Flash did not shoot the two armed guards. He had incapacitated and disarmed them in a matter of seconds without inflicting any major injuries on the pair. Nick was looking at someone who was operating at a completely different level of skill than anyone he had encountered before.

Nick had Izzy pull up the ATM camera footage. The angle cut out Flash's entrance and exit from the bank's parking lot but picked him up when he was about six feet from the guards.

Nick watched the monitor intently as Flash raised the gun, causing the sleeve of his shirt to pull back marginally. Izzy noted the black markings of what appeared to be a tattoo. She had already enhanced and enlarged the image. It was printed and rested atop of a stack of papers strewn across Darryl's desk. The image was clearly identifiable as a scorpion.

"Can you run that through our tattoo database? Maybe we will get lucky and it will be some local gang thing." Nick said this, knowing that Izzy had already done it. She was good like that.

"I sent it over to Greg at Digital an hour ago. He's working it and will let me know if something pops," Izzy said, referring to Greg Cranmore, of the Digital Forensics Unit. Izzy dabbled in the tech world and would be considered a whiz by a layperson's standard, but Greg was a master of that domain. Both Nick and Izzy had utilized the benefit of his expertise in the past with great success.

"I assume that the other tattoo on his neck has also been sent over?"

"Of course. You know how I work," Izzy said with a grin.

"Can you figure out what type of gun that is? It's hard to make it out, but it looks like a small caliber revolver," Nick said as he squinted at the paused image of the gun.

"Wait a minute!" Izzy said as she brought the image on the screen back several frames, looking for something specific.

"Look at that!" Izzy exclaimed, pushing her chair back to allow Nick to move closer to the monitor.

"Look at what?" Nick hated missing something, but he didn't notice anything of value on the flickering screen before him.

"Look at the end of the barrel. Do you notice anything out of the ordinary?" She was teetering on the border of giddy.

"Damn. How'd I miss that before?" Nick mumbled, massaging his temples as he noticed the capped muzzle of the gun. Nick now realizing that it wasn't actually a gun. It was most likely some type of starter pistol.

"The gunshot the guards heard was actually a blank. This guy went up against two armed guards with an inert weapon and seconds later walked away with eighty-seven thousand dollars in cash. Who are we dealing with Nick?"

"I have no idea, but whoever the Flash is, he's got some serious training in his background," Nick's tone betraying his awe of the man on the video. "Let's eat. I need to clear my head for a minute and get some fresh perspective."

The two told Darryl that they would be back later before setting off down the Silas Deane Highway in search of some good food. Nick had lost track of time and darkness had set in. Lunch would now be dinner. They saw the neon sign of a Mexican restaurant and pulled in, just as Nick's phone began to ring.

"The police just left, and Patrick is in his room." Nick's mother said with the frustrated anger of a parent fresh from disciplining a child.

"What did he do this time?" Nick placated, trying to figure out which time period he was dealing with.

"He crashed the car into a fire hydrant and walked away! Who does that?" She responded. Nick could hear the exasperation in her voice as if this was really happening.

"I will be home soon. Did you find the controller?" Nick said, hearing the familiar sound of the television kicking on in the background. Nick hung up, giving a discontented sigh. Izzy was the only person that he had felt comfortable enough with to share this piece of his life. She smiled in a way that softened the awkwardness, making him feel as though this conversation was normal.

Nick picked up his phone, making an important follow-up call.

"Hi Margaret, it's Nick. Can you stop over? I got stuck on a case tonight that will keep me tied up for a couple more hours." Nick had few resources to assist him and they were rapidly depleting as his mom's health status declined. Nick's next-door neighbor, a retired librarian, had come to relish visiting with Nick's mother. Over the years, the two routinely enjoyed a glass of wine in the evening as they discussed the ups and downs of life. The visits were more frequent before his mother's mental health had taken a more serious downturn. Now, Margaret usually only came over on Nick's request, but even that was becoming harder, with more excuses than acceptances.

"Sure, Nick. I can do it tonight. I will stay until she's asleep, but I think it's getting to be the time for you to get some professional help." Margaret said this with no hint of condescension, but with genuine compassion. "Sorry, I don't mean to preach, but you work a lot and it might be better for her."

"Thank you, Margaret. You're a saint." Nick clicked off, suddenly more tired than he'd been a few minutes ago.

"Food will help. Maybe a margarita or two couldn't hurt either." Izzy laughed, bringing Nick out of his momentary slump. The two made their way into the crowded restaurant, taking up a table in the bar area closest to the back wall covered in artwork depicting symbolic images of Mexico. The noise of the neighboring patrons seemed to drown out the disarray in his head that had surfaced from his mother's recent phone call. Nick focused his attention back to the task at hand. *Who was Flash?*

12

Nick had arranged for both of the armored truck guards to come into the office for an interview. Vincenzo Mangano was scheduled to go first, and he had arrived on time, entering the lobby of the FBI's New Haven Field Office at 9:55 a.m.

The interview room, or "box" as investigators commonly referred to it, was small and only contained one table with two uncomfortable plastic office chairs. The walls were covered with a stippled polypropylene beadboard to absorb sound, eliminating both internal and external intrusive noise.

Vincenzo was brought to the room by a civilian administrative assistant who had been employed by the Bureau for several years. Doris's conservative manner of dress gave her an air of professionalism even though she was only in her late twenties. Nick liked the quiet politeness of her demeanor. He always tried to use her to escort his interviewees to the box. This was done by Nick's design. He liked to make the environment somewhat uncomfortable, and Doris's silence aided that. It allowed him to apply controls that would subtly guide a person's behavior. The goal was to maximize Nick's ability to regulate the interview.

Nick was notified of Mr. Mangano's arrival and looked at his watch, noting that he was on time. A good sign. Showing up early is a potential indicator of nervousness. Arriving late can demonstrate a suspect's attempt to assert dominance.

Nick let Vincenzo sit for several minutes in the quiet isolation of the box. The armored truck guard was left in the uncomfortable plastic chair of the interview room with no distractions except for the thoughts inside his head.

Nicholas Lawrence knocked, entering the room with the presence of a congressman on a re-election campaign. He walked directly to Vincenzo, extending his hand. "Wow! You have been through an incredible ordeal. I am so glad that you are alright." Nick said warmly.

"It wasn't that bad," Mangano said with the false bravado that Nick had become so accustomed to. People, especially men, tended to minimize traumatic events.

"Tell me what you can remember. I want you to begin from the point that you approached the bank's parking lot. No detail is too small." Nick had said these words, or their equivalent, a thousand times before to suspects and victims alike.

"I remember that Shelly and I were driving up to the bank. We were talking about a show we watch. The Real Lives of Airline Stewardesses. Cheesy, I know, but it's our thing." He gave a sheepish grin, before continuing, "Everything was normal. We were running a bit late for the delivery, but our schedule gives a flex time of fifteen minutes. If we don't check on-site to our dispatch center within fifteen minutes of the scheduled arrival time, then they begin to try to reach us by radio. If that fails, then the local police are notified of our truck's GPS location. This is done in case we get hijacked or taken hostage." Nick scribbled some notes on his pad but already knew the general protocols, having been through this in previous cases. Each armored truck company had similar safety nets established to protect their assets.

Vincenzo sighed before he continued to retell his experience. Nick knew that this gesture was done in a subtle attempt to let him know that he had already told this story to the other cops. Nick said nothing and waited for him.

"We pulled around the bank and into position in front of the ATM. I ride shotgun and do the retrieval and reload of the machine. Shelly remains inside the truck and keeps it running."

"So, is it normal for Shelly to park the truck and get out?" Nick asked, knowing that this slight confrontation may put Vinny on the defensive, but it was essential to the interview process.

"What? No... but come on man, you can't blame this on her. She's a good employee. She has a family. We were just talking, and she got out of the truck so that she could hear me better. If you want to point the finger, then point it at me. I wasn't paying attention when that guy snuck up on me!" Agitation was clearly present in Vincenzo's voice.

"I am not blaming either of you. I may say things to you to get some clarification, but don't be offended. I am not looking to get either of you in trouble. My job is to understand how you guys do things so that I can figure out how our bad guy pulled this off. Please continue." Nick was calm, and he could see the tension in Vinny's face begin to release slightly. Nick was not the enemy and he needed the guard to register this.

"Okay. Well... yeah, Shelly was out of the truck talking with me. I opened the front of the ATM and detached the money container. Then I walked to the back of the truck and retrieved the refill. That's when it happened." Vinny's head slumped, projecting his defeat. Nick registered his embarrassment.

"And then what?" A subtle nudge to continue his explanation.

"You know what happened next. That asshole pistol-whipped me! The fucking gun went off in my damn ear. He could have killed me. I mean, shit, what would you have done? I thought I had been shot." Vinny responded, becoming defensive again.

Nick figured that Vincenzo was probably embarrassed because he had urinated in his pants when the gun went off. It was a very common reaction to this type of occurrence. If the brain becomes overwhelmed, then some of the subconscious controls shut down and very typically this came in the form of bladder or bowel release. Nick had seen it first-hand among some of his soldiers during combat engagements and held no judgment.

"I've never been in a situation like that and can't comprehend what it would be like." Nick, of course, was lying. He'd been in much worse scenarios with real bullets snapping past his ears. Several scars on his left shoulder told the tale of one such encounter, but Nick was not here to exchange war stories. He was here to listen to Vincenzo Mangano.

"Well... it was freaking terrifying. That's really all I remember. I never even saw the guy. I heard him say something about not moving and then he dropped me."

"What did his voice sound like?" Nick asked, seeking sensory details.

"Deep I guess. Kind of gangster like. I don't want to sound racist, but the guy sounded black." Vincenzo said timidly. Nick had learned long ago that there is no room for political correctness if it interfered with the progress of a case.

"Thank you for that Vinny. Is there anything else that you can think of that may assist me in catching this guy?"

"Umm. Not sure. I think that is everything." Vinny said flatly. He seemed to have suddenly been overcome with a wave of exhaustion, rubbing his pasty face with his hands. Nick was also familiar with this sudden fatigue, knowing the draining effect associated with reliving a traumatic event.

"I am going to give you my card and if anything else pops into your head, then please don't hesitate to reach out. You were very helpful today," Nick said, giving a reassuring handshake as he escorted Vincenzo Mangano out of the interview room. Doris quietly escorted him from the building.

"Not involved," Nick said to Izzy.

"Okay. Well, the female guard is waiting down in the lobby. I'll send for her," Izzy said, demonstrating the seamless teamwork of their partnership.

Nick seized this small break between the interviews as an opportunity to grab a cup of coffee. The k-cup was, in Nick's humble opinion, the greatest invention in history.

He exited the break room, observing as Shelly Lewis was being escorted by Doris into the same interview room that Vincenzo had recently vacated. Again, Nick allowed her to sit in the silence of the interview box for a few minutes before making his entrance.

Nick had a disarming smile as he entered. He gave her the nonverbal gesture of "*would you like a cup of coffee too*" pointing toward his paper cup.

She replied by shaking her head *"No."* Nick sat, placing his notepad and pen on the table.

"Are you sure that I can't get you a cup of coffee?" Nick offered again, easing the perceived tension.

"I'm good. Thank you," Shelly said.

Nick noted a rasp in her voice most likely caused by years of heavy smoking. She was thirty-one, but life had taken its toll, adding ten hard years to her features.

"I spoke with Vinny. You two have been riding together for a while now. I would like you to walk me through everything that happened on Thursday. Take your time and put in as much detail as you can remember. Let me worry about whether or not it's important. Whenever you're ready you may begin." Nick said as if he was a school teacher giving the directions to a test.

"Vinny and I got to the bank a little after five. You can check the dispatch records for the exact time. We pulled in and parked by the ATM, like we always do. Vinny got out and started doing his thing. He's responsible for the actual handling of the money on deliveries. I do the driving and dispatch communication. We've got our assignments." Shelly said, pausing for a moment to gauge Nick's reaction.

"Okay," he said, giving minimal encouragement. Interviewers like Nick used simple phrases or sounds to elicit a response by gently prodding the interviewee to continue.

"So, Vinny got out and walked around the front of the truck. He opened the ATM and went to the rear. He came back with the new canister and..."

"Sorry to interrupt, but where were you while Vinny was doing this? Remember that these details are important to me." Nick said this already knowing the answer but wanted to test the level of Shelly's honesty.

"Well, I parked the truck and got out to talk with Vinny." Shelly mumbled this statement as if she were a child fearful of being scolded.

"Shelly, please do not hold back anything from me. Assume that I know all of it. I just want to hear things in your words. I do not work for your company and couldn't care any less about procedures. Try to relax. I know that you have been through a difficult ordeal and I want to understand what happened. The only way that I can do that is if you open up to me," Nick said calmly. He could sense that he was establishing a connection with

Shelly. His tone and word choice were meant to break down the barriers of the interview.

"Okay. I'm sorry. Just nervous, I guess. So, as you know I got out of the truck. Vinny and I were talking about this silly show that we both watch. And then out of the blue, I see this guy appear out of nowhere, and he was pointing a gun at Vinny's head. It was so fast. And then the bang. I swear to God that I saw Vinny's head explode. He dropped." Shelly stammered, quivering as if shaking off a chill.

"Go on." Nick encouraged.

"Vinny was on the ground and the guy was yelling at me, but it was like I had earmuffs on. I heard the sound of his voice, but it was muffled, and I couldn't tell you what he was saying.

"I remember that at some point I was able to understand the gunman's words. He said something to the effect of *get on the ground*. So, I did what he said. I am no hero. I mean, Jesus, he had just shot Vinny. Well, I thought that at the time. I'm not dying for seventeen dollars an hour!" Shelly's reference to her salary was obviously something she had said numerous times before as if this was her mantra.

"I don't judge you. I have not been in your shoes and do not know how I would react. I want you to know that I think you were very brave." Nick reaffirmed, needing her to be confident so that her shame did not cover necessary details.

"Thank you." Shelly's shoulders went slack, and she stared at the wall. "I remember him telling me to look away and count. So I did. I felt him pull my gun out of my holster, and I was terrified that he was going to kill me with my own weapon. Then I heard a car drive off, but I stayed on the ground until I finished counting."

"Think about the bad guy and what he looked like. Try to picture him after Vinny was on the ground and you were facing him. Start at his head and mentally work your way down his body to his feet." Nick said, guiding her mind to a specific point in time to assist the recall process. This helped a witness organize their information, but even so, eyewitnesses were notoriously unreliable creatures.

"He had a black ski mask on. I remember that he had brown eyes. I would say that the guy had a medium-brown colored skin. He could have been black or Hispanic. I don't know. I remember seeing a black circle tattoo on his neck, but I have no idea what it was. That's pretty much it. I really couldn't tell you what he was wearing, and I never saw what he drove."

Nick listened and was impressed with her level of detail. Satisfied that Shelly Lewis was not involved, he closed his notebook.

"Shelly, I will be in touch if I have any more questions. You were very helpful. Thank you." Nick spoke in a reassuring tone that conveyed his appreciation, knowing that it was important to provide closure. "Take my card and reach out to me if something pops into your head that you think may benefit the case."

As Shelly departed the office area, Nick looked over at Izzy who was on the phone. She waved Nick over, thanking whoever she was talking with, and hung up.

"So, this is weird." Izzy loved to give a teaser and then stop. It drove Nick crazy, but he always played along.

"Are you going to make me beg?" Nick mocked, taking a kneeling position on the worn carpet of the office cubicle.

"I just got off the phone with the rental car agency that Flash's plate returned to. They said that they have a red Toyota Corolla with the matching New Jersey plates." Izzy paused, allowing time for Nick to process this information.

"That's not weird. That's great. Who rented the car?" Nick said with eagerness in his voice. He could feel that a shift in momentum was on the horizon. As of right now, the case was batting zero for leads.

"It hasn't been rented in over a month." Izzy let this information hit home with Nick.

"What? You're saying that someone stole a car, used it in an armed robbery, and then returned it?" Nick had never seen that done before and was thoroughly confused at this tactic.

"No. The manager reviewed the lot footage from the date and time of the robbery. The car was there the entire time."

"So, the car never moved?" Nick's eyes squinted, and his brow furrowed as his brain tried to sort out this new information.

"The car has only been moved one time in the last month, but that was for an oil change and car wash two weeks ago."

"We are dealing with a pro," Nick hissed, letting that hang in the air as he walked over to his desk and dropped into his chair. The phone in his cubicle rang and he looked at the visible display of the caller ID. It was his mother. He was tired and for the first time in a long time, he let it go to voicemail.

13

He had ridden this particular bus many times in preparation for this mission. Khaled had sat in the rear of this same bus several weeks ago and marked the rubberized backing of the seat in front of him with a small black "x". Every time he rode, he had walked to the rear and inspected the seat to make sure that the bus had not been changed. Each time the x was present.

It was Monday. He looked down at his watch and compared the time to the schedule, noting that it was running two minutes behind. He had found that this was very common due to the roadway congestion that marked the approach of the invisible boundary into the state capital of Hartford. Traffic accidents and road repair dominated the Connecticut landscape. The failed promises of politicians to improve roadways and public transportation increased with each passing election.

The bus pulled to a stop a few feet past where Khaled sat. He got up from the bench, entering as the doors folded open. Khaled moved past the tired faces of the few commuters already inhabiting the stained plastic seats. He found his place in the rear. Not many people took the morning commute. This would be to his advantage.

He waited for the bus to lumber forward and pull away from the bus stop that was conveniently located across from the Clover Leaf Federal

Bank. The same bank that his old acquaintance, Enright the Golden Man, had robbed the previous week. That recent development would add an extra level of chaos to the original plan. Khaled had a few adjustments to make before it began.

The ride to J's Pizza was uneventful. This time, only the heavyset man, known to him as Mustafa, met him at the door and brought him into the room. Khaled knew that this man's real name was not Mustafa. Everything had been arranged by the Seven so that no one could ever identify another if they were caught and interrogated. Khaled was known to them as Mohamed, but he knew that they also knew him by a different name, *Alghabar Alshaytan*, the Dust Devil. This was a moniker that had been bestowed upon him by terrified American soldiers. Even his FBI's wanted poster had no picture, only labeling him by his nickname. Khaled liked its anonymity. He really did not work for The Seven. In many ways, they worked for him, but none of that mattered. The only thing that counted was vengeance. His journey had begun in the rugged desert terrain of his homeland, but his masterpiece was soon to be unveiled on American soil.

"Mohamed. Good to see you again so soon," the man called Mustafa said as he pulled a hand-rolled cigarette from its rectangular metallic box. He offered one to Khaled who declined with a dismissive wave of his hand. Mustafa began the daily ritual of filling the small back room with a low hanging cloud of smoke.

"I need to get a message out." Khaled had no time for pleasantries and did not particularly like the fat man. Khaled felt that Mustafa had become too comfortable with American culture, adopting many of their despicable traits. Khaled decided that the fat man sitting before him would do nothing more for the cause than operate a business front, allowing safe harbor for the real soldiers.

"Of course, my friend. Please tell me what it is that you need." Mustafa said this with the feigned tone of cordialness that Khaled knew to be more done out of fear than respect. Khaled had come to learn that respect and fear caused men to act in similar fashion. In the years since his Sonia's death, he'd grown more accustomed to the latter.

"Tell them that it will be done to satisfaction, but at a new grid coordinate. I am deviating from the original location. I think that they will be pleased with my reasons." Khaled said, sliding a piece of paper to Mustafa with the hand-written coordinates 41.723158, -72.668059.

"Sure, my friend. It will be done." Mustafa said this as he retrieved the piece of paper. Khaled noticed that the fat man had registered that he was wearing gloves. Mustafa began to sweat, betraying his momentary terror.

"You will not see me again. I trust you know what to do with that piece of paper when I leave?" Khaled could see the dread in Mustafa's eyes. He did nothing to console him or ease his worry. *Let him think that I am here to kill him. He will work harder for me under that strain.*

Mustafa nodded. Fear had constricted his ability to speak. Khaled pushed his chair back and the screech of the metal against poorly laid tile caused Mustafa to jump slightly. Khaled walked out of the room and into the comparatively fresh air of the city. He knew that inside J's Pizza shop the fat man was already busy relaying the message to The Seven.

14

Declan had kept Val in the loop with everything that he was doing. She remained calm throughout the bank planning and its execution because she had a perpetual faith in him. This gave him strength, but also carried its own burden. The look of relief on Val's face after he told her that he had saved the house confirmed that he had done right by his family. Even with that, Declan felt conflicted by the robbery. He'd done some dark things during his time as an operator in the Navy, but it was always under the guise of the importance of the mission's objective as it pertained to national security. He had never crossed over his line of right and wrong. Until now.

Val was amazingly supportive. She had seen his torment when he talked about the robbery. He did not like taking advantage of the two innocent guards. She reaffirmed that he had done a great thing for their family and tried to provide further reassurance by highlighting that no one was hurt by his actions. She also tried to ease his worries by pointing out that the police hadn't knocked at their door. Declan was also a realist, knowing that eighty-seven thousand dollars was only a temporary fix for a long-term sustainability problem. This also weighed on him, but for the moment he dealt only with his immediate concerns.

Declan knew that he had to begin the process of slowly putting the cash into their checking account without drawing suspicion. Today would be his first deposit at the Clover Leaf Bank. It would serve two purposes. First, he wanted the bank tellers to see him in his filthy construction shirt, ensuring that the new cash flow would not raise any red flags over the next several months of deposits. Declan knew from his experience working drug distribution cases that banks would report activity that was outside of the norm for an account. He wanted to quell that suspicion before it arose. Secondly, he was hoping to catch an earshot of how the investigation was progressing. Maybe some small talk with a teller about the robbery would give him some insider information, knowing that people loved to gossip about such things.

He entered through the double doors of the bank at 11:45 a.m. Declan had parked his wife's minivan over at the gas station, purchased a Gatorade, and then walked to the bank with the sugary drink in hand. Everything he did was done for the specific purpose of blending into the environment. Declan portrayed himself as a hard-working construction guy who was making a quick stop at the bank during his lunch break.

There were only two people ahead of him in line at the bank and only one teller. Declan had decided to wait until he stood in front of the clerk before filling out the deposit slip. This would stall things a bit, giving him additional time and opportunity to talk. Silence was uncomfortable for people and Declan had seen people fill its cavernous void with things they shouldn't talk about. Many times, arrestees in the back of his police cruiser had confessed to their crime or given a critical piece of incriminating evidence in a desperate attempt to alleviate the deafening silence. He hoped that the bank teller would prove to be no different.

"Next please," the teller called. Declan noted her name was Melissa, evident from the name tag pinned above the breast pocket of her lightweight sweater. She sat on an elevated chair behind the wooden encasement of her workspace and pleasantly gestured for Declan to step forward.

"Hi there. I just wanted to make a cash deposit into my checking account," Declan said, pulling a crumpled dust-covered envelope from his pocket smudged with a little bit of dirt and grease. It had the mathematical scribblings like the one he used for the money order. Today's deposit would only be for $475. It was designed to look like a cash payment from a weekend job. This would allow him to make an additional deposit at the end of the week. Declan knew of the under-the-table payment system in the world of construction, exploiting its commonality with the teller.

"Did you fill out a deposit slip?" Melissa asked. She was distracted, looking out toward the entrance as she spoke.

"Sorry. I totally forgot," Declan said softly, cocking his head to the side and giving an apologetic smile. Melissa smiled back and didn't seemed bothered by his mistake. Declan had a rough masculine feature from years of hard physical training, but his light blue-gray eyes gave his face a warm element of kindness. Women found this quality attractive, and although he never had overtly flirted since being married to Val, he used it to his advantage when necessary.

"No worries. Do you have your license? I can fill it out for you." His charms had worked their magic.

"Thanks," Declan replied.

Melissa stopped filling out the deposit slip mid-pen stroke. She looked up as she heard the suction release of the front doors. Declan turned to see a man enter in a blue blazer jacket and button-down white shirt. As he moved through the lobby in the direction of the management area, Declan caught the glint of a badge and saw the back portion of the frame and rear sights of a Glock protruding from the right-side hipline of the agent.

"Sorry. It's been crazy here lately. Did you hear about the robbery?" Melissa blurted, attempting to calm her nerves by talking. *Perfect.*

"Yeah. I saw it on the news. Scary stuff. Were you at work when it happened?" Declan asked, giving the impression of genuine concern.

"No. I left early on that day, my son was sick. Thank God. It sounded terrifying," Melissa said, lowering her voice.

"I bet. So, did they catch the guy?" Declan said quietly, matching her change in volume. He tried to convey a level of interest equivalent to that of a nosy citizen.

"I don't think so. That guy who just came in is with the FBI. Nice guy. He's been here a lot. So, I guess he's in charge." Melissa whispered, acting like she was the president of the guy's fan club. "Your money is in your account. Here is your deposit slip. Is there anything else that I can do for you today?" she said, returning herself to business mode as the line behind

Declan grew with the lunch wave of customers. She slid the rectangular piece of paper across the lacquered brown wood over to Declan.

"No. I'm all set. Thank you," Declan said, taking the thin slip of paper. He walked toward the exit.

His hand pressed against the handle of the first set of doors. The door began to open when he heard Melissa call to him. "Mr. Enright, you forgot your license."

Declan turned, seeing that the yell from Melissa had drawn the momentary attention of the FBI agent who was standing with Janet, the bank manager who had recently denied his loan. A wave of disappointment immediately filled him. He did not want the investigating agent to take notice of him even if it was innocently done.

Janet smiled, recognizing Declan. "I am glad to see that you are working again. Sorry I wasn't able to help you out before but check back with me once you're settled in with your new job." Janet projected this to him from across the bank. It was only about thirty feet away, but it sounded to Declan as if she had used a megaphone. This total lack of professionalism by the bank manager caused a moment of panic for Declan. *Did she really just say that in front of the FBI agent?*

Declan noticed that this comment registered with the agent. A guy with financial problems is suddenly making a deposit within four days of a bank robbery. The fed was sizing him up. He watched as the agent visually scanned him, taking in his physical characteristics. *Time to go.* Declan turned and prepared to leave without saying a word to Janet.

"Oh my God!" Screamed Melissa. "Look!" she yelled as she stood up from her chair. She pointed frantically out toward the street.

Declan saw a CT Transit bus. It was stopped at the bus stop across the street. The same one that Declan had used for his reconnaissance during his weeks of preparation for the armored truck job. The rear compartment of the bus was engulfed in fire. He immediately pushed the exit door open, stepping outside from the silence of the bank into the raucous sounds of the street.

Declan instinctively began to run at the chaos taking place at the bus stop, moving on autopilot. As he did so, he realized that beside him, running step-for-step, was the FBI agent from the bank.

Traffic had begun to gather on all sides of the bus. Most people sat in their cars gawking at the scene before them. Those onlookers not frozen by the mayhem had taken their cellphones out, recording the rapidly unfolding events. People typically stood by and recorded tragic events, rather than getting involved. Everyone looking for the next viral video. *A world of useless voyeurs*, Declan thought as he scanned the crowd. He continued sprinting toward the burning bus.

Declan and the agent moved quickly, crossing the sidewalk nearest the bank. He could see that people were continuing to gather near the fire, like moths to the flame. Out of the corner of his eye, he caught a glimpse of the man he'd seen at the bus stop a few weeks prior. He had recognized something familiar about the man but couldn't place it then. Now, with the intensity of the situation heightening his perceptual awareness, it hit him like a twenty-foot shore breaker. The man from the bus stop was the translator from a village used by his SEAL Team in Iraq. There was no such thing as a coincidence of this magnitude in Declan's world.

Declan's brain went into overdrive as he instantly and without thought reverted to the mindset that had earned him the nickname Ace. Declan began a rapid-fire assessment of the situation unfolding in front of him.

"Stop!" Declan shouted as he extended out to the agent who was within arm's reach, grabbing him by the wrist. "Get back!" Declan yelled, pulling the agent to the ground.

"What the hell?" The agent yelled in response. His question was drowned out by the explosion and shock wave that followed.

Chunks of metal and debris accompanied the blast. Declan couldn't hear much as the ringing in his ears intensified. He looked down at his left shoulder and saw a jagged piece of metal sticking out. Blood saturated his shirt, steadily rolling down his arm and dripping from his fingertips. The agent was unconscious but appeared to be alive. Bypassing the pain, he grabbed the agent, pulling him behind a small retaining wall near the bank where he began checking his vitals.

Declan's head was on a swivel, scanning the area for the Translator, but he was nowhere to be found. *No coincidences.* Declan determined that the initial threat had passed and turned his attention back to the unconscious FBI agent on the ground in front of him.

15

The bank lobby had become a makeshift triage center for the wounded, and Nicholas was just now starting to take stock of his circumstance. Izzy was kneeling by his side there as he awoke on the floor of the lobby. A medic from the local Emergency Medical Service told him that he had a concussion and recommended that he be seen by a doctor. Nick avoided hospitals when possible and today would be no different.

"Nick, you should really listen to the medic. Get yourself checked out. I've got this until you get back," Izzy said, sounding genuinely concerned for his well-being.

"Look around Izzy. I'm not taking up a bed at a hospital when we have people here that are truly injured. I have been through much worse and had to push past it," Nick retorted, thinking back to that day when his shoulder was peppered with bullets from an enemy rifle. He had stayed in the fight for twelve hours with shredded tissue and bone. He got some chest candy for his bravery that day. The sum of his valorous efforts now lay at the bottom of a desk drawer at home. Nick had never been one for accolades.

"The locals are running the bus fire. It's not our scene to work," Izzy said, motioning to the expansive efforts out on the street.

"Bus fire? Don't you mean bombing?" Nick was confused. He remembered running in the direction of the burning bus with the construction worker. Why did the construction guy yell *Get Down*? *What did he know?* Everything else after those words faded into a blur.

"If you don't remember then I definitely want you to get yourself to the doctor. A brain injury is nothing to minimize," Izzy said, looking worried.

"I remember running toward the bus. And there was a guy with me. A construction worker. He was in the bank when I was speaking with the manager. Someone yelled and we both ran out to the bus." Nick rambled, feeling the fog in his head begin to lift, but only marginally.

"I didn't notice anyone in our casualty area wearing construction clothing. Maybe he's outside." Izzy ominously gestured out to the sea of yellow body blankets strewn across the road.

Nick looked out in the direction of where he last saw the bus. It was like looking through a magic mirror into some third world country. Twisted blackened chunks of metal were scattered everywhere with mangled cars surrounding the roadway in front of the bank. And then Nick saw the yellow plastic tarps covering the bodies, knowing that the dead needed to stay in place until their positions were photographed and marked.

"How many?" Nick said in a vacant tone.

"They're still working on the official number," Izzy said, sounding grave.

"Well give me the unofficial," Nick grunted as frustration set in. Compounded by his concussed brain.

"Thirty-two dead. Sixty-seven injured with some people transported in critical condition. The death count is bound to go up."

"Holy shit. So, they are listing this as a bus fire?"

"That's what they're saying. Something about a fire in the engine that ignited a fuel line. I'm no mechanic and that's beyond my technical expertise in that area. Tragic. I am so glad that you are okay," Izzy said, taking up his hand in hers before quietly continuing, "When I heard the explosion, I ran from the PD. It was the craziest thing I have ever seen. I was terrified that you were in that blast." Izzy's voice exposed her panic as she mentally revisited the trauma.

"The construction guy definitely knew something," Nick said this more to himself than to Izzy.

"We can pull the footage from the bank's ATM camera. It should give us a good angle to view the bus."

"Good idea. Where's Janet, the bank manager?" Nick asked, still a bit disoriented from his temporary period of unconsciousness.

Janet was seated in her office. Nick registered the signs of shock. She was paler than before and had a light layer of sweat on her forehead. She stared off into oblivion, and it took her a moment to register the two agents standing in front of her desk.

"I need you to pull up the footage from the bank's external cameras just prior to the bus fire," Nick directed, speaking clearly and slowly, allowing Janet to register this request in her current state of stress.

Izzy and Nick had taken over Janet's office and the manager now floated aimlessly in the lobby. Nick had given her the task of making a list of all bank personnel currently inside and to note any injuries. He knew that by giving her this responsibility, it would ease some of the emotional impact of the situation. People who were unaccustomed to these types of events benefited from tasks that distracted from the overwhelming nature of the ordeal.

The footage on the screen in front of them showed an image of Nick darting through the bank's parking lot close behind the construction worker wearing a fluorescent work shirt. The bus was already on fire and the brightness of the flames washed out some of the image at the far corner of the screen. They watched as the construction worker turned and grabbed Nick, pulling him to the ground. The blast followed immediately after.

"Run it again but slow it way down," Nick said, directing Izzy who handled all things technological for the two as he leaned in more intently.

"Okay. What are you looking for?" Izzy asked, seeing that Nick didn't even register the question. She had worked with him enough to know that he was in his investigatory zone. He could hyper-focus, excluding everything else around him. She had learned that it was better not to interrupt this process.

Nick slid his hand over Izzy's without speaking, taking control of the playback functions for the surveillance system. With the replay slowed down, Nick saw what he was looking for.

"Do you see that?" Nick asked, swiveling his head back to Izzy.

"See what?" Izzy replied, still trying to figure out what he had noticed.

"There." Nick pointed to a still image on the screen. He tapped the screenshot of the construction worker's head. It was turned away from the direction of the bus.

"So, he turned his head. What's the big deal?" Izzy said, still confused by this detail that she was apparently missing.

"He saw something. Look how he turns his head and then a split second later he's pulling me to the ground, right before the big explosion. Whatever he saw made him react." Nick got quiet and Izzy waited, knowing that he had more to say. "He saved my life."

"I'm not going to lie. That guy moved like a ninja. Look how much we had to slow this feed down just to catch all of this. He pulled you to the ground with one arm and then used his body to shelter you from the flying debris. It looks like he was injured in the blast too." Izzy said, scrolling a few frames ahead as she resumed toggling the playback controls and pointed to the blood-soaked shirt of the construction worker. "Even with those injuries, he managed to pull you to safety before heading back toward the carnage," Izzy said, sounding impressed.

"He pulled me to safety with one arm. The guy is strong, but beyond that, it looks like he's got some skills." Nick's brain was on fire again. He was trying to comprehend all this new information while dealing with the pounding headache that was forming.

"What do you mean by skills?" Izzy was lost again.

"He's got to be ex-military. No civilian has the wherewithal to react with composure in that level of bedlam without having been exposed to it before. Look how he swiveled his head back and forth while pulling me to safety. He was scanning the area. He never turned his back to the bus. Skills." Nick said this with an air of respect.

"Okay, so you are saying he is an ex-military guy who now works construction. That's a pretty common thing. Why are you looking so hard at this guy? Do you want to find him and thank him?"

"I definitely want to thank him, but I also have some serious questions." With that said, Nick got up and walked over to the teller counter. He saw the bank clerk he was looking for. Melissa. She was rocked back in her chair away from her window, talking on her cell phone. "Where is the driver's license from the construction guy?" Nick interrupted.

"Huh?" She too was unaccustomed to this level of stress and couldn't initially comprehend the question.

"The construction worker who forgot his license. Remember? You called him back to you when he was leaving... right before the bus fire." Nick was patient. There was no reason to get angry with someone in her condition. She just required a little extra time to process the questions.

"Oh yeah, right, I remember. Sorry. I put it over here," she said, handing him the license, and then without another word went back to her phone call. Nick noted that she never even inquired as to why he wanted it.

"Thanks," Nick said softly out of courtesy, realizing that she wouldn't register the comment. He looked down at the Connecticut driver's license belonging to the construction worker that had saved his life... Declan Enright of Wethersfield.

16

Declan pulled into the small driveway of his gray Colonial. Cold winters and warm summers had taken its toll on the exterior. The peeling paint revealed the original white undercoating. He sat for a moment as the blood continued to pour from his left arm. A torn strip of his shirt that was wrapped in a makeshift bandage did little to ebb the flow. The inside of the minivan would require a serious cleanup. A thick pool of blood was being absorbed into the floorboard carpet around the center console. Declan shut the engine off and heard the screams resonating from inside his house. The sound was audible through the closed doors of the van.

Laney's meltdowns were legendary and could unnerve a Tibetan monk. Before he and Val had learned anything about Autism they had thought that she was just an extremely temperamental child. Both Val and Declan had taken their turns trying to soothe her, most of the time without success. Each episode was an experience that left them both physically and emotionally drained.

Even now that they had learned techniques and routines designed to minimize the outbursts, Laney would occasionally explode. Sometimes these crisis points would happen in the privacy of their home. It created an additional level of stress when in public. As parents, they had become jaded toward the judgmental eyes of passing strangers. They wanted to scream *You try and do this! I'm a good parent!!* But usually when some "good Samaritan" tried to intervene and help by dispensing some parenting advice all that usually came out of their mouth in response was *screw off!*

Patience. Laney required patience. They would hold her tight to keep her from injuring herself. Her back would arc in a guttural response to the physical contact. Laney's arms and legs would lash out with a force that equaled a bullwhip. On more than one occasion, each had been caught off guard with a strike to the face or body. The impacts from these strikes were surprisingly powerful when contrasted to the size of the tiny assailant.

Declan walked to the side entrance of the house. The front door was inaccessible since he sealed a gap in the storm door with duct tape. One of many projects that required fixing once they got back their financial footing. As he opened the side door, the sound of Laney's scream penetrated the air. The blast had temporarily impacted his ability to hear, muffling the volume of her tantrum as if he had covered his ears with a plastic cup.

He walked into the living room and saw Val cradling Laney. To a layperson, Val looked like she was using some type of UFC grappling hold, but Declan knew better because he'd been in that position many-a-time himself. Val wrapped Laney up using her legs and arms. Val's mouth was pressed close to Laney's ear and she was humming. The repetitive noise helped soothe her. It was their way of bringing her back to them. They envisioned that she was lost in the woods and that the sound of their song would guide her home. Thoughts like that gave them a modicum of peace in their delicately balanced world.

Declan passed them, moving up the stairs to the bathroom without saying a word. He needed to get a better assessment of his injuries before he alerted Val.

He had dealt with worse wounds, under much harsher conditions, and had lived to tell the tale. Today would be no different. *The only easy day was yesterday.* A saying that carried with it the indoctrinated mindset that kept him going at the worst of times.

Declan slowly peeled back the shirt from his arm. Some of the blood had already begun to coagulate, adhering it to his skin. Pulling the cloth free had opened some of these fresh lacerations causing blood to run more profusely down his arm.

Laney's final high-pitched wail had managed to cut right through the fog in his head before subsiding. Val had become aware that he was home. She must have noticed that the minivan was parked in the driveway.

"Hey babe, are you home?" Val called from downstairs.

"Yeah. Upstairs. When Laney is totally settled I may need your help with something." Declan's voice did not betray the pain he was attempting to conceal.

"Okay. Give me a minute." Val's voice was calm. "Hey by the way, did you hear that loud bang earlier? It sounded like a transformer exploded."

Declan did not respond to his wife's comment. She would know the actual source of that sound soon enough. He grabbed a towel from the hallway closet, wet it and began the process of clearing the area around his gashes. Most of the cuts could be sealed with some butterfly stitches once they were cleaned, but four of them would require some suturing. He located a piece of metal sticking out of his shoulder. It was hard to tell how deep it was buried, but Declan knew that it had to come out.

"Val, can you bring me the Jameson?" Declan asked, knowing he was going to need to self-medicate. Their health insurance had pretty much dried up when he was terminated from the police force. Traditional medicine was not an option right now for the Enrights.

"Sweet Jesus! What happened to you?" Val said, trying to process the man standing before her in the bathroom. Only a half-hour ago he'd left her to drop some money at the bank, and now he stood blood-covered in their bathroom. Looking at her damaged husband covered in blood, she took a pull from the bottle of the Irish Whiskey before handing it off to Declan.

"Long story, but I need you to help me get this bleeding under control. I have cleared out most of the shrapnel from the cuts. Can you grab the peroxide? I am going to have to flush 'em out." Declan said this, managing a forced smile. There was a peculiar piece of his psyche that enjoyed testing the limits of his ability to endure pain.

Declan hung his arm over the sink's basin, wincing slightly at the discomfort as he pulled the metal shard out of his shoulder. He had to manipulate it in several directions to free it from the muscle tissue. The pain was intense, causing him to grunt through clenched teeth. With the jagged piece of metal removed from his arm, the blood began to quickly vacate the wound, soaking his shirt and further darkening its once bright color. Declan applied direct pressure to the open gash and within a short amount of time, the flow of blood slowed.

"Can you do the needlework?" Declan asked of Val as simply as if he were asking her to pass the salt during dinner.

"Of course. I'll go heat the needle. Be right back. Flush the big one again and then put some more pressure on it until I return," Val said, already in motion moving toward their bedroom to grab her sewing kit.

She returned after sterilizing the needle. "Ready big boy?" She jested, batting her eyes.

"Do I get a lollipop when you're done?" Declan retorted and gave her a quick once-over, eyeing her in an overtly flirtatious manner. A needed distraction from the current circumstance. Val was beautiful. The fact that she could stand there looking at him covered in blood as he sucked whiskey out of the bottle and still find a way to make a game out of this made him love her even more.

Seventeen stitches in total had sealed the wound in his shoulder. The sutures closed the two largest gashes and the rest were patched up with adhesive butterfly strips. Val placed loose sterile gauze over the damaged area, providing an extra layer of protection.

The whiskey had given ease to some of the pain, but it also had induced a rapid onset of fatigue. Declan needed to rest so that he could process what to tell Val about the event that just transpired. He sat on the couch watching as Laney played quietly, lost in her own world. He looked on, wondering if she knew how much he loved her. His eyes grew suddenly heavy and Declan allowed himself to drift off to sleep, knowing that this might be the only rest he got for a long while.

17

"Success." Khaled answered the phone and said this evenly to the man on the other end. The number used to call Khaled would be changed as soon as the conversation was over.

"Allah is proud of you," the man on the other end said softly. Khaled chose not to respond to this statement. He had long ago lost his belief in anything beyond the life he lived. The irony that any god would be proud of someone killing a group of people was never lost on him. Khaled was convinced that more people were killed in the name of God than any plague.

"I leave for my next destination soon. I have one thing left to do before I go. You understand our deal. Make sure that everything is set." Khaled said this with no hostility. He spoke briefly and with purpose, but not out of any concern of a governmental wiretap. His phone that had been provided by the Technician contained a level of encryption that would eliminate any interception.

"It has already been done, my friend. Good luck in Colorado." The man's voice carried an optimistic tone. "By the way, The Seven were very impressed with your decision to change the location of the bus attack. The fact that it was done during an FBI bank investigation made the iconic

American law enforcement agency look weak. It was an unexpected bonus and one that will be exploited to our advantage."

"I serve The Seven," Khaled said, ending the call with the middleman. Khaled thought to himself about the reality of the situation, *The Seven served him.*

Khaled took out a second phone from the center console of his nondescript Honda. He tapped the icon with a blue and white shield. The application opened, and the screen filled with a live feed showing footage of the front of the gray colonial home. A blue minivan and red Toyota were parked in the driveway. He double-checked his notebook, more out of habit than necessity. Enright's wife would be leaving in a few minutes with their youngest daughter. The time on his watch showed 1:20 p.m.

Khaled had been watching the house for a while. He had arrived midday three weeks ago dressed as a cable repairman. He had climbed the telephone pole that was positioned directly across the street from the American military man's home and attached a discreet digital surveillance camera. It was motion activated and had provided a clear picture of the comings and goings of this family. The camera would activate and record for thirty seconds whenever movement was detected by the sensor. This feature enabled the camera system to operate for an extended time with minimal battery drainage, negating a need for replacement. This remote view enabled Khaled to fill his notebook with the daily routines of Enright's family.

During the course of his preparations for the bus attack, Khaled had monitored the family's activities, focusing particularly on the littlest child. She was brought to a doctor's office, located on Main Street, every weekday. Like clockwork, the mother would leave the house at 1:20 p.m. with the little girl in tow. She had only been late on two occasions. *Tomorrow would be the last time that the two would ever make that drive.*

18

"Jake, I think there is more to this bus thing than we originally thought." Nick said with a sense of urgency. His boss was like many who had achieved the rank of administrator, in that he only liked ideas that had originated with him. Nick had come to realize that bosses were much like children. They needed to feel special, to be coddled to give them the impression that the world revolved around them. Nick had developed a skill for planting ideas in Jake Nelson's head. Nick would wait patiently, allowing it to fester until it took. Nelson would seize hold of the planted idea, sharing it as soon as he could take credit for it. Nick didn't care for this type of narcissism. Today, he didn't have time to play games with his supervisor. Time mattered and his boss's under-developed ego would have to be put on hold.

"We have our crime scene guys heading out to assist. If they notice anything, then I'll let you know. Otherwise, work the robbery and let the locals handle the bus incident." Nelson had put on his "I'm in Charge" hat and was already impeding Nick's ability to communicate his observations.

"You're making a mistake. This is going to be our problem very soon. You'll want to get out ahead of this before someone else figures this out... like the press," Nick said, knowing that by throwing out the potential for media coverage, Nelson would begin to sweat. His boss hated seeing something on the news before the Bureau knew about it. Nelson had a disdain for receiving a call from his supervisor with a question for which he did not know the answer. Shit rolled downhill.

"What? Why do you think the bus fire investigation is going to involve the Bureau?" Nelson reacted, showing his frustration at the implication. He was the type of man who tended to wear his emotions on his sleeve. As far as Nick was concerned, that was a terrible trait in a superior. Over the years, Nick had seen worse and he'd worked with better. Nelson was a mediocre leader, but Nick tolerated his shortcomings to a limited degree.

"Well, there was this construction guy in the bank at the time of the bus incident. He actually saved me from the blast by shielding me." Nick said as he took a breath, letting this sink in with Nelson. "Anyway, I don't think the fire and subsequent explosion were accidental. It reminded me of some things I saw overseas in the Sandbox," Nick said, knowing that his boss hated when Nick referenced anything military. Jake Nelson had never served, and like many in that category, felt in some way slighted by anyone who had.

"Please tell me why you think this! Because if you are going to start a shit storm in the little town of Wethersfield, then I want to be the first to hear about it," Nelson exclaimed, bordering on anger.

"I'm not starting any shit storm. It's already begun. I noticed something in the way the construction guy reacted just before the blast. And then there was the blast itself. I've never seen a vehicle explode like that except during wartime." Nick dropped the military connection again, knowing regretfully that he had added to Nelson's psychological roadblock as soon as he said it.

"Listen, Nick, I get it. You have just been through a crazy ordeal, but is it possible that you are overreacting? Maybe it's like a PTSD thing." Nelson said this for effect, knowing that Nick's brother had committed suicide after his combat tour. Nick had first-hand knowledge that post-traumatic stress disorder was real and attacked its victims in different ways.

"What did you just say?" Nick spat the question, teetering on earning some unpaid vacation. Hopefully, Nelson would register the rage in Nick's tone and recant his last comment.

"Sorry. No offense intended. I'm just under a lot of pressure about progress in this armored truck case, but you've shown good instincts in the past. So, I am going to give you some wiggle room today. You and Izzy take the rest of today to investigate your bus theory, but if you don't have anything tangible, then first thing tomorrow I want you back on the bank. Got it?" Nelson said, placating him. Nick didn't really care about the imposed deadline. Confident that by tomorrow morning he would either be wrong, and the world would continue to spin, or he was right and that meant things were about to take a dramatic downturn.

"Got it. Thanks. I'll keep you posted." Nick had learned that saying thank you took the edge out of any confrontational compromise regardless of whether it was genuine. Nelson hung up and the line went dead.

"Izzy, it's time to rock n' roll," Nick said, already moving. He had walked out of the bank and into the sea of police, fire, and EMS. Additional aid had been called in from the neighboring agencies of Hartford and Rocky Hill to assist with the scene. Nick saw who he was looking for and made his way over.

"Hey Lieutenant Patterson, got a quick minute?" Nick said as he approached, shaking hands with the local police commander.

"Sure, Agent Lawrence, what's up?" Patterson asked, obviously distracted by the carnage surrounding him. He was a man clearly more comfortable in the controlled, air-conditioned environment of his office than out on the street.

"It's just Nick." Nick smiled as he said this, reducing his status as an agent and humbling himself to Patterson. "I know that you guys are swamped with this bus fire and I don't want to be in the way. I will be running down some leads, but if anything unusual presents itself in the investigation please let me know." Nick was being intentionally vague.

"What do you mean by unusual?" Patterson asked in a half-interested tone.

"You will know it if you see it. Our crime scene guys should be here within the hour to assist. Hit me up on my cell if you have any questions. Thanks." Nick projected his voice over the noise as he walked away from the Lieutenant. He pulled his cell phone out and was already dialing as he and Izzy headed away from the bank to their government vehicle parked two blocks away.

"Hi Janet, how are you holding up?" Nick asked.

"It's kind of surreal. Like being in a movie," she responded, the remnants of the shock still present in her voice.

"Can you do me a favor? I need you to review the camera footage for the past five or six Thursdays. Just look at footage from the time frame of 4:30 to 5:30 p.m." Nick said this slowly to make sure that Janet comprehended his instruction.

"What am I looking for?" Janet asked. This was a good sign to Nick because it showed that she was paying attention.

"A red Toyota. Let me know if you find it. Thanks." Nick hung up.

"What's the plan?" Izzy asked, still trying to figure out where this was leading. She trusted in Nick's judgment and followed him, even if blindly.

"We're going to do a little digging into our construction worker who saved my life. Then we're going to pay him a visit," Nick said, tossing Declan Enright's driver's license to Izzy.

19

Khaled sat on the worn fabric seat of the blue Honda, enjoying the isolation of the rear parking lot of the Department of Motor Vehicles. The dilapidated old government building and expansive concrete lot stood out in contrast to the historic homes of Wethersfield. He was only a few blocks from his intended target.

He opened a pack of Parliament cigarettes, removed the cellophane wrapping and repeatedly slapped the top of the box into his hand, using the force to pack the tobacco inside. Drawing a cigarette from the box, Khaled stepped out from the car and lit it. He leaned against the hood, looking out at the tranquil water of the Cove. There had not been much water in the arid climate of his homeland and because of this, he tended to appreciate its beauty more than most. Khaled had spent many afternoons walking the Charles River while attending Northeastern University in Boston years back. It felt like a lifetime ago. He was a different person then. That person had burned with his Sonia.

Khaled allowed himself to take this brief mental hiatus from the final preparations to reflect on the moment that brought him to this point.

His beautiful Sonia. She would always ask him about his time in America, fascinated by a land so different from theirs. Khaled would tell her about the colors and smells. She loved when he would describe how the setting sun looked reflecting on the Charles River. Khaled had promised her that he would take her there someday, but that opportunity was stolen from him. He looked down at her aqua-blue bracelet wrapped tightly around his left wrist, feeling as though she was here with him now. A tear began to form, but Khaled took a drag from his cigarette and stared out at a group of geese meandering by the Cove's tranquil shoreline. He pushed back against his emotions. Sometimes he felt as if there was a paper-thin wall holding back the coming tidal wave of grief. There was no time for sorrow.

Rage had consumed Khaled early on in his desert village, driving him to take his vengeance on members of the elite American soldiers. He was a man that would appear out of nowhere and without warning, reign chaos upon the enemy. Khaled would disappear just as quickly as he arrived, leaving a wake of death and destruction. Thus, he became known as the Dust Devil, a reference to the unpredictable and devastating sand storms of his homeland. He had allowed himself to be recruited and trained by the Muqawama but quickly saw that they were limited in their ability to reach the Americans. Through a series of successful missions, Khaled had caught the eye of The Seven.

The Seven wielded incredible power. The financial backing and resource that they provided gave Khaled the support he needed to exact his revenge. He was trained by mercenaries with many of his instructors coming from a pool of U.S. ex-special forces operatives. In their defense, they never knew Khaled's true purpose. He received expert level training in the art of death from these military elite men, under the guise that he was a high-level bodyguard of a Saudi prince. These tacticians valued their high salaries and did not question his backstory too deeply. In time, Khaled had developed a skill set that would put many trained special operators to shame.

His attacks on U.S. forces stationed in Iraq were impressive but left him with an emptiness that they could not seem to fill. It was in that void that Khaled had hatched his plan. He knew that The Seven were men who had lost much in war, but also felt that they could never truly know the depth of pain that he had experienced, watching his Sonia burn to death under the rubble of her school. He had approached the emissary of The Seven and told him of the plan that he'd developed. One that would forward their cause, but more importantly fill the cavernous gap in his heart.

The only face-to-face meeting Khaled had with The Seven lasted a few hours, but when it was done the funding for his operation was met and all the resources he could fathom were at his disposal. To The Seven he became known as *Rasul* رسول,The Messenger.

Khaled felt conflicted as he leaned against the cracked front bumper of the Honda smoking his second cigarette. The pain of Sonia's death was as boundless today as it had been years ago, but yet he wondered if he would be capable of completing this next task. *Could he give that pain to another? Intentionally drill an unfillable hole in their heart?* He had relived this moment over and over again in his mind in the years since his Sonia's death. Now, on the eve of his first strike, he lamented his ability to complete the task. The bus had been easy. This would be something else. It would be personal. That meant that it would also be emotional. Devoid of human emotion is how Khaled typically conducted his operations. It would be a departure from the cold, calculated methods of his previous missions.

He pushed himself off the car and walked down the short gently sloping hill to the gravel, walking the path that surrounded the cove. In the brisk fall air of New England, Khaled lazily strolled along the trail, taking in the bright colors of the dying leaves. In the distance, he could still hear the sirens that perpetuated the fear and turmoil he'd created earlier, striking deep into the heart of this quaint, suburban town.

20

Izzy ran Declan Enright's information through the usual channels, trying to gather as much about the hero as she could. Nick took this opportunity to reach out to a different source.

"Jay. It's Nick. Been a long time, but I am into something that may require your skills," Nick said, hoping that this call would be well received. It had been a long time since he had dialed this number.

"Long time indeed. What's it been? Five years?" Jay said in a tone that showed that he was genuinely excited to talk to his old friend.

Nick and Jayson Barton had crossed paths on the battlefields of Iraq, a place that Nick "lovingly" referred to as the Sandbox. Nick's involvement with the Rangers put him in the circle of the military's elite special forces groups, and with that came Tier 1 missions. Those operations were linked to various intelligence agencies, requiring a high level of security clearance. Jay had been his "spook" connection on more than a few ops, and they had become fast-friends, as people do when life hangs in the balance.

Over the years since his time in the military, Nick had discovered that he never felt as close to coworkers as he did to the people he went into battle with. *War was funny that way... you never feel more alive than when you are so close to death.* Maybe that is why for the first time in a very long time Nicholas Lawrence now felt a resurgence of energy.

Nick and Jay had kept in touch after their time together overseas and last met a few years back for a night of drinking at an Irish pub in Old Towne Alexandria. As things went with friendships forged in combat, time left little to talk about when back stateside. Some veterans could reminisce about their war experience for the rest of their lives as if time had stopped for them. For many, like Nick's brother, it had. Some of the warriors never truly left the battlefield. As for Nick and Jay, they had both moved forward after the war and found that neither really wanted to talk much about their past engagements. That ultimately left them with less to talk about. Nick had moved on to the FBI and Jay had stayed in the CIA. Although both agencies typically crossed paths on television, in the real world it was far less common.

Nick had needed Jay's resources when he was assigned to the Austin office, but that was an extreme circumstance. Jay had put himself out to help Nick, testing the boundaries of their friendship. That was the only time he had requested his assistance outside of Iraq. Until now.

"Sorry to hit you up out of the blue, but I have come across something that you may be able to help me with," Nick said with some hesitancy in his voice. Jay had risked his career and potential jail time when he helped Nick with an international human trafficking ring out of the Austin area a few years back.

"Tell me what you've got, and I will tell you what I can do, or better yet, *if* I can do it." Jay was always a straight shooter when it came to his job, and that's one of the reasons that the two had gotten along so well in a combat environment.

"I'm working an armored truck robbery in a town called Wethersfield, here in Connecticut. I was at the bank doing a follow-up when a bus caught on fire while stopped in front. When I exited the bank, the bus exploded." Nick spoke, knowing that brevity was the key and the details would come later.

"Shit man sounds like you had a really bad case of the Mondays," Jay said with a slight chuckle. To an outsider, this comment would have sounded inappropriate, but a warrior's sense of humor was as key to survival as food and water.

"Like old times. I don't think the bus was an accident. More importantly, there was a guy present who saved my life and may have some of the answers. And that's where you come in," Nick said, hoping that he had secured Jay's support by inferring the bus explosion may have ties to his special set of skills. Nick was not sure if Jay was still in the counterterrorism game anymore.

"What do you have for a name?" Jay asked, alerting Nick that he was in.

"His name is Declan Enright. My partner, Isabella Martinez, did some digging on our side and found out that he was recently terminated as a police officer. She is coordinating with his former department to gather the details, but the human resource person she spoke with mentioned that Enright was former military. Specifically, he was a Team guy." Nick said knowing that Jay would understand this reference to the Navy's elite SEAL Teams.

"When you say that he may know something, are you really saying that he might be involved?" Jay asked, aware that pulling files on a spec ops guy could result in some immediate blowback.

"No. I don't think he has anything to do with the bus, but his actions on scene are leading me to believe that he may know something about it," Nick reassured his friend. No one liked when an operator, past or present, went rogue.

"What's your take on the bus? What is it that you aren't telling me?" Jay asked, demonstrating that he had immediately picked up on Nick's innuendos. *He was a smart guy.*

"I don't think it was a bus fire. I'm not getting much in the way of support from the brass here, but I've been given a day to bring forth some evidence before I get tossed back on the armored truck robbery," Nick answered knowing that Jay was familiar with the politics of such things. Probably better than most.

"Okay. So, you think this was..." Jay trailed off, wanting to hear it from Nick's mouth.

"I think it was a planned attack. This had a similar feel to the things we experienced in the desert. The fire drew in onlookers and stopped nearby traffic. It was a smart move because it increased the nearby populous at a rapid rate. Once the people were close, a secondary device must have been activated, causing the bus to explode. I'm guessing that it was a remote detonation and not a suicide bomb. I think that this is what our ex-SEAL realized and reacted to." This is the first time that Nick had said his theory out loud, and he caught Izzy staring at him out of the corner of his eye. Her reaction was not pessimistic, but more one of shock.

"You know that if you are right, then this would be the first truly successful stateside attack in years?" Nick noted that Jay's voice carried with it an element and tone that he had not heard from his friend before. Fear.

"I know. I hope I'm wrong, but something tells me that I'm not. If I have any chance of getting ahead of this thing, then I've got to move fast. See what you can find out about Enright's military time. I'm going to make a surprise visit soon and want to know who I am dealing with before we meet."

"Will do. I'll be in touch. Stay low and watch your six." Jay said, ending the call.

21

The morning air was crisp and clear. Khaled sat on the soft brown leather chair located in the back of the bustling Starbucks sipping from the thimble of white porcelain. The espresso he was drinking best resembled the strength and bitterness of his homeland's brew but lacked the balance of sweetness provided by the green cardamom that his palate had become accustomed to. He took in the movement of the people lost in the frenzy of their own world. Most of them hypnotized by their cell phone. Completely devoid of human interaction. It assisted his ability to blend in and disappear into the scenery. The pull of social media and digital communication had left the average person disconnected from the present.

The apartment provided by his network was now vacant. He'd spent the morning scouring the surfaces with bleach, removing any evidence of his time there. Khaled knew that The Seven would send someone to erase his presence, but he trusted nobody more than himself. It gave him peace of mind knowing that in the remote possibility that anyone would link him back to that place, they would find no physical trace of his existence. Plus, the cleaning gave his mind a break from the day's upcoming task. He had not slept well on his last night in Connecticut as he replayed his plan over and over again. Khaled did not pay attention to the news because he had to focus on his next step. The bus attack was still being listed as a terrible accident. The information regarding the attack was in the hands of The Seven for dissemination. Soon their voice would be heard.

Khaled pulled out of the parking lot of the small strip mall and drove the back roads of Wethersfield to his preplanned waiting position. The device had been set a week prior, but the challenge to this operation was the proximity he needed to be to detonate. Enright, or the Golden Man as his beloved Sonia had affectionately referred to him, was married to a very schedule-oriented person. Her routine with the youngest daughter was like clockwork. Today, that would be her downfall. This would turn out to be the worst day of their lives. *They would soon feel the burn.*

He sat in the blue Honda, checking the mobile application that allowed him to oversee the house of his enemy. Patience was at the core of who he was, and it had served him well up to this point. He understood that there was no reason to rush the process now. Although, he knew that these last few hours would feel longer than the previous eight years he'd waited, leading up to this moment of vengeance. His Sonia would have been sixteen now.

As he strolled the gravel path that encircled the Wethersfield Cove, Khaled allowed his mind to momentarily drift as he envisioned what type of young lady she might have grown up to be.

22

They had been up most of the morning running down information and reading Enright's personnel file. It was voluminous and carried with it an impressive listing of awards. He had excelled on patrol and was quickly brought onto the regional tactical team. His military experience had obviously contributed to the SWAT team's interest in him. The tactical team only operated on a part-time basis, enabling Enright to continue his patrol responsibilities. He was selected for the department's narcotics unit where he had spent his last two years prior to his termination.

The investigation file for Enright's use of deadly force was very thick and took up the space of an extra-large three-ring binder. The summary documented that Enright had responded to assist patrol units with a mentally disturbed party holding a gun to his head. The notes of the case stated that he had been conducting surveillance of a street-level drug transaction only a few streets away when the call came out. Due to his proximity to the call, Enright arrived on scene first.

Enright's picture had been taken by a bystander and used by the media. The photo showed that he was not wearing a uniform, and at the time he looked more like a homeless person than a cop. Enright had grown a beard and let his hair slip way past regulations, but all of this was accepted by his department because of his role as a narc. His grungy appearance was used by the family during the civil suit, claiming that it made him unrecognizable as a police officer. The media had jumped on that aspect of the story and numerous opinionated articles were generated around that debate.

Enright's report documented that his badge had hung from a metal chain around his neck and was exposed against his chest during the standoff. The media's focal point was on the fact that the gunman was a young black male in his early twenties. Multiple officers reported that Anderson had begged Enright to shoot him. Nick read this, perceptive that this trend of "suicide by cop" had become increasingly more common. The fallout in the media for any officer involved shooting was never good, but the soundbites of news panel experts buried Enright's reputation.

Enright had written in his report that he observed that Jamal had a small black handgun pressed against his temple and was yelling for someone to shoot him. Enright had held his position which was noted in a diagram to be seventeen feet from Anderson. Enright's report, which was corroborated by two other officers, said that as additional police arrived on scene that Anderson removed the gun from his temple and pointed it in the direction of another cop.

Enright had fired his department-issued Glock 22 three times at Anderson, striking him twice in the chest and once in the head. The body diagram and photocopied image of the deceased Anderson from the Medical Examiner's report showed that the two body shots penetrated left of center mass and had entered the chest, destroying the heart. The head shot was placed in a portion of the skull that tactical guys commonly referred to as the T-intersection, an area directly between the eyes above the bridge of the nose. Nick knew from personal experience that a shot to this region of the head immediately rendered a person's motor functions useless. Thus, it was the choice location snipers used on someone holding a detonator or hostage. Nick reflected on his own use of this technique and knew the difficulty of this shot.

This three-shot group is trained by military and SWAT operators and is commonly known as the failure drill. This shot placement almost always guarantees a fatality. Nick was thoroughly impressed with Enright, aware of the complexity of that shot group on a paper target under low-stress conditions. Enright had stopped the heart and brain of his target in a split second under extreme conditions. Speed and deadly accuracy were the signs of a true operator.

"Izzy, you're seeing this right? I mean this guy handled that situation perfectly. What the hell did he get fired for? He should have received a damn medal." Nick blurted, smelling the distinct odor of administrative bullshit in the handling of Enright's shooting.

"I know. The cops I spoke with all said that Declan was "the man" around that PD. Not one of them spoke ill of him. They each complained about their leadership, in particular, their Chief, as being more concerned with public opinion than the backing of his officers." Izzy said this shaking her head in disgust. The thin blue line had gotten a lot thinner in the past years, but some leaders had drifted so far that the ever-fickle public opinion guided more of their decisions than anything else. At face value and without any other facts it appeared that this had been the case with Enright's termination.

"It looks like the gun Anderson had been holding was empty and contained no magazine. The media experts provided analysis on this point, claiming that with Enright's combined military and police tactical proficiency that he should have been able to recognize the empty magazine well. At that distance and in low-light conditions, no one would be able to tell that." Nick said frustration was evident in his voice.

"I Googled the incident. Enright was buried in the press coverage. It was chalked up as another incident of racial injustice where a white officer shot a young black male. His Navy SEAL background only seemed to fuel the fire with some of the media sensationalists, claiming that he used his skill to serve as an executioner. What happened to the days when a chief would get in front of a bunch of cameras and verbally slug it out with reporters? What happened to standing up for a good man?" Izzy said this repugnantly.

She'd become accustomed to comments at family get-togethers regarding police brutality and race relations. As a Hispanic female, she had never been the recipient of racial injustice within her profession. The twenty-four-hour multi-billion-dollar media machine drove American opinion and right now they did not have a high one of law enforcement professionals. This opinion also appeared to have shaped the direction of Enright's internal affairs investigation.

"Those days are dead Izzy. Look at our boss. He's no different and would bury us in a minute if it would boost his career or keep his ass out of the fire." Nick said, the disdain resonating in his words.

"So, basically our humble opinion doesn't count for shit! It appears that Enright is a good guy. What do you want to do now?" Izzy asked as Nick's phone began to ring.

"Hey, sorry for the delay. I had to run a little interference when I started digging. You pull a decorated SEAL's file and people ask questions." Jay sounded tired.

"No worries. I appreciate anything that you can do." Nick didn't ask because he knew the answers were coming.

"So, his military record is interesting. He has the normal progression of basic training at Great Lakes to Basic Underwater Demolition/SEAL training in Coronado. Enright made promotions above grade and had excellent FITREPS. That is the Navy's term for fitness report which is basically performance documentation in layman's terms." Jay added the additional explanation, knowing that Nick was a former Army guy and might not be familiar with the acronym. "He was assigned to Team Two out of Dam Neck, Virginia and that is where things get a little weird. After one deployment to Afghanistan his file empties out with no details until he discharged under honorable conditions in June of 2011," Jay said. Nick could hear him shuffling some paperwork on the other end of the call.

"What do you mean his file emptied out?" Nick figured there might be some redactions from his military record, for security reasons. Nick's record had a few of those, but he had never heard of what Jay described.

"Well, there was nothing. So, I reached out to a source." Jay said, never divulging where his information came from. Part of his tradecraft was to protect his sources. "This operator knew Enright personally and shared some things with me. I would not be sharing them with you now if I did not think it was critically important." Jay paused.

"I understand. It stays with me and my partner."

"You've heard of the Navy's counter-terrorism, super-secret unit formerly known by the popularized name SEAL Team 6 and more discreetly known as DevGru?" Jay asked, speaking quickly.

"Yes, of course. The stories of their unit's success have been touted worldwide, especially after they took out Bin Laden." Nick responded.

"So, that's what I am getting at. The Navy's special ops people must have realized that the Hollywood status of their top unit was becoming its own issue. A middle-aged school teacher in Eastbumfuck Nebraska should not know about a secret mission team, but they do. These guys have become celebrities, doing talk show interviews, writing books and working behind the scenes on movies. The day of the silent professional seems to have gone by the wayside." Jay said, pausing for effect. "That was until a few years ago when some special operations purists got together, and they created a new group pulled from the Teams' absolute best." Jay knew that he was really putting himself in a compromising position by sharing this information but continued regardless.

"The new group operated completely outside of the normal channels. They set up their base of operations at Fort Devens in Massachusetts. The location was apparently selected because it was closed in 1996 as part of the post-gulf war one downsizing. The base re-opened as an Army Reserve training complex. Some of the property had been sold off and redistributed. This newly formed SEAL team liked the location because of the terrain and the fact that they were physically separated from the other Team guys. The base had been home to the U.S. Army's 10th Special Forces Group, but they had since been relocated. So, it had the ranges and training facilities in place necessary to support their work-ups. This new SEAL detachment had truly gone off the grid."

"You are saying that Enright was one of those guys?" Nick asked. His interest was peaking.

"I am going to say yes, but even with my resources, I have been unable to confirm anything official. That's never happened to me. These guys were true ghosts. My source told me that the group was rumored to have been called Alpha One, but there is nothing in any database with that callsign." Jay said, sounding impressed. This is something that did not happen easily.

"I really appreciate you putting yourself out there to get this for me. If this bus thing breaks the way I predict that it might, then I might see you down this way soon." Nick said this as a means of feeling Jay out to see if he still worked on the CIA's Counter-terrorism Unit.

"It would be good to see you again. Be safe." Jay said, not biting on Nick's unspoken question regarding his status with the agency. Then he was gone.

Izzy had caught the gist of the conversation. She was now staring at Nick waiting to hear what the next move was going to be. Nick registered this, turning his body toward her.

"It looks like it is time to go see Mr. Enright." Nick checked his watch. It was almost 1:15 p.m, as they drove through the historic district of Old Wethersfield, passed the wood-lathed exteriors of the homes toward Declan Enright's house.

23

The Seven had supported Khaled's plan through financial backing and logistics, but one of the great assets was the Technician. Khaled had met him overseas and was the only familiar face left in his world. The Technician understood the pain and suffering Khaled had faced in Sonia's death. Their unlikely bond had only been strengthened by her tragedy. Recently their relationship had become strained due to Khaled's personal agenda, but the Technician would continue his assistance until the end. *He had no other choice.*

The Technician had an uncanny ability to create electronic devices. Khaled deployed these with deadly efficiency. Khaled would call the one number in his phone and explain what he needed to accomplish his task. The Technician would then design the tool to achieve his vision. The devices were delivered through the expansive network of The Seven. The implements used in the bus attack had been a design of pure genius.

The FBI would soon discover that two devices had been installed on the bus. The first, a small rectangular metallic box the size of Khaled's thumb, had been clamped to the fuel line on the undercarriage of the bus. When activated it sent a charge that split the tubing. A spark would be created after an internal timer initiated its function. This spark ignited the gas exposed from the severed line. It was this chain of events that caused the bus fire.

As was Khaled's intention, the fire on the 53-54 CT Transit bus had halted traffic in all directions and drawn in the curious pedestrians. The second device had been planted in the rear of the bus earlier that morning. It was slightly larger and built into a stainless-steel thermos that Khaled had left wedged between the rear bench seat, marked with an "x", and the frame of the bus.

Khaled had patiently waited, outside of the blast radius that The Technician had factored into his design. The original plan had been to detonate when a large group of people had surrounded the bus, guaranteeing maximum casualties. Khaled was forced to speed up the timeline because ironically Enright, the Golden Man, had been at the bank and his attempt at heroics had interfered slightly with the timing of things. Khaled had at least hoped that a fire truck and some police would be in the kill zone before activating the secondary device, but when he saw Enright running toward the bus fire he triggered it. Khaled needed to keep him alive, otherwise, he would not suffer as intended, and all of his meticulous planning would be a waste.

After the blast, Khaled waited around long enough to verify that Enright was still alive before departing on foot. Khaled had moved through the crowd holding his head, as if injured by the blast, deflecting any suspicion in his rapid escape. He stumbled his way through the despondent faces of the onlookers until he was around the corner and took on a normal gait. He walked up Jordan Lane to his nondescript Honda parked in front of a liquor store. He got in the car and drove slowly into Hartford as police cars and fire engines rushed to the scene.

The Technician's newest devices were now affixed to the beat-up blue minivan of Enright's wife. A piece of duct tape held the left taillight of the minivan in place, showing the wear and tear of their financial hardship. Khaled took simple pleasure from the fact that Enright's fall from grace with the police department had taken its toll on his family. He was disappointed that the Golden Man would never know how instrumental Khaled had been in that downfall. *It's about to get a lot worse.* Enright's job loss and financial struggle would soon pale in comparison.

The first device developed for this mission had been a work of pure genius. Khaled had explained to the Technician what he needed. He didn't think, given the complexity of the design, that it would actually work, so he did a test run of its effectiveness on his own car. To his amazement, it worked flawlessly. The Technician gave specific instructions, telling him exactly where to attach the small magnetized box within the engine compartment.

The second device adhered to the gas tank in a similar fashion. Khaled had attached these items on two separate occasions while Enright's wife was with her daughter at the therapist. It did not take long, and each time Khaled had parked next to the van and pretended to drop his keys. He prided himself on deploying these subtle facades as an extra layer of protection in case some observant person noticed him reaching around under the van. No one had noticed.

The time was drawing near, and Khaled could feel the adrenaline beginning to pump throughout his body. His training had taught him how to disperse it so that it did not interfere with his control. Khaled began methodically tensing and releasing his muscles while taking in long, controlled breaths, enabling him to maintain a physiological balance under the intensity of these circumstances.

Khaled activated the mobile application on his phone and instantly had a view of the front of Enright's house. Both detonator triggers, disguised as retractable pens, sat on the passenger seat under a folded newspaper. The red pen trigger was designed to activate the first device and the blue would engage the second. The color coding was important to Khaled as he could not afford a mistake in the plan's execution. He observed that both of the family cars were there. The minivan and the sedan. Years of patiently waiting led up to this moment in time. Khaled reveled in its significance. He took a deep breath, waiting for the triggering event.

24

"How's this conversation going to go?" Izzy asked showing concern in her voice.

"Well, from where we sit this guy is a damn hero. Everything we know about him points in that direction. So, as far as questioning goes, I just want to know what he saw that caused him to redirect his attention. It might be the lynchpin in determining if the bus was an accident or something more." Nick said this knowing that he didn't have to explain further the other possibility.

They turned onto Declan's street. Nick saw a female exit the house that the GPS was indicating belonged to the Enrights. The woman had a little girl in tow, presumably her daughter. The little blond-haired girl walked with her head down and arms intertwined as if in an embrace. She followed directly behind her mother and waited until the sliding door of the minivan opened. The child entered, disappearing into the interior. The girl's mother leaned in, assisting her into the car seat.

Nick pulled to the side of the street. He decided to wait until she left before approaching the house to speak with Declan Enright. There was no need to alarm his wife and young daughter. She had probably become jaded toward any law enforcement officials since the internal affairs inquisition into her husband that led to his termination.

Nick registered Izzy's silent approval, demonstrating her understanding of his thought process. She looked over giving him a knowing glance. At that moment, Nick thought for the first time that maybe there could possibly be something more to their partnership. The notion was fleeting as his attention was immediately redirected to what was transpiring before him.

Using his surveillance camera, Khaled watched as the two walked out of the house. He'd witnessed this same routine over the past several weeks. The daughter would follow close behind the mother, never holding hands and never talking. He thought of his Sonia and how different this girl was in comparison. Something was amiss with the littlest Enright girl, but none of that would matter now.

He observed the mother leaning inside the side door of the minivan to secure her daughter into her car seat. After tending to her, Khaled watched as the Golden Man's wife entered the driver's side and closed her door. The brake lights illuminated, indicating that the engine had started.

Khaled silently counted to three, reaching down he grabbed the first detonator that looked like a red pen and pressed the button on top. As expected, the brake lights of the minivan went off. He could see a slight sway in the van, indicating that Enright's wife was moving around. Probably trying to figure out what had happened and why the engine had just died. Khaled waited.

He saw what he was looking for. The van was shaking much more visibly now. Panic had set in because the first device worked as designed, rendering the electronics of the minivan useless. More importantly, the Technician's creation had engaged the locks, disabling the ability to open the door from the inside. *Trapped. Panic-stricken. Just like his little Sonia had been eight years ago.* Khaled waited.

Declan's cell phone rang. He saw that it was his wife. He answered, assuming that she must have forgotten something. In the chaos of their life, this happened more times than not.

"Hey babe, what's up?" Declan said casually with a little curiosity in his voice.

"We're locked in! Something happened to the van. Laney and I are stuck in here." Val's voice was steady, but there was a hint of panic. Declan assumed that the tension in her voice was probably from the fact that this break in routine might send Laney into an uncontrollable screaming fit.

"Okay. Where are you guys?" Declan asked, figuring they were somewhere close.

"I'm in the God danged driveway." Even under stress Val kept her composure and refrained from language that was inappropriate for their children. Declan had failed in that regard many times.

"I'll be right out," Declan said, and immediately began rummaging the kitchen drawer for the spare set of keys to the minivan.

Nick could not figure out exactly what was happening in the car, but it looked like Enright's wife needed some help. He watched her banging on the windows of the minivan and could see through the light tint that she had climbed into the back seat area.

"Let's go give her a hand," Nick said this almost simultaneously as Izzy was making an ushering gesture for him to go.

They were only a few houses down, enabling the two to close the gap quickly between them and the van. As Nick and Izzy popped out of their Impala things rapidly deteriorated before their eyes.

"Shit! Look!" Izzy yelled, pointing in the direction of the left wheel well of the blue van.

An orange ball of fire ballooned out from underneath the rear of the vehicle. Flames licked at the blue paint, spreading up the side. The two agents exchanged a quick glance. No need to speak. They were in sync. Moving swiftly, Izzy ran to the side door and pulled hard. It didn't budge. Nick popped his trunk and was digging under the spare tire. He came up a moment later with a black tire iron in hand. The left side of the van was already engulfed in flames. He rounded to its right where the fire was beginning to continue its assault. The heat was intense. The combination of melting paint, metal, and rubber created a thick black smoke, obscuring the van's occupants.

"Cover your head!" Nick yelled into the van at Enright's wife as he reared up with the tire iron. Enright's wife covered her screaming child as they huddled down on the floorboard of the passenger side. Nick swung at the window with tremendous force just as Declan Enright exited the side door of the house in full stride. Confusion and fear were apparent on the face of the former frogman as he took in the sight.

Khaled watched in disbelief as the FBI agent from the bank and a dark-haired female pulled up to the Golden Man's house. He had activated the second device moments before their arrival. By design it had punctured the gas line and ignited the exposed fuel, triggering an intense fire that quickly covered the van. He witnessed in shock and disbelief as the two agents ran out of their car toward the burning minivan. The black and white images on his mobile app displayed the failure of his plan. Years of work fell apart before his eyes. *This was Enright's time to feel the burn! It was to be his Al Harq!*

He looked on as the FBI agent shattered the side window of the van with one heavy swing of a tire iron. The wife and child were pulled to safety. The group frantically ran toward the rear of Enright's house with his daughter, unharmed. The minivan burned. Flames ravaged its metal frame throwing the acrid black smoke high into the air. Khaled turned off the phone and sat in a dazed silence.

Khaled was only a few streets away, watching as the black smoke climbed above the rooftops as the roar of a fire engine on approach came to life in the distance. It was time for him to go. The Colorado timeline had already begun.

25

The combination of sounds from the approaching sirens and the inconsolable screams from Laney combined to create an additional layer of chaos. Declan had pulled his wife out of the burning van, using a fireman's carry. He saw the FBI agent reach in through the broken glass, grabbing for his daughter. Declan observed as the agent ran into difficulty extricating Laney from the floorboard. She had curled herself into a ball. The agent from the bank persevered, climbing partially into the burning van to save his daughter. Declan noticed that the agent was bleeding from his arms and chest where the shattered glass fragments had slashed through the sleeves of his button-up shirt, penetrating his skin.

The group had all collapsed onto the grass of the fenced-in backyard. Laney was lost in a fit of writhing screams. Declan held her in the same manner that his wife had yesterday, rocking gently back and forth with her in his tight embrace as he hummed into her ear. Sadly, this was one of the rare times that he ever got to hold his sweet Laney and he cherished the opportunity, regardless of its circumstance. She did not react well to human contact, even from her parents. Ripley, their five-year-old, seemed to be the only one that had broken the no-contact barrier and could hold Laney's hand.

Declan surveyed the turmoil, trying to piece together how all five of them had suddenly come to be in his backyard together. His ability to comprehend anything was hampered by Laney's wailing and convulsing body movements. Declan continued to hum.

"Who the hell are you people?" Val's question was said in a combination of anger and confusion. Her mind was obviously still reeling from the very recent trauma that she and Laney had just endured.

"We're with the FBI. We were driving to your house to meet with your husband when we saw that you were in trouble." It was Izzy that spoke first. She had a way of calming people down.

"Okay. Sorry, I am just... well, I have no idea what just happened." Val softened her tone and shot a quick glance of concern to Declan. He gave a slight nod demonstrating that he registered her uneasiness with the FBI's arrival so soon after the robbery.

"I am just glad we got here when we did. Your van ignited fast. What happened to your vehicle?" Izzy asked, genuinely perplexed.

"I don't know. Nothing seemed different when I started it. I was taking Laney to her daily therapy session. Then, all of a sudden, everything just shut off. I heard the doors lock and I couldn't get them open. I mean aren't doors supposed to automatically open from the inside?" Val's voice trembled as she spoke.

"I'm no mechanic, but I've never heard of a malfunction like that before," Izzy reassured.

Laney had started to calm, and Declan loosened his hold on her. He gingerly righted her, lifting her off the ground. She stood and then followed him, arms folded, to the swing set where she sat and rocked, soothing herself further. Declan returned to the group, who looked like survivors of some campy '80s horror movie. Each of their shirts was covered in some variety of soot and blood stains.

"I can't thank you enough for what you did back there." Declan's arm outstretched taking Nick's hand giving it a firm shake.

"It was nothing. I'm truly glad that we happened to be there. And besides, I think that it is I who owe you the debt of gratitude. You saved my life yesterday. If it hadn't been for you I would have been laying on the M.E.'s slab." Nick pushed himself off the ground and stood before Enright.

Izzy took in the sight. Both of these equally impressive men standing face to face had left her somewhat awestruck.

"You're bleeding pretty good," Nick observed, pointing at Declan's shoulder.

"Damn." Declan looked down toward his left side, realizing that he must have ripped open the stitches when he had carried Val from the burning van.

"You should have the medics take a look," Nick said.

"Can't. I have no insurance. We can't afford the bill. I'll be fine. Had worse." Declan was short in his responses. The fact that the FBI just happened to stop by was not lost on him. *Maybe he had missed something that these agents had found.* All these pleasantries seemed genuine, but they could just be trying to lull him into a false sense of security before they asked about the armored truck. Declan kept his guard up while maintaining his affable demeanor. Declan subconsciously glanced at the area where the money was buried.

"When things calm down, I need to talk to you about yesterday. I think you may be able to help me out. Get your family settled. I'll go speak with the fire and police guys to get them up to speed." Nick and Izzy walked back toward the front and stood by as the fire department got the blaze under control.

Powerful streams of water produced by the firetruck doused the fire, quelling the rising black smoke of the charred minivan. He had not noticed it during the fire, but now Nick saw that a red Toyota Corolla was parked under the tree on the other side.

26

Police and fire units had cleared the street surrounding Declan's house. Many of the emergency personnel had worked the bus explosion from the day before. The physical and emotional toll was etched on their faces. Nick had requested that the Enright's minivan be towed to the FBI satellite office in Meriden, Connecticut for additional evidentiary processing. He wasn't sure yet if the two incidents were connected, but as Nick's college lit professor used to say when quoting Linda Poindexter, "Coincidence is a plan in disguise." It appeared to him that the last couple days might be a testament to that adage.

Nick and Izzy were seated on the small corner bench in the Enright's dining room. The house was small but well kept. It was only a two-bedroom, one-bathroom home and yet somehow, they had managed to fit three girls and two adults into this quaint colonial.

"I have a really important question," Nick said as Declan fired up the Keurig.

"Shoot." Declan played it cool but was concerned where this questioning could eventually lead.

"What is your morning bathroom routine like with three girls and a wife?" Nick chuckled. His smile eased the tension.

Declan laughed softly, shaking his head. "I'd rather be dodging bullets in the sand on some days than fighting for a moment of peace here," Declan said as he blew a kiss at his wife.

Everyone in the room laughed, and for a moment it seemed that everyone forgot that Val and Laney had just barely escaped a fiery death inside of the family's minivan.

"You guys couldn't have come at a better time. I don't think that I would have been able to gain access to them in time if it hadn't been for you two," Declan said. The sincerity in his eyes further acknowledged the efforts of Nick and Izzy.

"Like I said earlier. I owe you and was glad to have an opportunity to repay my debt," Nick responded, deflecting the accolade.

"Obviously, I'm glad that you came to see me when you did, but what was it that brought you my way in the first place?" Declan spoke calmly, but he could feel a palpable pressure rising inside him.

"I'm not sure how much your wife knows about yesterday's bus incident. Do you feel comfortable speaking about it in front of her?" Nick was offering Declan an opportunity to speak in private.

"I keep nothing from Val. Not ever. So, whatever we need to talk about can be done in her presence." Declan also knew that it was good to have witnesses present during any questioning and wanted her to be there as a safety net if the Bureau agents were trying to set him up.

"I meant no offense. I just wanted to make you as comfortable as possible." Nick gave Val a friendly smile as he said this.

"So, what's up?" Declan wanted to get it over with.

"I was reviewing the video footage from the bomb yesterday. I watched it over and over again at various speeds. I didn't catch it at first but later noticed that right before you pulled me to the ground you turned your head to the left. Something caught your attention and I need to know what it was." Nick said this as his mind momentarily relived those intense few seconds before the explosion. His pulse quickened, and he could feel the adrenaline begin to activate in his system. Nick knew that this was a common physiological reaction when rehashing a recent traumatic event.

"Okay?" Declan said this in a tone that made the statement more of a question than an affirmation.

"What did you see that caused you to react the way you did?" Nick now asked more directly, but still maintained a non-accusatory tone.

"Someone who shouldn't have been there," Declan spoke softly.

"I don't understand," Nick said flatly. He was quickly realizing that Declan Enright did not give up any amount of information easily.

"I saw someone from my distant past who was out of place in little old Wethersfield. I saw him two weeks before near the bus stop, but it didn't click then. It wasn't until I saw him standing by the fence line that separates the bank from the gas station that it dawned on me who he was." Declan paused. Fearful that his disclosure about being at the bus stop two weeks ago had potentially exposed something he shouldn't have.

"A guy from your past causes you to stop running mid-stride and redirects you to react by pulling me to safety?" Frustration was setting in as Nick saw that Declan was putting up a wall. Nick had an uncanny ability to read people and could see that Enright was holding back. "Tell me what I'm missing here."

"My past is not that of your average citizen. When someone from it appears, I become concerned."

"We did some research into your background before heading over for our visit. When you say *your past* are you referring to your life as a police officer or your time in the military?" Nick asked this assuming it was the latter but didn't want to jump to conclusions.

Declan registered no judgment to Nick's question. "It was someone that I crossed paths with when playing in the sandbox," Declan said, making a second reference to gauge Nick and determine if he too was ex-military. If he didn't ask what he meant by the term sandbox, then he could plausibly assume that the FBI agent had also served.

"It's like pulling teeth with you." Nick exposed a hint of frustration. "I did a little digging into your military past and I understand your background. I'm not trying to gather information from classified missions. I'm simply trying to figure out who this guy is and if you think he was involved with the bus's explosion." Nick's face had hardened and was more serious now.

"Sorry, old habits die hard. People start asking me questions about my past and I revert to my counter-interrogation training. It's like a reflex reaction." Declan gave a soft chuckle. "I don't know the guy's name, but I am more than willing to tell you whatever I can remember about him if you think that might help."

"Anything you can tell me would be better than what we have right now. Please go on," Nick said, softening his facial expression.

"Some of the guys in my team referred to him as the Boston guy or just plainly, Boston. He was a village translator in a small town located twenty miles east of Choman and set in the foothills of the Cheekha Dar Mountain. My unit had taken refuge there as a waypoint between objectives. It was challenging terrain but was a thoroughfare for an Iranian insurgent group that had sprung up in Iraq. He was a great asset to us. We had a guy in my team, Hook, that spoke Arabic, but it was always better if a local assisted. And that is what he did."

Nick took this moment to interject while Declan was paused in thought. "Why did you call him Boston?"

"He had been educated at Northeastern University in Boston. My unit commander, Moose, got along really well with him. He also went to school in Boston. Both had similar degrees. I guess they bonded on those points. They maintained a friendship until the village elders pulled their support for us."

"I know that you probably aren't supposed to talk about details for Opsec but give me whatever you can." Nick used lingo knowing that Enright would pick up on this and realize that he too had some military experience. Nick also did this because he knew that using similar terminology or gestures encouraged communication.

"I assume that you have some experience over there too. Who were you with?" Declan asked. Two knights raising their visor to gauge friend-or-foe.

"I was with the 3rd Ranger Battalion. You and I were overseas around the same block of time. Shit, we may have been on the same base, but I wouldn't know because your service record has some holes," Nick said, raising one eyebrow in mock suspicion.

"So, you have been doing some digging?" Declan responded, sounding impressed.

"Of course we did. I had to figure out who we were dealing with."

"You could have just asked." Declan smiled.

"Yeah, that's worked out well so far," Nick sarcastically blurted out. "Back to this translator, you mentioned that things in the village changed with respect to their support?"

"The acceptance of American military troops in an Iraqi town is a careful balancing act under the best of circumstances. The politics of those relationships was not something that I involved myself with and avoided as much as possible. But after we pulled out, a terrorist group moved in. Without going into details, we assaulted the bad guy stronghold in the village. During a heavy firefight, the translator's young daughter was killed," Declan said softly.

"Shit," Nick said, letting out a sigh. His mind was already heading down a dark path.

"Yeah, shit. The translator was never the same. Physically he carried scars from the fire. He was found in the smoldering rubble of the school holding his burned daughter. But psychologically he was a broken man. I'm sure that you can now understand why his presence outside the bank yesterday completely caught me off guard."

Nick was quiet. The reality of the bus explosion was sinking in. Sometimes he hated being right. "It was him. He blew the bus." He wasn't sure if he was saying this aloud for his own benefit, but he noticed that everyone in the room was looking at him with a hint of fear in their eyes. Everyone except Declan. Nick saw the rage that lay just beneath the surface. The operator inside of Declan Enright had been awakened.

Val broke the silence when she walked out of the kitchen and returned with her sewing kit. Declan grimaced knowing what was in store for him.

Izzy got up to help. "I was a medic in the Army. Not a warrior elite like the two studs over there, but I patched plenty of them up during my time. I can help with that."

"Thank you. I really wasn't looking forward to doing it again so soon." The two set to work, sterilizing the needle and cleaning the area around the wound.

"I've got to make a quick call." Nick pulled his cellphone from his pocket and held it to his ear as he walked outside.

"Jake. I'm at the ex-military guy's house, and it's what I thought. The bus was no accident." Nick let this information sink into his supervisor's brain before continuing.

"Holy shit. How sure are you? If I run this up the chain and it turns out you're wrong..." Jake Nelson let the veiled threat go unsaid. Typical bureaucrat, more worried about his potential backlash than doing the right thing.

"I am as sure as I have ever been. Make the damn call." Nick Lawrence very rarely spoke like this to a supervisor and because of that, he knew that it would have the intended effect.

"Nick, you and Izzy are reassigned as the primaries on this thing as of this minute. The armored truck investigation can wait. Tell me what you need. You two are going to have to come in and give me a full workup on what you have so far. I don't want to sound like an idiot in front of the SAIC." Nelson was always concerned about Special Agent in Charge Emily Watson's opinion of him. Not a great quality to have, especially when lives hang in the balance.

"I will get in when I can, but we may have to do the briefing on the move. I may be sitting at a secondary attack location right now." Nick had realized this when Declan mentioned the translator's daughter having been burned alive. He had just witnessed Declan's daughter almost face the same end.

As Nick ended the call he found himself again staring at the red Toyota belonging to Declan Enright. *Coincidence is a plan in disguise.*

27

Declan leaned out the side door and called over to Nick who was standing on the sidewalk in front of his house, "I need a few minutes to make a call. Feel free to help yourself to anything in the fridge." He looked at his two nurses who were cleaning up the bloody mess left in the wake of his in-home shoulder surgery. Val and Izzy were chatting like old friends. War had that effect on people. And that's what this was quickly becoming.

"DJ. It's me." Declan had stepped outside and stood by his girls' playscape that was out of earshot of the house.

"Holy shit. Declan 'Ace' Enright calling me! And to what do I owe this honor?" Alex Morales was Declan's closest friend and the person he trusted most in this world, besides Val. Alex's luck with the ladies had long ago earned him the nickname *Don Juan* from his Teammates but was shortened over time to DJ.

"It's been too long, my friend. Lots to catch up on, but we're going to have to leave that for later. Right now, I need your help."

"Absolutely. What's going on?" Alex answered without any hesitation. They had not been in contact much since Laney's birth. The challenges that came with raising her had taken much of his time and energy, leaving little for anything else. But no amount of separation, chronologic or geographic, could sever the bond that Declan and DJ had forged.

"There was an attack yesterday here in my quiet little town. It hasn't hit the news yet because no one has figured it out. A serious shitstorm is on the horizon."

"What kind of attack?" DJ knew it was better to ask than assume.

"Bus. Dual-event sequencing. The first event was a fire. That drew in the crowd. The second was the explosion. If I had to guess I would say C4 or Semtex. The blast radius was short range, but the result was devastating. The metal fragments from the bus acted as fléchettes and did most of the damage." Declan had responded to his friend's inquiry devoid of emotion. He methodically laid out his assessment using a brevity of words. He had learned the importance of emotionally detaching himself so that his judgment was not clouded.

"What's the count?" Alex asked. The initial jocularity of the conversation was gone, and his tone was now more serious.

"Thirty-two is what the FBI agents said. That number will probably change. It was bad. Like being back over there." This last statement needed no further explanation between the two men.

"Jesus! Did you just say thirty-two? The last bombing attack to yield any casualties was in 2013, at the Boston Marathon, and I think the count was around three people. If what you're saying is true, then this is the deadliest explosive attack in recent history." Alex sighed quietly after processing the reality of what he had just said.

"I am sure that it will be playing out that way on all the news stations very soon," Declan said, knowing that a wave of panic was about to befall the nation and somehow, he was at its epicenter. "Do you remember the Boston guy from the village just outside of Choman?"

"Of course. Good guy. He kind of lost it after his daughter died, but who wouldn't? Why are you bringing him up now?" Alex sounded somewhat confused by this new direction in the conversation.

"I saw him a few weeks ago at a bus stop in town. I couldn't place him then, but he was there yesterday at the time of the explosion." Declan's voice was composed, but the pulsing in his re-injured shoulder activated a deep source of rage, and he could feel his adrenaline kick in.

"He was there?" Alex questioned. He was slowly getting up to speed on what Declan was overtly hinting at. It was a hard transition to make when sitting on his back porch in the Texas sun, drinking sweet tea.

"Thank God I recognized him when I did, or we wouldn't be having this conversation now. I caught him out of the corner of my eye as I ran to help the people on the bus. He had something small in his hand and kept it down low by his waistline. I realized that it was a detonator with just enough time to drop to the ground and shield myself from the blast." Declan had been out of practice and could feel his breathing rate change as he retold the events.

"Just like old times. You're a dang shit magnet." Alex chuckled. Men in their line of work tended to find humor in the gravest of circumstances. It was part defense mechanism and part genetic makeup.

"Have you seen him out your way?"

"Who? The Translator?" Alex questioned. He still wasn't connecting the dots that Declan had.

"Yeah. I think it had something to do with me or maybe us. Today, my wife and daughter got trapped in our van. The doors locked, and the power was cut making it impossible to get out. Right in our driveway! Then it caught on fire. The fire was engulfing the van when I came out. If it hadn't been for the two FBI agents that showed up, Val and Laney would surely be dead." Declan knew that he was throwing a lot at his friend, but the last twenty-four hours had spun him up and his mind was racing.

"So, wait a minute. You're saying that he bombed a bus and then attacked your family?" Alex's tone conveyed the seriousness of the implication in this question.

"Yes. I have no proof that the attack on my wife and daughter was done by the Translator, but the FBI agent, Nick, is in agreement that it is a real possibility. He sent the van off so that the Bureau crime scene techs can take a look at it."

"You're asking me if I saw him because you think he might be planning something out here too? Do you think the Translator is coming for me? Is this about his daughter dying? You think he blames us? How the hell would he even know who we are? I mean we're ghosts. Steak Sauce baby!" Alex's last comment was made in reference to the nickname given to their unit, Alpha One. Hook had said it one night after many beers, *"Do you guys realize that we are named after a steak sauce?"* The Team had laughed and from that point forward the nickname stuck.

"There aren't many of us left to come after," Declan said.

"I know. Hook's still in Colorado and Moose is doing his thing in D.C. But that's it. Eight hard men are now down to four." Alex didn't need to list the fallen. Those names were forever etched into all of their hearts. "I don't have any kids if you think that's his motive. I have my niece and nephew out here, but that's it."

"I don't know his angle. I just know that a bus blew up and a lot of innocent people are dead. Then one day later my wife and daughter were almost burned alive. Every fiber of my body is telling me that the Translator was behind it." Declan's wiry muscles tensed, and his teeth clenched as he continued, "I don't give a shit why he did it! I am going to make sure he doesn't have a chance to do it to anyone else."

"What do you think his next move is going to be? I haven't seen him out this way, but that doesn't mean he hasn't been here."

"I don't know yet. Who knows? Maybe he is still lurking around my neck of the woods. The FBI agent, Nick, is getting the information out through law enforcement channels. The problem is that no one knows the Translator's real name and we have no picture of him."

"Moose may be able to help with the name. He and the Translator were pretty close before things went sideways. He might remember. I think I can help with the photo. I've got a couple boxes filled with memorabilia from our days in the Teams. Some of the photos are with the natives. I know that I have some pictures from the time when we were in the good graces of the village. I'm pretty sure there has to be at least one picture with the Translator in it. When I find it, I will text it to you."

"Good thinking. I will reach out to Moose." Declan thought for a moment and then said, "Maybe I'm wrong about him coming after our team, but just do me a favor and watch your ass."

"Will do, brother. I know you got your hands full there, so I will call Hook and give him the heads up. Stay frosty and watch your six."

"Thanks. Good hearing your voice bro." Declan hung up and returned to the house. Nick was in the kitchen with Izzy and Val. Laney was on the couch in the living room using her tablet with the headphones on, oblivious to the visitors.

Nick looked down at a text message he'd just received. His head came up and he said, "Where's your TV?"

Declan and the group stood in the living room and stared at the one television in the Enright house. The room was silent except for the voice of the news anchor.

"This video was just received by our agency. Please be advised that what we are about to show you is graphic in nature."

The video that followed was taken by a cellphone. The user's unsteady hand coupled with the canted angle created a Blair Witch effect in the production quality. The footage began just as the bus fire initiated and continued until the blast.

The video then cut to a long table with seven men all wearing the traditional ghutra headdress, but their faces were obscured by a black cloth. Only the man in the middle spoke. His English was clear with minimal accent.

"It has been too long that the American people have used their military forces to destroy other countries in the name of national security. Yesterday we demonstrated how easy it is for us to do the same to you. There is more to come, and the timeline has begun. The only way to stop the next attack is the complete withdrawal of the occupying troops in Iraq. There will be no further communication. Your President always says that he doesn't negotiate with terrorists. We agree with that statement. Your government is the biggest terrorist organization in the world and we will not negotiate with them either. We are The Seven. No place is safe."

The news cameras faded back to the Barbie and Ken look-a-likes that sat behind the anchor desk. The journalists continued the broadcast with a combination of fear and disbelief. They quickly cut to a press conference. At the podium was FBI Special Agent in Charge, Emily Watson, and behind her stood Jake Nelson with an ensemble cast of the usual characters. This had become a law enforcement protocol in recent years when tragedy struck. A panel of bigwigs would get together in a show of solidarity between state and local law enforcement. They each would thank the other agencies as if receiving an award at a banquet. Usually, after all the pleasantries were exchanged nothing of real importance would be said. The real work was being done behind the scenes by people who didn't talk to the Press. Sadly, these clips would be repeated and analyzed ad nauseum by panels of experts until the next update. Declan clicked the television off. They had work to do and he needed to pitch something to the agents.

"I reached out to an old friend and he may be able to help us in getting a name and photo of the Translator," Declan said in the hopes that sharing it would help the investigation, but he was also secretly wishful that they would see his potential value in the manhunt. He needed to piggyback off the FBI if he was ever going to get a chance to personally ensure that the Translator paid for what he did to his family. Nobody had ever attacked Declan Enright's family. *That was a mistake and the Translator would pay a tremendous consequence.*

"Fantastic. Should I even ask who you are getting this help from or is that a waste of breath?" Nick said this half-jokingly, but there was an underlying truth to that statement.

"I could tell you, but I would have to kill you," Declan retorted with the stereotypical line and a smile. "On a serious note, the guys from my former unit would probably only speak with me. They aren't as trusting of law enforcement as I am."

"Okay. I'm not going to push it, but as soon as you get any info give me a call," Nick said as he and Izzy made their way to the door. Nick's phone began to ring, and Declan noticed that he seemed hesitant to answer.

"Hey. What's going on?" Nick held up one finger to Izzy and exited out the side door of the house. Izzy stayed behind with Declan. "Where is Patrick now?" Nick said, moving out of earshot of the house's occupants.

"His boss?" Declan asked, breaking the awkward silence left by Nick when he walked out.

"Ummm. No. His mother. Nick's got some personal shit going on with her. He's a great guy. Gave up everything and came to Connecticut to take care of her." Izzy stopped herself. "I don't know why I just told you his personal business. That's not my place."

"No worries. Everybody has their burdens. It's nice to see that you FBI guys aren't all robots," Declan said, easing the awkward tension that arose from Izzy's disclosure about Nick's mother.

"Thanks."

"I was about to ask Nick before he took the call, but I have an idea that I want to run by you guys." Declan was speaking in a more hushed tone obviously trying to keep this conversation from Val, who was in the other room tending to Laney.

"What's up?" Izzy seemed open to suggestion.

"I think that I can really help your investigation. I've done investigative work before, but more importantly, I have hunted guys like the Translator. With success." This last statement carried another message. Success in his old life meant target elimination.

"We read your history and know that it's both extensive and impressive. I'm not exactly sure what you mean by help though."

"Your agency hires consultants all the time. People with special skills. The Bureau pays them like the contractors used on overseas security gigs. I have skills and connections that will benefit your investigation. If you really want to get this guy, then you're going to need me." Declan realized this last part sounded cocky and tried to soften the blow. "That came out wrong. I just think that if I worked side by side with you and Nick then things would move quicker."

Izzy was pensive and seemed to be absorbing what he had just said. "I want to get this son of a bitch. If Nick can convince our boss, Nelson, then I'm good with it."

"I could obviously use the money too. Things have been pretty tight in the Enright house since I got canned from my police department," Declan said.

He thought that this potential opportunity would remove any suspicion about the robbery money if he could generate a legitimate source of income. The irony was not lost on him that the income would come from the same governmental agency investigating the crime. In light of these recent events, the robbery was recessed in his mind, but he couldn't allow himself to forget that these two were investigating him... even if they didn't know it.

Izzy shot a glance back at Laney and Val. "Hopefully Nick can convince Nelson to overlook your termination from law enforcement. It wouldn't be the first time the Bureau partnered with someone who had a tainted past."

Declan said nothing.

"Shit, that came out wrong. I meant we've worked with criminals to help solve other crimes. Damn. I just keep making it worse." Izzy shook her head. "Listen, we read your file and for what it's worth, you should have received a damn medal for that shooting and not a pink slip. Nick feels the same way I do about it." Izzy blushed, fumbling with her words.

Declan relaxed a bit after hearing what their take had been on his shooting. "I hope that Nick can get this worked out with your boss."

"Tell you what. Let me bounce this off him when we are alone so he doesn't feel the pressure. I know him better than most and he always needs a little bit of time to decompress after dealing with his mother." Izzy put a hand on Declan's uninjured shoulder and smiled, knowing that he would understand.

"Thank you."

Nick had ended his call. The Enrights and the agents shook hands and said their goodbyes. The Impala drove off and Declan returned inside his home hoping that the decision on his involvement would be made quickly. Regardless, if he would be officially or unofficially working on hunting the Translator, he needed to get his gear. In the partially finished basement, Declan went to an area near the bulky oil-fed steam boiler. He pushed aside some cardboard boxes exposing a large safe. Inside were relics of a past that he never thought he would need again. Especially on his home turf.

28

The drive to Colorado was uneventful. The radio stations were playing The Seven's manifesto on what seemed like a continuous loop. Fear was spreading as predicted. All the "red-blooded Americans" were using social media and radio call-in shows to make their powerless threats of what they would do to the terrorists. Khaled passed by many cops and state policemen during his three-day road trip from Wethersfield, Connecticut to Colorado Springs. None of these *men-of-action* had given Khaled a second thought. Some had held doors for him and exchanged pleasantries when at the various gas stations along the way. There was no face put to the monster that lurked their lands and so he was able to move among the people with anonymity. There would be no additional warning. Soon the seriousness of The Seven's message would be delivered again and the panic to follow would be crippling.

Routinely scheduled events offered up unique opportunities for people like Khaled. The support provided by The Seven enabled him to do things with ease that would have been otherwise impossible to accomplish without exposing himself.

Jeremiah Wilks was the only Golden Man that Khaled had communicated with using his native Arabic tongue while in the village. The others in his group called him Hook. Khaled had once asked him why they called him that and Wilks deflected, telling him that it was a long and embarrassing story. The story of Wilks's nickname came up again during an impromptu night of drinking with the Golden Men where Khaled had shared a homemade Arak. Wilks apparently had made the mistake of bragging to his teammates that his penis bent slightly to the left and from that day forward he was known as Hook. He recalled how funny it had been that night. *How different things were before they took his Sonia away.*

Khaled had learned through information gathered by The Seven's extensive sources that Wilks had moved to Colorado Springs after getting out of the military. Wilks had become the owner of a medicinal marijuana dispensary in the downtown area. He only had one child, a teenage boy. Wilks was divorced but from the surveillance camera installed outside of the house, it appeared that he spent a lot of time with the boy.

Khaled called one of the two numbers in his phone. He could hear the rhythmic click of the encrypted line. Routed to its destination, ringing only once before it was answered. The person on the other end of the line waited silently for him to speak. "Is it confirmed?" Khaled asked simply.

"Yes. Your new identification and vehicle registration will be at the apartment. The Technician has supplied the other items that you requested and they are secured in a false wall under the kitchen sink." Khaled wondered if the man on the other end even understood what was going on or if he was just reading a script supplied by The Seven. *It didn't matter. Those details were beyond his control. And therefore, superfluous.*

"Then Saturday is a go. Everything is on schedule," Khaled confirmed.

Just as Khaled was about to hang up, the voice on the other end of the line said, "What was your delay to leave? You should have been on the road yesterday."

Khaled took a deep breath and exhaled slowly, clearing the anger from his voice. "I had something come up. It was nothing that I can't resolve at a later date." Click and the phone call was ended. *They serve me.*

There was a cleanness to the air around him. During his first reconnaissance visit to Colorado Springs, Khaled had experienced some difficulty adjusting to the elevation and dryness. He suffered from headaches and nosebleeds but found that drinking the local tap water helped. During Khaled's operator training, he'd learned that he was quite athletic. As an academic and later the village's school teacher, sports had held no interest to him. But after Sonia's death, he realized that a change was needed, and the Dust Devil was born.

Khaled enjoyed hiking on challenging terrain and found his current location to be reminiscent of the Cheekha Dar mountain training grounds. Colorado Springs, or the Springs as the locals called it, provided some excellent trails to explore. The foothills of the Rocky Mountains were temperate, and the views were breathtaking. *I will move out here when this is all done. If I can manage to survive the next few weeks.*

Khaled arrived early, but he saw that some of the event planners were already moving about the grassy expanse of Memorial Park. He hung the staff parking pass from his rearview mirror and exited his Honda. The license plates had been changed since his arrival and by DMV standards his vehicle and driver's license were valid. The level of detail that The Seven had put into his backstory and credentials was beyond his expectations.

The identification card encased in plastic hanging from the lanyard around his neck listed his credentials as the safety inspector. Khaled entered under the awning flapping in the light breeze of the cool mountain air. It read "Welcome to the Labor Day Launch." It was a Colorado Springs tradition going back forty plus years. The colorful hot air balloons were a symbolic icon of Colorado and adorned many postcards and billboards throughout the state. It was a free event that drew thousands of locals and tourists each year. An impressive sight to behold.

"Good morning, "Khaled said as he passed by several of the behind-the-scenes personnel. They waved to him and smiled. *Nice people*, he thought. "Just doing a once over on the tethering lines before the crowds get in here." One of the passing staffers responded by giving him the thumbs up.

This morning's launch would be an event simultaneously releasing over seventy balloons. Khaled walked over to a row of deflated balloons and began inspecting the lines. He was actually ensuring the devices that he had attached to seven of these monstrous contraptions were still in place. He'd been on location the previous night and assisted in the preparations for today's event. Darkness still shrouded the grounds as the sun hadn't begun its morning ascent. *All in place.*

The challenge for the Technician was the effective range of the detonator. Khaled was initially told that he would need to be in one of the balloons for it to work. This was impossible. Khaled had a debilitating fear of heights and demanded an alternate solution. As always, the Technician came through. Hand-held walkie-talkies were used by several of the staff members. One of these had been converted into the detonator and the long antenna enabled the Technician to give Khaled the range he needed so that he could remain on the ground. The other challenge for the Technician was creating a container for the explosive that could withstand the heat from the balloons' flame until detonation. That too had been accomplished by the genius of his gifted friend.

The seven balloons targeted for destruction were intermingled with the others. It was done intentionally to add to the shock value. One of the balloons held special significance for Khaled. The Technician was aware of his side projects and did not approve. This was why Khaled had the Technician send him the needed materials in advance for his next two operations in the event that he got cold feet. Some assurances were in place to continue the Technician's support, but Khaled believed in redundancy.

The crowds began pouring in. Sounds of the propane supported flames roared to life with each balloon's crew doing their part in preparation for the sunrise launch. Khaled stood back, scanning the field until he saw who he was looking for.

"Pretty cool huh?" Wilks had asked his son.

"Yeah," Wilks's son, Trevor, said nonchalantly. He had hit that cool-guy stage of his teenage years but was never disrespectful. Wilks knew that Trevor was excited because he saw his facial reaction when the invitation arrived. Wilks had assumed that it was a bullshit marketing scheme, but when he called the number on the postcard stating that he'd won a free balloon ride, he learned that it was a legit offer.

Wilks got excited when Trevor asked if he could bring another person on the ride. The two were close, but as teenage boys and dads go they had grown a bit distant lately. Wilks asked, and the balloon people said that one guest was acceptable. Then Trevor immediately asked his best friend Adam. Wilks didn't show it, but the blow to his heart was heavy. He had hoped that the plus one request would be used for him and was disappointed when Trevor chose to bring his friend.

"Dude, check out that chick," Adam mumbled to Trevor.

"I know, right? She was totally checking me out." The two boys pushed at each other, pretending to square off.

Trevor didn't lack for confidence, but neither had Wilks back in the day. He was glad to see that this quality had rubbed off on his son.

"Alright studs, let's get over to your balloon before you go off and get married." Wilks said this just a bit too loud and could see that his son's face flashed with a hint of embarrassment. He redirected them and pointed to the balloon. "There it is."

Trevor and Adam walked a few feet ahead of Wilks, pretending to be there on their own. Wilks laughed to himself, wondering if he had been as awkward around his parents when he was this age.

The boys entered the large basket that fit six additional people. The teenagers stood with the group listening to a safety briefing from the pilot. Wilks noted a trace of fear on his son's face but also observed that he hid it well. Just as Wilks had done many times before in his previous life. *Like father, like son.* Wilks never pressed his son to follow in his footsteps, but watching him standing there, he was confident that he could do it.

"So, what do you think?" Izzy had just finished passing along Declan's request to be involved in the case onto Nick.

Nick rubbed his head and looked at his partner. "Nelson is going to throw a fit." The thought of this brought a smile to his face. "I'm in. I'll make the call."

"Well, Nelson put you in charge. It's your show to run and in my humble opinion you should be able to pick your team."

"True. Hopefully, our politician of a boss will see it that way." Nick said this with a hint of optimism.

Nick also had an ulterior motive for his decision to vouch for Declan's assistance. He wasn't quite ready to share his thoughts with his trusted partner just yet. Nick felt that bringing Enright into the hunt for the Translator would give him an opportunity to monitor him more closely. It wasn't lost on him that a man of Enright's skill happened to be a member of the recently robbed Clover Leaf Bank and that he drove a red Corolla.

The call went as expected. Nelson had initially balked at the idea, mostly due to Declan's recent termination as a police officer. Nick laid out the facts surrounding the shooting and the political fallout that ended Declan's career. If anyone understood this process it would be Nelson, but Nick also knew that deep down his boss sided with the troops on the ground. Nick had also discussed the military skill set that Declan possessed without going into detail or compromising Jay's trust in him about the Alpha One info. Nelson authorized Declan to be brought in as a consultant only, and that he was to remain clear of any fieldwork. Nick had agreed to the terms even though he wasn't sure that he would be able to follow them.

"He's in. Consultant status only, but we will keep him close." Nick looked at Izzy's face. She seemed excited, almost happy. "You can call your new boyfriend and let him know the good news," Nick said this jokingly but felt a note of jealousy just beneath its surface.

"Don't worry, he's married." Izzy said this with a playful batting of her eyes.

Declan was excited when he received the call from Izzy. He had already packed two bags. One with enough clothing to get him through a week and the other duffle contained his gear. Hoisting the bags to his shoulder as he walked out to the waiting Impala, he felt like he was heading out on deployment again. He looked back at Val and his three daughters. When Abigail and Ripley had come home from school to the charred driveway and empty space where the minivan was normally parked, they were concerned, but he and Val told them that the car had malfunctioned. *No need to scare them.* Declan registered the look of despair on their faces when he told them about leaving to work with the FBI on a case. They were very perceptive. He did his best to quell their nerves, telling them that it was a good thing. He kissed his two eldest. He moved in to lay a gentle kiss on Laney's forehead. She turned to the side. Maybe it was her way of showing that she understood his departure and was upset by it. He hated leaving them all, but Laney in particular. Declan told them he would be back soon. *A promise he intended to keep.*

Ripley started to cry. She was the most emotional of his three girls. Declan kneeled face to face with her in a futile attempt to console her. Val intervened and put a gentle hand on his shoulder, signaling that she would deal with it. Declan stood and held Val in a tight embrace. He was single when he was in the service and now felt a new-found respect for those who deployed leaving behind their families.

Val had told the girls that they were going on a trip to Georgia to visit their Aunt Gretchen, Val's sister. The FBI had contacted the U.S. Marshals service and arranged for a protection detail to be assigned to Enright's family until the Translator could be located.

U. S. Marshal Whitney Rodgers had been tasked to Val and the girls. Declan immediately liked her when they met. Whitney had been a competition shooter long before she joined the Marshals. Beyond her resume, she was loud and outgoing and didn't appear to take any shit from anyone. Whitney was born and raised in Augusta, Georgia, and was elated when she learned that Val's sister lived in Martinez. Rodgers got approval for the family to go. They planned to depart shortly after Declan.

"Jesus, what did you throw in the trunk? A small elephant?" Nick jested as Declan entered the small government vehicle.

"Just some odds and ends." Declan broke into a slight grin.

"Khaled is the name of the man we are looking for," Declan announced, adjusting himself to the confining space of the Impala's back seat.

"So, all we have is the first name?" Izzy asked.

"Yes. That photograph I sent you yesterday is the only one that I could locate using my sources. Otherwise, he's a ghost." Declan didn't like people that he couldn't find. It was a disadvantage that left him feeling unbalanced.

"I already sent it to someone I trust that may be able to provide some insight. Nelson has a copy as well and it will be circulated in law enforce-ment circles, but I doubt it will be released to the public. We don't want to spook our bad guy and alert him of the manhunt," Nick said as he looked at Declan through the rearview mirror, gauging if he agreed with this tactic. Declan nodded his approval.

"Does the Bureau have any leads on where we think he may be hiding?" Declan wanted to find the Translator and share the contents of his heavy duffel bag with him.

"No idea. Hopefully, my friend will get back to me soon with something for us to work with. As of right now, we are flying blind."

29

The National Anthem had just finished being sung by a rising country music star that Khaled did not know of or care about. He was focused intently on the speaker's words that followed the crowd's cheers. "Fly high and enjoy the sky," the announcer proclaimed over the loudspeaker, and the tethering ropes were released. The glow of the canopies lit the cloud-covered dawn. The colorful dance had begun as the massive balloons began their gentle ascent.

He focused on one balloon. The massive rainbow-colored canopy made it impossible to miss. Inside he could see Wilks's son giving a slight wave to his father on the ground. Unbeknownst to them this would be the last communication the two would ever have.

Most of the hot air balloons had made their slow climb into the morning's light. Some of the teams were still on the ground, but the seven target ones were airborne. The walkie-talkie was held up to Khaled's ear as if he was listening to someone. He keyed the push-to-talk button on the side activating the detonator.

Simultaneously the seven wicker baskets erupted in flames. The effect was immediate and devastating. Screams of the onlookers below rippled across the grassy expanse of the park. Cell phones recorded the tragedy that was unfolding before their eyes. Khaled watched intently—focused solely on only one bystander's reaction to this event. Jeremiah Wilks.

Wilks said nothing. The horror of what he was witnessing had dropped him to his knees, Khaled observed only twenty feet away, as the former SEAL crumpled on the grassy field in helpless agony as he watched his son burning alive in a slow descent to the ground. Wilks let out an animalistic yell that momentarily seemed to drown out all others.

Khaled allowed himself a moment to absorb the broken Wilks before turning and walking back toward his car. His mind was already preparing for his next destination and the work ahead as he navigated a path through the onlookers.

30

Every news channel was running the same story. Nick, Izzy, and Declan sat in the second-floor conference room of the Wethersfield Police Department. The television mounted on the wall was muted. They decided that there was no need to have the background noise of an anchor reading teleprompter information that wasn't accurate. No commentary would do the scrolling images justice. They watched as the Labor Day Launch Festival had become the next target. Multiple videos shot from the witnesses on the ground showed the devastation in raw perspective provided by the amateur filmmakers.

The group knew without saying that this latest catastrophe was the work of the Translator. The slow descent of the falling hot air balloons looked like they were moving in slow motion making the scene even more horrific. When the canopies of the seven rigged balloons caught fire, it shifted them in the sky and rendered the controls useless, sending them crashing into other crews. Some of the desperate balloonists, facing a painful fiery death, chose to jump from their baskets hundreds of feet above the ground. It was a sickening sight.

In their collective experiences they had seen a lot of bad things involving the untimely death of others, but what transpired on the screen in front of them had shocked them all into silence. The news ticker running across the bottom of the television listed the ever-growing body count to be holding now at forty-eight. No new declaration from the terrorist group called The Seven, but they knew that was only a matter of time.

"How on God's green earth are we going to keep ahead of this guy? First, little Wethersfield and now he's hitting a festival in Colorado. I don't see a pattern and there have been no sightings of Khaled by any federal, state, or local law enforcement." Nick seethed and subconsciously gritted his teeth as he spoke.

"I know this attack fits the profile, but I need to make a quick call to confirm my suspicion," Declan said, and stepped to the corner of the room with his phone in hand.

"Hook?" Declan questioned, unable to discern if the voice he heard on the other end of the line was his long-time friend and former teammate. His speech was low and barely audible. A far departure from the larger-than-life, gregarious Jeremiah "Hook" Wilks of his past.

"Ace?" Wilks questioned despondently. "He's gone. Gone, bro. All the shit we've done back in the Teams and all I could do was stand by, helpless." Wilks's voice cracked. He was barely keeping it together as he spoke.

"What do you mean gone? Who are you talking about?" Declan showed genuine concern for his friend, but didn't understand the incoherent ramblings.

"Trevor!" Wilks lashed out.

Declan exhaled and felt the pain of his friend's loss. No parent should ever have to bury their child. He could think of no worse fate. "Brother, I'm so sorry. How?" Declan asked, assuming that he knew the answer, but needing to hear its confirmation.

"We were at the Labor Day Launch. He won a free hot air balloon ride. He went up..." Wilks couldn't finish, and Declan didn't need him to. "I mean how could this happen?" His voice a shadow of the man Declan remembered.

"It was no accident," Declan said. He was afraid of Wilks's reaction but knew that his friend needed to hear it.

"Wait a minute. I got that message you left on my phone about seeing the Translator in your town. You think he was behind this?" Wilks said desperately, instantly regretting not calling Declan back, but life often got in the way and a recent argument with his ex-wife had trumped the call.

"I know he was. He tried to kill my wife and daughter. He's the one behind the bus bombing here in Connecticut, and I'm sure that we will hear from the group calling themselves The Seven very soon about their involvement in this latest attack." Declan said this in the hope that this information would snap his friend back into the operator mindset by giving him an enemy to focus on.

"I'm going to find and kill this asshole," Wilks said in a strange, disconnected tone. He was capable of doing what he said, but Declan could hear how distraught his teammate was and knew that he needed time to process his son's death before he could be effective. Wilks was now a shattered man, and a lifetime would not be long enough to reassemble the pieces.

"I'm working with the feds on this. I promise that I will keep you in the loop," Declan said. He hoped that the next time he called his friend it would be to inform him that the Translator's threat was eliminated. Permanently.

"My Trevor. What am I supposed to do without him?" Wilks's voice trailed off. The brief bout of vengeful rage he had displayed was now replaced by an inconsolable sadness.

As the phone call was ending he could hear the muffled sobbing of Wilks through the receiver. It was a sound he had never heard before from this hard man and one he never wanted to hear again.

"I have my confirmation. This has to do with my old unit. The targets are centered on my teammates and their children." Declan interrupted a quiet conversation that was taking place between Nick and Izzy when he said this.

"How so?" Nick asked trying to assimilate this new information.

"We obviously know about the attack here and the probability that The Translator was also responsible for what happened to my family. The Labor Day Launch falls into that same category of unlikely coincidence. The son of one of my former teammates was among the forty-eight killed in the hot air balloon attack."

"As tragic as that is, we at least now have a pattern of behavior established that we can use to direct the focus of our efforts. Where do you think he's going next?" Nick was energized. It was the first potential lead in the case.

"Well, there are only two other living members of my team. Alex Morales and Mason Richards. So, we have a fifty-fifty chance of picking the correct location. Texas or Virginia. I hate the thought of being wrong with so much at stake."

"It's better than nothing. I need you to reach out to your guys and let them know we'll be coming their way."

"Already done. Alex is the one that located the picture you used, and Mason gave us the Translator's name," Declan said, and could see that Nick and Izzy were connecting the dots on the source of his intel.

"It's good that they are aware of the threat. Maybe they will be vigilant enough to spot Khaled. That would be a definite advantage so that we can determine the next target area before he strikes again." Nick said this and was caught in a wave of dread. Out of the corner of his eye, he saw the graphic images from Colorado being replayed. The country would be spun into a frenzy, dealing with two devastating blows that had occurred within eight days of each other. Nick felt desperate knowing that potentially more carnage was on the way unless they could locate and stop the Translator.

"They're aware and have been looking out for him. So far nothing has turned up. Khaled seems to be going after the children of my teammates."

"Then I think we should start close to the families and work outward from there to find any potential larger scale events that would serve as suitable targets. Tell me what you know about your guys and let's see if we can start to increase our probability of finding the Translator." Nick's eagerness was palpable. Declan liked him. He decided that Nicholas Lawrence would have been a good guy to have on his team. Declan was impressed with the agent's calm resolve that he was demonstrating under the incredible weight of their circumstance.

"Alex doesn't have any children. Mason has a large family with two ex-wives and five children ranging in age from twenty-three to six," Declan said.

"I guess that it makes sense that we put the primary focus on Mason and his family. We could send a team to watch Alex, but without children, he seems to be the odd man out. And in this situation, that's actually a really good thing," Nick interjected, quickly applying his threat assessment.

"That makes sense to me," Izzy spoke up for the first time after a long period of silence following the incident in Colorado. Nick also noted that she seemed to be slightly intimidated and reserved around Declan. That thought brought the return of that increasingly frustrating pang of jealousy.

"I would agree too, but part of me feels that the Translator has a plan for each member of my old team. We can't exclude Alex just because he doesn't have any children of his own. He has a teenage niece and nephew that he adores. It's actually the reason he moved out to the Austin area. He wanted to be closer to them after he left the military." Declan never liked to pick the obvious answer. He was a legend among his former teammates for being able to see possible solutions and outcomes that no one else could conceptualize. That was one of the reasons he had earned the nickname Ace.

"Well, we need to pick one of the two locations to focus our efforts," Nick said somewhat deflated, realizing that Declan was right.

"Being wrong will be catastrophic. Even if we pick the correct city, how are we going to pinpoint the attack location? The targets are not related and the only link we have is to your former team. If you are looking at it from a strategic standpoint, what is The Seven's purpose behind the attacks?" Izzy puzzled.

"What if that's the point?" Declan muttered quietly, looking at the agents. "By attacking random soft targets, they create a sense of unpredictable fear. Think of 9/11 and the effect it had on transportation. We still feel its impact a decade later. When has there been another successful domestic plane attack? If The Seven continues to attack small targets that can't be protected, then the fear would be crippling to the general public. Places like New York and D.C. have always been the epicenters of disaster, but the average American can psychologically distance themselves from those places by saying, *that would never happen here.*" As Declan spoke, Izzy and Nick seemed to register the impact of his words.

"With that being said, my educated guess is that the next target will be in the Austin, Texas area." Declan continued. "Mason was also closest to the Translator when we were overseas. The two had both been educated in Boston and were in the city around the same time frame. It was Mason who had nicknamed Khaled, Boston. Mason's relationship with Khaled seemed to strengthen after the death of his daughter. Mason invested a great deal of time and energy into trying to make him whole again. I would venture to say that destroying his old friend might be something that Khaled, the Translator, might avoid altogether."

"I trust you." A statement Nick used with very few people. The small conference room of the Wethersfield Police Department contained the majority of people in his life that were on that list. "I will bring Nelson up to speed. We can do that from the road. Nelson can arrange a private jet out of Bradley Airport. Let's plan on meeting back here in an hour. I have to take care of something before we go." Nick was up and moving. Time was not on their side and he had to make arrangements for his mother's care before he left.

As Khaled drove, he listened to the newscast on the talk radio channel. The Seven had released their latest statement. Purposefully disseminated to the media.

You have felt the power and reach of The Seven a second time. Yet, your government has failed to begin its troop withdrawal. They will tell you that it takes time and that they are working on it, but this is a lie. They have no intention of pulling out and we have shown our resolve in continuing our assault on your country until they do. Your government doesn't care about you and they can't protect you. The FBI was at the location of the bus attack and could do nothing to prevent it. There will be no further warning. The next message you receive will come if our demand is not met.

Khaled was impressed with the psychological impact of the message. The Seven were turning the vacillating American public against their leaders.

He knew that the media would be flooded with images captured by bystanders of the FBI agent running toward the bus prior to the secondary explosion. This would weaken the confidence in their law enforcement officers' ability to protect them. It was a brilliant strategic move in this game.

He began his drive south, crossing from Colorado into the northeast corner of New Mexico. Khaled was confident that all traces of his presence during his short stay in Colorado Springs had been erased. Everything was on schedule as his small, nondescript Honda merged among the sea of eighteen-wheelers.

31

Nick used the hour to check on his mother. He met with his neighbor, Margaret, and explained that he'd be out of town for a few days. She agreed to look in on Nick's mom. She had begun to inquire about his reason for leaving. He deflected, and she dropped it. Margaret was clearly becoming frustrated with her ad hoc role as caregiver. Nick could tell that she wanted to discuss this with him but tactfully avoided the topic. There was no time for that conversation under the pressing circumstance. But he knew that she was right. Nick contacted the Bureau's health insurance liaison and scheduled for a nurse to visit his mother daily. He knew that she needed more consistent care. A care that he couldn't provide. Nick promised his dying father that he would step up. He felt that he was slowly failing to honor those words and it did not sit well with him.

Nick packed a small bag. He kissed his mother goodbye and turned to leave. Nick heard his mother call after him, "Have a good day at school sweetie."

"Love you. See you soon," Nick mumbled. Emotionally deflated, he headed off to rally with the others.

. . .

The hour had passed quickly. They regrouped and the three rode north to Bradley Airport.

"We'll be teaming with agents from the Bureau's satellite office in Austin. The Hostage Rescue Team has been on standby since this became a counter-terrorism op. The lead tac guy will be at the airport when we land," Nick said.

The FBI had regional SWAT teams. These guys were tactically trained and assisted in apprehensions or stand-offs when needed. They did this in addition to their primary investigative responsibilities. HRT operated at a totally different level. A full-time tactical team comprised of skilled operators. Deployed from their home base in Quantico, most of them former special forces. Nick had passed selection for HRT. He turned it down. The unit's operational tempo was intense. His mother needed Nick's stability.

"Who's running the show?" Izzy asked.

"Apparently we are. I know the ASAC in Austin. We worked together for the few years I was stationed there. Good guy. He'll give us the support and freedom to get things done," Nick said, attempting to ease Izzy's unspoken concern.

"And where do I fit in?" Declan asked. He needed to know his role. He needed to get close enough to get his shot at The Translator.

"You're going to be strapped to my hip. Whatever you know I want to know. The only way we keep up with Khaled and have any chance of getting ahead is to be synced up."

"Anything to help," Declan said dryly.

They entered the airport through a secure gate. Nick was directed to the hanger. They exited the Impala, grabbed their gear, and headed in the direction of the only plane in the bay.

The pilot called out from the small jet, "Wheels up in fifteen!"

The three approached the plane with bags in hand. The unspoken tension and burdensome weight of their responsibility clearly visible on each face.

Declan used the plane's phone onboard the jet to update his former teammates.

"Hey bro. We're on the move. Five hours out. We're heading to you as soon as we land. The agents that I'm with want to sit down and talk." Declan wanted to prep his friend on what to expect.

"No problem. But like I told you before, Mason seems like a better bet. I think you're wasting valuable time and energy on me." Alex said this obviously conflicted by the decision to pick him over Mason Richards.

"I've got a good handle on this. You've got to trust me," Declan said confidently.

"You know that I do, but I hope that you're not choosing me over Moose because of our friendship."

"When it comes to decision making, you know that emotion has zero to do with my thought process," Declan reaffirmed.

Part of him wondered if maybe his friend was right. Their bond was unbreakable. Forged quickly during the hellish conditions of Basic Underwater Demolition/SEAL training. Initially partnered because of their comparable physical skills, the two became fast friends. As swim buddies, they were responsible for each other, but Alex went above and beyond. He saved Declan from a potentially career-ending injury.

Rock portage training evolutions challenged exhausted SEAL trainees tasked with disembarking their rubber inflatable boats and climbing the jagged rocks of the Coronado beach with the boat in tow. Choppy waves added to the misery. Everything was a race. The prize for winning came in the form of a brief respite from the physical torture.

During one of these portages, Declan's right foot had become lodged between two rocks. The surf was rough that day as it was every day during southern California's unpredictable *El Nino* weather pattern. Declan stood trapped, unable to release himself. Rocks on one side, the unmanned boat on the other. The ocean's swell forced the boat at Declan. An impact that would most likely end his chance of completing training. He struggled to free his encased ankle. Alex had recognized the perilous situation that his friend was facing. Without hesitation Alex dove from the rocks. He struck Declan in the chest. Alex's actions freed him from entrapment before the boat made its impact.

That moment epitomized their friendship that was further strengthened during their time together in the Teams, especially while in Alpha One.

"Have you briefed your sister that we are heading your way?" Declan asked his friend.

"Cassidy is terrified for her children's safety. She's willing to do whatever is needed. She wanted to pull them out of school until we catch the Translator, but I convinced her otherwise. I explained that any sudden change in routine might spook him. Cassie's at my house. So come here when you land."

"Sounds good. I'm going to bring Moose up to speed. He seemed okay with us heading out to Texas and agreed with my threat assessment."

"Well that's a first," Alex said with a laugh.

"I know, right? Maybe retirement has softened him," Declan said. When Mason Richards commanded their team he always challenged Declan's op planning. The perpetual devil's advocate. It served a purpose. Declan felt that it was healthy to voice opinions during operational planning. Mason usually gave in to Declan's influence, but not without a fight.

Declan was not able to assert his will over Richards for the mission that took place in the Translator's village. The one that subsequently resulted in the death of the Translator's daughter. Declan had planned for the assault to take place under the cover of darkness. Riskier in the potential for close quarters battle or CQB. But stealth assaults minimized the potential for civilian casualties. Mason opted for an overt daytime assault using heavy firepower. The results had been catastrophic. Now they were facing the ramifications from that day.

"See you soon but keep your head on a swivel. If he's there, then we may already be too late," Declan said gravely.

"Don't forget, I'm a hard man to kill," Alex replied. No truer statement had been said. Declan had seen Alex walk away from many near-death experiences, most of the time with a smile on his face.

Declan ended the call and immediately dialed his former commander.

"Moose, it's me."

Mason Richard's extreme size had earned him the nickname. Movies had the American public believing that Navy SEALs looked like Arnold Schwarzenegger. A Hollywood misstep. Most operators were of average height and build. Physically fit, yes. But more like an elite class triathlete than a bodybuilder. Moose broke the mold. Six feet four inches and weighing nearly two hundred eighty pounds. His impressive bulk made him unforgettable, giving way to folklore. Although Mason's most impressive asset was his intelligence. The huge SEAL was a thinking man. Educated at the legendary Massachusetts Institute of Technology, MIT, Moose put his mechanical engineering degree to work in the Teams. He designed some of the equipment for their missions. Explosives were his forte and his creations were nothing short of genius.

"Ace, is that you? I can barely hear you. You sound like you're in a wind tunnel." Old habits die hard. The team rarely used real names when speaking on the phone. Even after years of civilian life.

"In the air. Heading to DJ. Anything on your end?" Declan spoke louder to compensate for the background noise of the jet.

"Quiet here. I haven't seen any sign of him. The Bureau guys assigned to my family are pretty green. I'd be better off doing this on my own. Just my humble opinion." Richards laughed. Picking apart tactical shortcomings was second nature to him.

"They all can't be bold and spicy like a Steak Sauce guy," Declan jested. The two men chuckled softly at this.

"Keep me posted. I should be on the ground in Texas in a couple hours. I briefed you on the lure he used on Hook's son at the balloon festival. Keep your eye out for anything that seems out of the ordinary. Especially regarding your children," Declan reminded him.

"Nothing so far on my end. If something comes up, you'll be the first to know." Mason paused. Continuing in an anguished tone, "I can't believe that Khaled would come after our families."

"The Bureau guys are looking at the bus and balloon attacks. Nick said that the devices used had some advanced tech. If their guys run into a road-block, would you be willing to apply that big brain of yours to the problem?" Declan asked, knowing that Mason had gone off the grid after his military time ended. His willingness to help a government agency was questionable.

"Normally, I would tell them to go screw, but this is different. Anything I can do to help."

"Thanks. I'll pass it along. I hope to have a better handle on this once I meet with DJ. Until then stay safe. Hopefully, I'm not wrong on this." The implication of that statement did not require Declan to elaborate. If he was wrong, then Mason Richards was in serious trouble.

"Don't worry about me. My little compound is well protected." Mason said this with confidence, referring to protective measures designed into the construction of his home in Virginia.

Declan was sure that his old commander's home defense was a maze of countermeasures that would rival the best operatives.

"See you when I see you. Steak Sauce out," Declan said.

He returned to the plush seat of the small aircraft. Nick and Izzy were brainstorming conceivable target locations in the Austin area.

"Steak Sauce. What's that supposed to mean?" Izzy asked this as Declan returned to them.

"Eavesdropping?" Declan raised an eyebrow in mock suspicion.

"Hard not to in this little space," Izzy retorted sheepishly.

"It's a reference to my former unit's call sign," Declan explained no further. "Did you guys come up with a list of possibilities?" he continued, diverting the conversation.

"Yes. The problem is the Translator's unpredictable target selection. If he was operating in the traditional fashion then we could harden some prime landmarks, but he's random," Nick answered, sounding exasperated. The two agents had obviously reached a frustration point with the topic.

"Let's start with the obvious first. Then we can look at the more obscure ones," Declan said.

"Okay. Sounds good," Nick reaffirmed his receptiveness to Declan's input. "I just want to have something to give HRT when we land."

Declan had a knack for breaking down seemingly insurmountable tasks into workable equations. The solutions to these were usually at a catastrophic loss to his enemy. It didn't seem that Nick took his input as an attempt to usurp his authority. Thankfully, because the last thing he needed was to butt heads with his new team.

32

Khaled had navigated the Georgetown Independent School District's Athletic Complex with ease. He wore the tattered coveralls of the custodial staff. The uniform fit loosely. It gave his wiry frame more bulk. The donor of the uniform had been out sick for several days. Khaled knew that Alfred Humble would never return to work.

Humble had lived alone in a modest apartment. Little evidence of family adorned his bare walls. It did not appear that he would be missed by many. At least, not before it would matter. Death came easily to Khaled. Humble's unremarkable life ended simply. His body rested in his porcelain tub. The large groundskeeper's bodily fluids would go down the drain rather than seeping into the floor and into his downstairs neighbor's apartment. The air conditioning set the room temperature to forty degrees. Decomposition would be slowed. After removing the evidence of his presence, Khaled used Febreze plug-ins in every room. Several buckets of bleach and ammonia surrounded the tub. The low concentration mixture released chlorine gas. A clean smell to mask his rotting flesh. All done to buy time. Everything was on schedule.

His credentials clipped to the front breast pocket of the faded gray shirt, Khaled, or Larry Jenkins as the name tag indicated, an interim custodian, moved about the stadium. A large black plastic bag was slung over his shoulder, a trash grabber in his left hand.

Khaled walked the bleachers of Birkelbach Stadium, a massive expanse of metal and concrete that seated thousands of fans. Over twelve thousand at max capacity. The Williamson County Sun, the local paper, listed the upcoming game as one of the most important of the season. The Georgetown Eagles would face off against the Hutto Hippos. Both teams were potential contenders for this year's title of State Champion. *How trivial a thing.* He'd learned that in Texas, football was second only to religion.

Khaled looked different. Nothing like the image plastered on the news. A thick goatee distorted his jawline, changing his face's dimension. His head shaved. The Beats headphones added to the intended illusion. The cord extended into his pocket but wasn't attached to an MP3 player. He needed to hear if someone approached. It gave the appearance that he was listening to music and thus would discourage unwanted conversations from other employees in the area.

Two devices were planted on the home team's side. The magnetized boxes containing the explosives clicked into place under the metal lips of the bench seats. Khaled bent low, ensuring that they were not visible. He then crossed the Astroturf field, the crunch of the artificial grass uniquely different from any surface he'd felt. He made his way to the visiting team's bleachers. There, he placed the third device before exiting the stadium. There was more to do. But that would have to wait.

He threw the black trash bag into one of the large bins located at the stadium's side exit. Khaled walked directly to his Honda, now bearing valid Texas license plates. He drove off toward his safe house. His mind raced, double-checking his plan.

Finding that Morales's sister was staying at his house meant that the FBI had tracked him to Texas. He had planned for this possibility and had a contingency in place. Khaled did not fear his own death. In many ways, he welcomed it. He had died with his Sonia years ago.

33

"Mike Haggerty, HRT Team Leader." He gave each a firm handshake. His eyes were an intense shade of blue with flecks of gray. His chiseled physique exposed by the tightly fitted under armor shirt. Modesty appeared to be a foreign concept.

"Good to meet you. I'm sure you've been briefed. We'll fill you in on anything the leadership may have left out," Nick said. There would be no secrets among them. *No holding back.*

"I never take what the big wigs say as gospel. I'd rather hear things from the boots on the ground," Haggerty responded.

"Glad to hear that," Nick said. A slight smile accompanied his words.

"I wouldn't trust a damn word that comes from a former squid," Declan snapped, stepping from behind Nick. He moved toward Haggerty as if he were going to pounce. An uneasy tension immediately settled over the two agents.

Haggerty boomed a contagious laugh. "You son of a bitch! Declan Enright! What in the hell are you doing here? Been a long damn time."

"Too long. You look like shit. Don't they have any gyms in Quantico?" Declan poked Haggerty in the chest, goading him. The backhanded compliment of hard men.

"You know the saying: A good soldier makes a fat civilian." Both Haggerty and Declan laughed at this.

They walked the tarmac away from the jet. Nick leaned over to Declan and asked, "What was all that about?"

"Hags was a couple classes behind me at BUD/s. We spent a little time together on Team Two before I was reassigned. He's a solid operator." Declan vouched for Haggerty's ability. And Nick was confident that the tactical side of the mission was in good hands.

Haggerty brought the three over to a black Chevy Suburban with heavy tints. Nick was glad. Anything to reduce the relentless Texas sun.

Nick laid out everything they had to Haggerty. The potential target list was extensive. Everything was hypothetical. Bad odds if you were a betting man. They drove to Leander. A small city, ever-growing in population due to Austin's urban sprawl. It was home to Declan's former teammate, Alex Morales.

Declan paused as he exited the SUV. He stared at the large house belonging to his longtime friend. Impressed. Compared to Declan's it was a mansion. Hard not to feel slightly envious of his friend's situation. The thought of his family crammed in the one-thousand square foot colonial with one bathroom. Their planned extension never built. Maybe it was time to move but their financial downturn had put that on hold. He then thought about the money secured under the flowerbed in his wife's garden. *Buried treasure. Maybe after this was over it would be time to move.* All these thoughts dissipated the moment the door swung open.

Alex "DJ" Morales stood on the front porch, arms wide. He shouted, "Declan Enright! You sexy son of a bitch get over here and give me some sugar!"

"Way too long brother," Declan said. The two embraced followed by some hearty back-slapping. Declan turned to the agents standing behind him. "This is the team. Nicholas Lawrence and Isabella Martinez of the FBI."

"Agents," Alex said, shaking hands.

"Just Nick and Izzy. No formalities here." Nick spoke as Izzy sized up

Alex. His bronzed skin and thick muscles were clearly visible under the white linen button-up. Nick shot a glance at Izzy. She stood star struck. He understood how this guy had earned the nickname of Don Juan. *Girls must throw themselves at him.* He suddenly felt insecure. He was angry at himself for caring that Izzy had noticed him. *They were partners. Nothing more.* He was aware that this was becoming something that he had to convince himself of more and more lately.

Declan continued, "You remember Hags? He's our chauffeur." He thumbed in the direction of Haggerty. "He's now with the Bureau's HRT. He'll run tac ops for this thing."

"Well, we're in good hands then. Come in and meet my sister, Cassidy. She's pretty upset by all this so try not to overwhelm her." Alex said this last part quietly as they walked into the kitchen area.

Cassidy was attractive. Her dark shoulder-length hair gave way to gentle features. Her hands were tightly wrapped around a cup of coffee. She gazed out through the French doors into the expansive backyard, lost in thought.

"Cassie, this is the crew," Alex announced as they approached, startling his sister.

She regained her composure and stood awkwardly. "Thank you all for coming. I hope that I can help in some way, but I have to be honest with you. I'm terrified. Not for me, but for my children. Alex told me that it was better they stick to their routine, but if this guy is planning on hurting them then shouldn't they be in protective custody or something?" Cassidy rattled off her concern. No time for small talk. Everyone felt the pressure. Especially with her children's lives at stake. Her initial meekness gone. She was a lioness. Nick was impressed by her assertiveness. He guessed that having a Navy SEAL for a younger brother probably had something to do with her lack of timidity.

"I totally understand your concern. But, your family might be one of the last possible opportunities to end this. We have some very good people keeping a distant eye on your kids. The last thing we want is for any harm to come to them," Izzy responded. She was good at disarming people. She spoke with a gentle firmness. Her voice was calming, while simultaneously instilling confidence.

"We're going to need your children's schedule. Are there any big events coming up? Anything that you can think of that may help?" Nick asked. They needed a plan. A focal point to direct assets. Something to give them traction in this manhunt.

"There's a football game this Friday. I'm sure Alex told you that we live in Georgetown. It's not too far from here. Both of my children go to high school there. Mitch is in his senior year and Mandy's a sophomore. Mitch is on the football team. Football is a big deal around these parts."

"He's pretty amazing. He could give us a run for our money," Alex said to Declan with the pride of a father.

"Mandy's a cheerleader," Cassie continued. "I guess that's the way of things in Texas. Boys play football and girls cheer." She chuckled to herself. "That's how I met their dad. He cut tail and ran after life got too real." Her face grimaced at this last disclosure. Nerves acted as a truth serum to some.

"Okay. That is definitely a start. Where's the game being played?" Nick asked, avoiding the pitfall of digging into Cassidy's failed marriage.

"Georgetown has a huge sports complex. It's really impressive. This Friday is a home game. So they'll be playing there." She paused. She looked at Alex, concern on her face. Her flicker of confidence dissipated. "Do you think this guy would attack a bunch of kids at a football game?" Cassie regretted asking. The silence by the others in the room only compounded her growing fear.

"That's why we're here. To be honest we're not sure where he'll strike next. That's why this conversation is so important." Izzy stepped in to ease her tension.

"We received this in the mail yesterday," Cassie said, holding up a large envelope. She handed it to Nick.

Nick read the contents of the glossy card stock. It was an invitation addressed to her son Mitch. A voucher for a river cruise. Scheduled for Saturday afternoon. Valid for up to ten persons.

"Did you call the number?"

"Yes. I spoke with someone from Capital Cruises. He said the voucher was purchased by a booster club member who wished to remain anonymous." Cassie's voice quivered. She was overwhelmed by the stress. Anyone would be. A trained assassin had potentially targeted her children. Her world.

"We'll have to consider the football game as a possibility too, but I think our efforts should be concentrated on the boat," Haggerty interjected. Hard decisions came easily to him. And he made them with unquestioned authority. It was no surprise that he led the FBI's elite tactical unit.

"I agree. This sounds very similar to the lure he used with Wilks's son. Get a surveillance team to the cruise company's docks immediately. Find out how many boats the company uses, and which ones are going to be in operation Saturday." Nick's mind was at full throttle. It felt good to have a solid lead for the first time. Before there were any more bodies to add to the count. Before another message from The Seven. Nick knew what rested on his shoulders. He bore its weight dutifully.

"I'm on it." Izzy stepped away from the table and punched the cruise company information into her phone.

"My guys will make a soft approach and look for any signs of him. I'll hit you up if we find anything. I've got a bomb guy in our unit that was a former Delta. If something's there, he'll find it," Haggerty said.

"Soft approach?" Cassie posed this question to the group. The terminology was foreign to her.

Declan answered, "They're going to blend in. They'll make themselves look like dock workers or employees of the boat company. This way if the bad guy is watching, then he won't know that we are onto him. We don't want to spook him. He's unpredictable enough without making him nervous."

"Don't worry. A protection team will remain assigned to your children. I can't afford to be wrong." Nick let this statement hang in the air before he continued, "Did you tell the cruise company that you'd be going on Saturday?"

"I didn't. I wasn't sure what to do. Do you want me to?" Cassie was eager to help. A need to feel useful. The lioness and her cubs.

"Yes. We need him to think that your children will be going."

The group made their way to the door. The oppressive heat of the afternoon Texas sun was a brutal contrast to the interior of the house.

Alex whispered to Declan as the two lagged behind the others, "Let me know when you need me."

Declan nodded. "Will do."

Dirt kicked up as the black SUV pulled away with Haggerty at the wheel. A lot of work needed to be done before Saturday.

34

"What else do you need?" Jim Fitzgerald, the ASAC in charge of Austin's satellite office had welcomed the newcomers and was already up to speed on things.

"I think we're good for now. I really appreciate the support. The HRT guys are already on site. They're searching the docks. They'll hopefully be checking in soon with their assessment. The anonymous booster was a dead end. He paid in cash. The manager doesn't have any surveillance cameras in his ticket office. We're checking the area for other possibilities. Maybe we'll get lucky and get him on video, buying a soda at a gas station. Nothing so far. And I'm not hopeful," Nick said, rapidly pushing this information onto his acting supervisor. Nick knew that Fitzgerald could keep up. Past experience taught him that he was a sponge with new information and very rarely needed it repeated.

The quick debrief completed, Nick shook hands with his former boss and headed out the door.

"Keep me updated," Fitzgerald called out to Nick.

"Of course." Nick said this over his shoulder, never breaking stride. Izzy and Declan were in tow.

"And Nick. It's good to have you back. Even if it's only temporary and under these conditions." Fitzgerald didn't expect a response. Nor did he get one. But the message was received.

All three pulled out their cell phones, almost in unison, while standing outside of their newly assigned government vehicle. A light wind gave a brief reprieve from the heat, giving promise of cooler evening temperatures.

"We might have a lead on him. He used a similar tactic with Wilks. Hopefully, HRT will find something soon," Declan updated Mason Richards. He wanted to keep his former commander in the loop. Plus, he needed a little reassurance that he had made the right decision in going to Texas.

"Everything is copacetic on my end. Thanks for the update. I hope you nail this bastard. Beers on me if you vent his frontal lobe with a hollow-point. Sounds like you made the right call. Good job. Steak Sauce out." The call ended. Declan turned his attention to Izzy.

"Anything from the cameras?" Declan asked, assuming that is who she was talking with from the small bit he'd overheard.

"Nope. They are still checking. It would be nice if we could confirm that it was Khaled who bought the tickets, then I would be more confident that we are focusing on the right target." Concern was evident in her voice.

"Awesome. Thanks. I have a guy that may be able to help if you can send me a pic when you get a chance." Nick slipped his cellphone back into his pocket and smiled for the first time in a week.

"What do you have? Don't keep us waiting," Izzy prodded.

"The bomb guy found a device. Apparently, it is attached to the fuel line of the boat. They're not sure what they are dealing with yet. It's possible that there may be more and so the pace is slow. Haggerty is going to send me a pic in a minute." Nick knew that this was huge. It finally felt like they were gathering some advantage over the enemy. The next steps would be critical.

The cell phone vibrated, alerting Nick of the incoming message from Haggerty. The three put their heads together and looked down at the image.

"It doesn't look like much," Izzy said unimpressed.

"That's the thing about these weapons; they seem innocuous until they go off." Declan said this ominously and then continued, "Can you forward it to me? Mason was our tech guy and still does this kind of work on the civilian side. He may be able to give us some insight."

"An extra set of eyes never hurt, especially in a case like this," Nick said in agreement. "I've got a guy who should have a look too."

"Hard to tell from the picture. The container looks fairly advanced, but I would need to see the components inside to give you a better feel for the maker. I disabled something similar, but that was years ago. I kept a notebook with photos, diagrams, and notations. Give me a little bit to dig it up. I will call you back if I find something. Tell whoever is on location to be careful. It's definitely going to have a remote detonation capability, but the maker may have also put in a tamper trigger." Mason said this with an edginess in his tone.

"The bomb tech on scene is ex-Delta so he should be good, but I will relay it. Thanks." Declan ended the call and passed this information on to Izzy because Nick was on the phone.

"Have you seen anything like it before?" Nick asked hoping for some confirmation.

"Unfortunately, yes. Overseas we were tracking a high-value target that had been disrupting special ops teams in the area. He was known only by his nickname, the Dust Devil. Somewhere along the way, he had been given the name because of his reputation for moving in and out of an area with the speed and ferocity of those wind-whipped desert tornadoes. His devices crippled several missions and the Dust Devil had accrued a considerable body count. Only one device had been found intact. Apparently, one of the cauterized wires had detached rendering it inert. I will pull the file and let you know what I find. Whoever analyzed the bomb might have some information about your Translator or his associates." Jay's information hit Nick like a sledgehammer. Khaled had successfully assaulted some of the military's best with success and managed to elude capture.

"What happened to the Dust Devil? How did he escape apprehension?" Nick was wrought with the stress of this new development.

"From what I remember, they thought he was dead. There was information that he had been killed during one of his attacks. I'll gather what I can. This might be more difficult than pulling your friend Declan's background. As soon as I know, you will know. This is a game changer. Be at your best." Jay said this and hung up.

"Shit." Nick was reeling from the blast of information from his CIA connection.

"What's up?" Declan and Izzy asked almost in unison.

Nick was silent for a moment. He always found it important to pause and absorb new information before reacting to it. He looked up at his two partners who waited patiently for him to speak.

"Apparently these devices may be the work of a terrorist who goes by the nickname Dust Devil. My source has some personal experience with this maniac and he warned me that his skill set is as good as it gets. He is doing some more digging on it and will hit me up as soon as he gets more." Nick scanned their reactions to his news. Declan's eyebrow flickered momentarily before returning to its stoic norm.

Nick had learned in his extensive interrogation training that a brief physical response, like Declan's twitch, was a subconscious reaction. The barely perceptible movement had immediately followed the information that Nick had just shared. In the world of Interview and Interrogation, it was referred to as a micro gesture. And it usually meant that a person was hiding something.

"So, it's worse than we thought. Any ideas on how to stop this guy?" Izzy threw her hands up, feeding off Nick's frustration.

"I don't know. What do you think?" Nick's question was accusatory and directed at Declan. Izzy caught this and looked back and forth between the two men like a child standing between arguing parents.

Declan was quiet this time. He seemed to be selecting his words carefully, "I know the name if that's what you are getting at."

"There is no time for your secret squirrel bullshit here. If you know something, then give it up or you are heading home," Nick said, letting his anger show.

"Easy. You obviously have a little snapshot into my past, but you need to understand there are things I can't share. Regardless of the stakes. I will tell you what I can remember about that asshole, the Dust Devil. I just won't tell you how I know." Declan showed restraint. No emotion was present in his voice and this seemed to soften Nick slightly.

"Sorry. There are so many things in play right now. I just need to get a feel for what this guy is capable of doing and how effective he is at doing it."

"For starters, whoever provided you that information is probably more knowledgeable on the subject than me. It seems like you are well-connected." Declan paused. "If it's the same guy then we are in some serious trouble. I assume now that you may know more about me than you should which is troubling, but we will come back to that later. I don't know what your source told you, but this guy targeted special operations teams operating in Iraq. He did this with deadly precision."

Declan composed himself as he prepared to share some secrets with Nick and Izzy. Things that he had never even shared with Val. "Did your source tell you how he earned the name Dust Devil?"

"Yes," Nick said plainly.

"I've never been up against someone like him before or after, until now. Overseas he orchestrated an attack that left four of my teammates dead." Declan paused. He had never spoken about this to anyone except for Alex, and the raw emotion of it caught him off guard, causing his eyes to water as his throat suddenly constricted. He looked away briefly and took a deep breath before he continued. "The Dust Devil had initiated successful attacks on military convoys and small forward operating bases, referred to as FOBs. And then he turned his sights on the military elite. He actually targeted special forces groups operating in the area." Declan shook his head and continued, "Do you realize how insane that is? He went after the best and came out on top. Time and time again."

"Jesus." Nick exhaled having realized the audacity to take on SEALs and SF operators willingly. It went against the mentality of most of the combatants he had faced overseas.

"Our unit operated outside of the normal channels. We were tasked with finding and neutralizing the Dust Devil. Our operational success rate was beyond reproach. We had some good intel on him and developed a plan... We didn't know what hit us." Nick and Izzy could see that Declan's mind had gone somewhere distant. The unshared recall of that memory played out in the empty look in his eyes.

"The only reason everyone else on my team isn't dead is that the secondary explosive device he had set malfunctioned. It appears that he has worked out the kinks since that day," Declan said gravely.

"What happened after that attack?" Nick asked curiously.

"He disappeared. We'd heard that he was killed during another engagement. A report we received had documented it, but I'm sure that paperwork has long since been destroyed. I remember seeing a picture of a blown-up body. Unrecognizable to me, but someone in the intel world identified him as Aziz Mohamed. He was part of the village council that our unit had visited from time to time." Declan thought for a moment and then continued, "It made sense to me back then. It was the same village that Khaled, the Translator, had lived. I knew that Aziz was anti-American military prior to our attack so it seemed to match up that he would take up arms against us afterward. Hindsight is always twenty-twenty."

"So, this guy blew up another villager to throw your team off the scent?" Izzy questioned, trying to keep up with Declan's condensed recap.

"I guess so. It worked. After Aziz was killed, the attacks on special forces operators stopped overnight. So, our unit focused on other missions until we disbanded and came home." Declan finished detailing his past exposure to the Translator.

Declan's phone vibrated, snapping him back to the present. It was a text message from Val. *We are almost to Gretchen's house. The kids are good. Laney too. Whitney's awesome! We're in good hands. Be safe. We love you. Call me later tonight if you have time. Get this bastard and come back to us!* He'd been so focused on the mission that he had failed to contact Val. He shot her a quick response while the agents digested what he had just said. *I'll call tonight. Love to you and my girls.*

"If what you told me holds true, then Khaled has been holding out for years developing this plan. We are trying to play catch up in a matter of days," Nick said as Declan looked up from his phone. Whatever excitement they'd experienced when HRT located the device was quickly dissipating.

35

Khaled sat in the parking lot of the Starbucks watching the mobile application on his cellphone. The black and white images clearly displayed the FBI men and women as they moved around the boat. They had quietly evacuated the area. The agents had attempted to blend in with the cruise company's staff. A failed effort. *Amateurs.*

They took precautions, moving methodically. Exactly what he'd hoped. Everything was on schedule. And why wouldn't it be? He was smarter than these people. Sadly, they assumed that the tide had shifted. He envisioned that the senior leadership were now sitting around in their respective offices high-fiving each other in an early celebration of their hard work.

Khaled assumed that the FBI team would try to mask their retrieval of his device, building inert look-a-likes to replace the ones on the boat. They had located three bombs in total. He anticipated that it would have taken longer for the Bureau to locate the devices. Khaled was impressed with the man who found them. He was obviously experienced. Khaled had placed them all in spots that he would have used if he had actually planned to blow up the boat, but that had never been his intention.

Locating the bombs was step one for this team. He knew that they would spend several more hours ensuring that they did not miss a fourth device. They would not find one because there was none to be found.

Step two would be the removal of each device. This too would take time because an appropriate level of caution would be taken to verify that no triggers would be activated.

Step three would be to analyze each one. Khaled knew that normal protocol dictated that they destroy them on site, but he knew that there would be pressure to understand the design in the hopes that this knowledge might lead them to the maker. Hand-crafted bombs typically held structural elements that are unique. Khaled had implemented a roadblock to this step. Each device's box was lined with lead which would block the x-ray of its contents. The bomb technicians would need to examine the devices in a blast-proof lab. The closest facility was located in San Antonio. The slow transport of the bombs would add hours to the process.

The FBI would replace the missing devices with well-made facsimiles in the event that Khaled returned to do a final check before Saturday's cruise. The area surrounding the marina would be jam-packed with agents for the next two days.

Satisfied, he minimized the window showing the marina and tapped the screen bringing up another live-feed video. This time the camera was split screen and showed both main entrances to the football stadium.

With two days to go Khaled took a moment to relax. He reclined in his car and listened to the newscaster on the radio. He was speaking rapidly in a nasal voice about the failures of the current administration's ability to handle this situation. The FBI was being bashed as the picture of the agent photographed on scene at the bus bombing had gone viral. Callers chimed in their two cents. Each one louder than the next. Panic had struck deep and the country was becoming unhinged.

Sound bites from the President and representatives from the FBI and Homeland Security were interspersed throughout the radio program. The messages from the country's leadership were all hollow promises of increased law enforcement presence and recommendations for safety precautions. Each ended with the false assurance that "Every resource available is being used to bring this terrorist to justice." Based on the flurry of responses on social media and news channels, those words were not being believed.

The law enforcement entities across the country were bleeding out overtime budgets assigning more officers to security details of listed potential targets. Some called for Congress to amend the Posse Comitatus Act, allowing U.S. Military forces to operate within the borders of the United States. The National Guard were exempt and had already been mobilized. The footage of these military units rolling into the major cities, like New York, had the desired effect. People were outraged that these troops were only being seen in places like the big cities. Small town America was angry, and this was evident from the current caller's ramblings on the radio.

Khaled absorbed the impact of his two attacks. The Seven were pleased. The mighty United States was feeling the strain. He looked up, sipping his espresso and observed the tension in the faces of these people trying to go about their daily lives while their safety had been shattered. Khaled smiled and waved to a police officer entering the bistro. The gesture was returned without hesitation. Khaled looked nothing like the man in the picture that the media had circulated. In addition to the goatee and tight afro he also thickened his eyebrows and affixed a latex covering to his nose which widened his nostrils. The slight variations in his facial features had completely changed him. His valid Colorado license had his name listed as Darius Johnson and the picture on the government ID matched his current appearance. He drove from the parking lot with the angry shouts of a new radio caller in the backdrop.

36

With the three devices located and the trap set at the marina, Nick told the small contingent to take some downtime and recoup before the intended takedown on Saturday. The devices had been transported to the FBI's explosive evaluation testing facility located in San Antonio. Nick told Declan that they had to wait for the technician team from Connecticut to arrive. The agency's resources in that specialty field had been drained considerably during the events of the past two weeks.

Declan took this opportunity to meet up with Alex and take a small reprieve from the intense pressure of the manhunt. The two sat on the back porch of his best friend's house, facing east with the setting sun at their back. The cascade of light washed over the leaves that clung to the twisted branches of the Mesquite trees lining the backyard of his friend's property. Condensation quickly formed on the cold glasses of beer in their hands.

"You've got a good spread here bro. I'm proud of you." Declan said this genuinely and without the typical ball busting.

"Thanks. Life out here has been good to me, but I still miss it."

"Yeah. Me too. There are aspects of civilian life that never really fit after serving. I think part of me stayed over there." Declan and Alex had had this conversation repeatedly over the years since the two had left the military.

"Here now. The past should stay where it belongs." Alex laughed a little as he said this. "Listen to me Ace. I should be writing greeting cards."

The two spent the evening laughing about the good times and paying homage to the times that weren't. Their friendship had weathered things most couldn't fathom, and with that came a comfort. Night had begun to grab hold of the arid landscape before the two had shifted the conversation back to the present circumstance.

"Why is this asshole targeting our crew? Do you really think that it all goes back to that moment in the village?" Alex questioned, trying to process the hatred of the Translator.

"All things aside. What would you do if a missile attack killed someone you love?" Declan paused for effect, "I mean shit, look at me. He didn't get a chance to complete the task with my family, and I am going to drop him the moment the opportunity presents itself. If he had succeeded I would wipe anything he valued off the face of the earth."

Alex sat there and nodded, subconsciously agreeing with Declan's assessment. "Those FBI guys are never going to let you close enough to take that shot and you know it. You're here for your knowledge, not your trigger finger."

"You never know how things will line up. If our time together proved nothing else, it definitely demonstrated that Murphy's Law presents unique opportunities." The two banged their glasses together and swallowed the remnants.

"I'm calling it. Time for me to head for shelter." Declan yawned and stretched.

"If you think there is a chance to get some play on this, then I want in." Alex's eyes were deadly serious.

"Be ready to go. If the opportunity breaks, then I want you by my side."

"Hey, a little off topic but maybe you will be able to catch a bit of the football game tomorrow evening. Mitch is really impressive on the field. He's getting looked at for some big schools. Plus, there really is nothing like a football game on a Friday night in Texas," Alex said.

"I'll see."

The two old teammates parted ways. Declan drove into the Texas night wondering what the next couple of days would hold for him and his team.

37

"Mr. Lawrence, she's going to be fine. Her injuries were minor, but because of her age we would like to keep her here a few more days for observation." The doctor spoke to Nick in a calm and reassuring manner.

"Thank you, Doc. Please keep me posted on her progress." Nick cleared his voice. "I am out of state right now, but I'm hoping to be back by Monday."

"Of course, Mr. Lawrence. I have you listed as our point of contact. She's in good hands."

"Thank you." Nick ended the call and looked around at the modest hotel room. He had requested to be lodged in Georgetown because he wanted to have quick access to Cassidy's children in case of an emergency. Nick had been shocked when Nelson told him that arrangements had been made for the three of them to stay at the Sheraton. Normally the Bureau's travel arrangements were not so accommodating. *Big case equals big hotel room.*

Declan's room was adjacent to his. Nick had heard him return a few minutes ago and was tempted to stop over and discuss the case. Then decided that a mental break might help all of them gain a fresh perspective.

Without thinking, Nick opened the door to his room and stepped out into the hallway. Crossing the red and gold carpet runner, he approached Izzy's room. Nick just stood there, hesitating outside the door.

Why, suddenly, did he feel like a sixteen-year-old pimple-faced boy waiting for his prom date? He heard an internal door in her room close and felt a moment of panic. *This is stupid. What am I doing here?* He had just turned around to leave when the door to Declan's room opened.

"Hey, Nick. Everything good?" Declan said as he passed by with the beige ice bucket in hand.

"Yeah. I was just heading back to my room." Nick had to focus hard on his words, afraid of stuttering like a child caught with his hand in the cookie jar. Declan gave a slight nod, saying nothing as he continued to the cutout in the hallway marked Vending. But, as Declan moved from sight he shouted back, "Just knock bro. She won't bite."

Nick exhaled, trying to release the embarrassment of the moment. Just as he raised his hand to knock, Izzy swung the door wide open. Nick almost jumped in surprise.

"I knew I heard someone in the hallway." Isabella Martinez stood before Nick with a towel wrapped firmly around her and was using a second, smaller towel to squeeze the dampness from her long, dark hair.

"Sorry. I was just coming by to shoot the shit. Nothing important. I'll let you rest. Talk to you in the morning." Nick knew he was speaking a mile-a-minute and could tell from the warm feeling in his face that his cheeks had flushed. He turned quickly, wanting to escape this awkward moment as fast as he could.

"Come on in. I just opened a bottle of wine." Izzy said this in her normal, casual voice. But, as she lowered her head to the side and looked up at him from under her dark eyelashes, Nick thought he might have noticed something different in her smile.

"Okay," Nick said, stepping into her room.

But just then Declan passed by carrying his full ice bucket. "Hey Dec, do you want to come in and hang out, too?" When Izzy said this, she instantly deflated any hopes that her invitation was more than just a friendly gesture. He also caught Izzy's eyes run the expanse of Declan's body, his white undershirt exposing the dense network of tight muscles. Although Nick maintained his fitness level after leaving the service, he knew that he had become a little softer around the edges in his time with the Bureau. Declan Enright looked like he had just come back from a deployment. The two were close in age, yet the former SEAL looked ten years younger. Nick felt the wave of jealousy wash over him. Until a week ago, this feeling had been foreign to him.

"I'm gonna rest up and call the family, but you kids have fun." Before Declan closed the door, he threw Nick a quick wink.

Izzy slipped into the bathroom and came out a few minutes later in a gray T-shirt and running shorts. Her hair was still damp as she finished working it into a braid and casually sat down on the bed with her legs crossed. She patted the spot on the bed, inviting Nick to join her.

Nick tried to look relaxed but struggled to ignore his thoughts about where this might lead. He met her on the thick comforter with two plastic cups of red wine. After a mock cheers motion, they both took a sip. An awkward silence passed between them but was quickly broken by the image on the television.

"Do you think I will ever live that down?" The media was questioning Nick's competence because he was there at the scene of the attack and never even saw it coming.

"Nick, there was nothing you could have done. Everyone knows that."

"Apparently *that* guy didn't get the message." But behind his sarcasm, he realized that he was really letting the media circus get to him. He never used to care about the opinion of some news anchor, so why would he start now? This wasn't the first time he felt truly grateful for Izzy's friendship. He started to feel more relaxed and took another sip from his cup.

"More importantly, how's your mother doing?" Izzy asked with genuine concern.

"The doctor said a couple of days. Which is actually a blessing in disguise because it gives me some peace of mind that she is being taken care of while I'm out here."

"Listen, Nick. I know it's been rough, but how long do you really think that you can care for her in her condition?"

Nick knew where this conversation was headed, it had come up a few times in recent months. "I found a few facilities that I plan to visit when I get back. It's just tough to think about letting her go. I also promised my dad that I would take care of her, guess I reneged on that." He attempted to make light of the conversation with a quick, unconvincing laugh. But he couldn't hide from Izzy the vacant look in his eyes.

She took the wine from his hand and placed both of their cups on the bedside table. She leaned forward with an intense and determined look that somehow made her seem even more beautiful. Her voice was firm, almost angry, as she said, "Damn it, Nick, you have to stop being so hard on yourself! What is that saying... 'Have strength to accept the things you cannot change'? Whatever, you know what I am talking about! You are the most dedicated person I have ever met, and your mom is lucky to have you." Izzy paused, taking a deep breath before adding, almost inaudibly, "Anyone would be."

Nick was caught off guard. Izzy's comment completely derailed his train of thought. As he went to adjust himself on the bed, his hand accidentally grazed hers. That slight physical contact, like a match to a fuse, ignited something inside of Nick.

Nick's heart raced as he looked up to search for a trace of interest in Izzy's eyes. But before he was able to process her response, she reached out, grabbing him by his broad shoulders and pulled him on top of her.

38

"Good morning." Declan said to Nick and Izzy as they strolled in together to the hotel's Brix and Ale Café. Declan had already devoured a hearty breakfast and had moved onto his second cup of coffee before the two agents had appeared. He learned a long time ago that when you had a chance to eat, you did, because sometimes that next meal might be far off.

The two exchanged greetings and each poured a cup of coffee from the carafe that had been left by the waiter. Declan broke the silence, "Any word about the devices yet?"

Nick was glad for the question. His mind had been stuck on the previous night with Izzy. "I just got off the phone with Nelson. He said that the bomb tech was delayed but should be arriving sometime later today."

"I guess that really doesn't affect us. We are running on the assumption that Khaled is our doer. The discoveries made by the Bureau's technician will help the extended search for the maker but has little to do with us finding the Translator. Agreed?"

"Agreed," Izzy said, and Nick nodded.

"What's the next step?" Declan said, looking to gauge his opportunity for a crack at Khaled.

"We've flooded the area surrounding the marina with agents acting as employees and tourists. As of my last update, twenty minutes ago, no sign of the Translator."

"Where are we going to be staging?" Declan tried not to show his eagerness.

"The three of us should steer clear of the cruise boat and its surrounding area. Khaled knows our faces and I don't want to spook him when he arrives." Nick said this sounding slightly annoyed. Registering the deflated look on Declan's face he continued, "I don't like it either but getting this guy trumps all of our personal agendas."

"Well if we are not going to be near the scene then maybe we could stay near the kids. I heard there is a big football game tonight," Izzy interjected.

"I guess that would work. You good with that?" Nick posed the question to Declan.

"Anything beats sitting around twiddling our thumbs. I'll give a heads-up to Alex. He can meet us. I know that he was going to head to the game too."

Nick looked down at his vibrating cell phone and saw that the number calling had a Connecticut area code. He picked it up. Immediately recognizing the voice on the other end, he stepped away from the table.

"Good morning Agent Lawrence. This is Janet Morgan, the manager of the Clover Leaf Bank."

"Good morning Janet. What can I do for you?" Nick said, having put the bank case completely out his mind until now.

"I'm sorry to call you so early, but you told me to notify you once I had a chance to review the surveillance footage from the weeks leading up to the robbery." She said this with some reservation in her voice.

"Anything of value?" Nick's interest was piqued.

"The car that robbed the armored truck was a Toyota Corolla, correct?"

"Yes."

"Well a few weeks prior to the robbery; four to be exact, there was a Toyota parked at the bank." Now a hint of excitement was notable in her inflection. Nick found this common among civilians who thought they had cracked a case.

"Go on. What can you tell me about it?" Nick was patient, but Janet seemed to be holding back for some reason.

"Well, that's the thing. I know the man who drives it. He was there the day of the explosion too. I don't know if you would remember him." Nick listened and waited for her to continue, "His name is Declan Enright and he has been a patron of our bank for many years. I saw him on the video camera and he was leaning against the hood of the Toyota. It was around five p.m."

"He was at the bank then? And you're saying that this was on a Thursday correct?" Nick's head was starting to spin. He glanced back at the table with Izzy and Declan engaged in small talk.

"Yes, to both. I did some checking and found that was the day that he met with me to discuss some financial assistance options for his family." A quick pause and she continued, "You don't think it was him, do you? I mean the guy from the robbery was dark skinned with tattoos."

"I don't know, but I have to look at all possibilities until I have an answer. Could you tell me what the financial issue was that he discussed with you?"

"His family has been struggling since losing his job and he had requested a loan. He didn't qualify for it, but on the day of the explosion I remembered that he was wearing construction attire, so he must have gotten a job." Nick heard the concern in her voice. She seemed to respect Enright and sounded remorseful for not being able to help him through his financial hardship.

"Do you recall how much money he asked for?"

"I would have to check my files, but off the top of my head, it was somewhere between fifteen and twenty thousand dollars. He said he just needed enough to float the bills until he could get a job. He's in a tough spot, especially with his youngest daughter's special needs."

"Janet, can you make me a copy of the video footage and any paperwork regarding Mr. Enright's loan request and include his banking statements?" Nick said his name in a hushed tone so that he did not alert his new friend to the current topic of conversation.

"The footage is already on a DVD. The request for his financial records needs to be obtained by a subpoena or search warrant, but what I can tell you unofficially is that his checking account was closing in on zero when he came to see me." Her demeanor had returned to a matter-of-fact style.

"Okay. I will take care of it when I get back to Connecticut. The robbery case is going on the back burner until we get this other situation under control." Nick knew that he did not need to explain that any further. "Thanks again for all of your assistance on this."

"You're welcome. Be safe wherever you are."

"Will do and please don't share your findings with anyone else." Nick ended the call and returned to the table.

"Everything okay?" Izzy asked with a look of concern.

"It was my mother's doctor. He just wanted to update me and confirm that she was responding well to treatment." Nick hated lying to her, but he couldn't share the information with Declan present. Neither Izzy nor Declan seemed to note his deception.

39

The rhythmic thumping of the drums reverberated in Khaled's chest as he sat in his nondescript light blue Honda parked outside of Birkelbach Stadium. The sea of blue and white moved in droves toward the home team entrance area. The energy and chatter amongst the arriving crowd were electric.

Khaled ensured that the two detonators were prepped and ready before stepping out into the noise and lights that enveloped the parking lot. No one would recognize him. Khaled, or Darius Johnson as his current ID noted, had immersed himself in the football culture. Half his face was blue and the other white. He wore the official Eagles' windbreaker and carried two light wands; representing team colors. The wands were different than others that the fans brought... each of his contained a detonator.

He merged with the crowd and ambled into the stadium. It took a moment to adjust to the shock of the floodlights which bathed the field. The band played. Cheerleaders and players were conducting their warm-ups. He took his seat in the middle of the bleachers close to one of its many stairwells. Khaled sat and took in the sight. Impressive that a high school football game could draw such a crowd. *The more the merrier,* he thought as he scanned for his enemy.

. . .

"There they are." Alex pointed out toward the center of the field. "Mitch is wearing number twenty-eight. Mandy is over near the bench talking to the tall girl with the blond hair."

"This will be fun but remember to keep your head on a three-sixty swivel. He could be here too." Declan was trying to relax, but the circumstances prohibited that for him. He was in operational mode and trying to take in everything he saw. He needed to establish a norm so that if something changed he could catch it. Focus and patience were the two key ingredients to conducting any kind of surveillance. Declan leaned over toward Nick's ear to speak over the crowd's volume, "What's your take?"

"I've never seen a crowd like this for a high school game. I hope to God that we didn't point our assets in the wrong direction." Nick seemed awestruck by this potential realization.

"Nick, you have done everything you could. We are here now and can be the extra eyes, but all of the clues have led us to conclude that tomorrow is the day and the intended target is the cruise boat." Declan gave Nick's shoulder a firm slap and then continued, "For what it's worth I'd go into battle with you any day." Declan did not give that compliment lightly.

"That means a lot." Nick felt a surge of confidence imparted by Enright's words. At the same time, he had a sinking feeling in his stomach. What if Declan did the armored truck job? Just then his phone began to vibrate. It was Fitzgerald. He answered just as the stadium announcer began to call out the Hutto Hippos starting lineup.

"Hello? Jim, I am at a football game and can't hear a word you are saying. Give me two minutes and I will call you back." Nick gestured to the group that he would be right back. They nodded that they understood as they took their seats midway up on the left side of the bleacher area.

The announcer boomed out names and positions of the starters as Nick moved out of the stadium to the sidewalk by the home team's parking lot. The crowd erupted as the Georgetown Eagles exploded onto the field from their locker room. Once the volume subsided Nick re-dialed Fitzgerald.

"Let's try this again. Sorry about that. Texas football is something to behold." Nick had already briefed the ASAC that the three of them would be attending the game.

"They're decoys!" Jim Fitzgerald, a man known for maintaining an eerie level of calm was unhinged.

"What do you mean? What's a decoy?" Nick fell victim to Fitzgerald's intensity.

"The damn bombs! The ones from the boat. The technician spent all day trying to verify that they would not detonate when he opened them up. The maker lined the boxes with lead blocking the x-ray. There was nothing inside except some disconnected batteries and wires. A bit of Semtex so the bomb dog would hit. He set us up!"

The impact of these words caused Nick to stumble slightly. His mind raced. A volley of cheers from the crowd unleashed, causing him to become momentarily overwhelmed. "Oh my God! It's the game! Send everyone! Alert the ground team here. We have to shut the game down and get everyone out of the stadium! Now!"

Nick turned and ran back into the stadium his head scanning the faces of people he passed. He had always prided himself on the ability to compartmentalize any sense of fear or panic. Not that he didn't feel those emotions, just that he could push them aside to focus on a solution. It's what made him so effective leading men into battle, but this looming threat had challenged his ability to do this. He pressed on into the clamor of the stadium.

Nick stopped and stood at the base of the Eagles' bleacher section. The crowd focused on the action taking place on the artificial grass behind him, oblivious to the danger that loomed. He made eye contact with Izzy who immediately registered that something was wrong with his facial expression. She nudged Declan, getting his attention and the two stood, turning their bodies in search of the threat.

Nick grabbed a security officer who was standing by the concession stand, flirting with a woman working the register. He needed access to the announcer's booth. Declan, Alex, and Izzy navigated the bleacher's stairs, heading in his direction. Cassie had broken off from the group and ran toward the field. She ran toward her children.

· · ·

Khaled found the American football game entertaining. Although he didn't fully understand the rules, he liked the speed of the athletes. He had watched as Enright and Morales, two Golden Men, entered the bleacher area with the FBI agents. He assumed that they would be at the game. Actually, Khaled had planned on it. What he didn't foresee was Agent Lawrence's awareness of his plan. The phone call he received had alerted him. The FBI must have realized the cruise boat was a decoy.

He intended for the detonation to occur after the start of the second half of the game so that the security detail assigned to Mandy and Mitch would become somewhat complacent. Now he watched as Agent Lawrence was getting the attention of a security staff member. His timeline had been fast-forwarded. *Adapt and overcome*, he thought. It was ingrained in him during his sniper training, several years back.

Khaled stood nonchalantly and made his way down the bleachers and positioned himself at the concrete corner of the structure on the opposite side of the devices. He watched as Agent Lawrence was in a dead sprint for the announcer booth with the security officer lagging behind. The booth was located atop the opposing team's bleacher area.

Enright stood only ten feet away from Khaled. Tension was present in his body as he turned and twisted, looking in every possible direction for the enemy. He felt the Golden Man's eyes pass over his features in quick evaluation, dismissing Darius Johnson as he continued his relentless scan of the stadium's populous.

Khaled waited until Agent Lawrence had begun his ascent up the opposing team's stairwell in his futile effort to get to the announcer. *Too late.* Khaled activated the first detonator. The concussive effect was devastating.

As was the plan, the two devices on the Eagles' side and the one located on the Hippos' bleacher area erupted to life in sync. The shockwave from the blasts seemed more intense than he'd predicted, due in part because of the partial enclosure of the stadium's design. The panic was palpable as screams echoed through the debris.

The flood of Eagles fans in their blue and white and those in Hutto orange began moving toward the exit like a tidal surge. Khaled allowed himself to merge into the crowd of panic-stricken families as he was shoved and slammed through the concrete arched underbelly of the bleachers.

Khaled tried to keep a visual of the children, Mitch and Mandy, but the volume of people made the task difficult. Khaled needed to get ahead of the mass exodus departing from the stadium's parking lot before the authorities began to lock it down. The police working the stadium as an overtime job had moved toward the carnage but would soon redirect their efforts to containment.

Khaled began pulling away from the stadium and as he neared the effective range of the detonator he observed Mitch and Mandy being shuttled by their mother toward the exit. He activated the secondary devices with a click of the button located on the side of the glowing blue wand.

The large trash bins bookending the exterior of each of the stadium's exits flashed, throwing heat and fire into the tunnels filled with retreating fans. The crowd had wedged themselves inside, adding to its effect. Those not killed or injured by the fire would be trampled by the panicked onslaught of the frenzied mob.

Nick had been moving at breakneck speed, ascending the stairwell two and three steps at a time when the blast had hit him. It had taken him a moment to comprehend what happened. His brain had to connect the dots. He was running one moment and the next his body was thrown sideways onto the laps of a family who had been intently watching the game. As he righted himself the ensuing chaos was equally terrifying as the crowd reacted. The average citizen was not exposed to trauma and typically had a guttural reaction when confronted by it.

Nick changed directions, abandoning the announcer booth, and turned toward the field. He saw Cassie herding her children near the Eagles team bench area. Izzy and Alex were also running in her direction. It seemed that they all had the same thought, *this was not over.* Nick assumed that if there was another part to this attack that it would be directed at Mitch and Mandy.

"Are you guys alright?" Nick said this to everyone as he approached, but his eyes instinctively focused primarily on Izzy.

"Where is he? How the hell did we miss this?" Izzy was venting her frustration.

"The boat was a decoy. I got the call from Fitzgerald, but obviously, we were totally caught off guard. We have to get these kids out of here. Now!" Nick took point. Izzy and Alex each flanked Cassie and her children as they quickly made their way toward the exit. They moved like a small dignitary protection team attempting to shield the principal.

Nick moved the group toward the mass of people trying to exit. Out of the corner of his eye, he caught a glimpse of someone moving at them quickly. It took a second to realize that it was Declan. He was shouting something inaudible over the crowd's frantic screams. Nick slowed as he saw Declan flailing his arms, not sure of his message.

Declan closed the gap quickly and finally, his voice was heard, "It's a trap. He's sending us into a fatal funnel. Move!" Declan redirected Nick and the group back toward the football field against the flow of people just as flames roared through the tunnel.

40

The people pouring back into the stadium from the engulfed tunnel looked like something out of a post-apocalyptic movie. Nick watched in horror as a young girl emerged from the smoke with half of her face and body charred. The shock had blocked her brain's understanding of what had happened as she drifted in a daze into a police officer. Sirens had now replaced the previously joyous cheers of the football game.

Cassie and her children sat safely on the bristly Astroturf of the thirty-yard marker. The rest of the group took on the daunting task of attending to the wounded. Everywhere they looked there seemed to be another injured person. Within a matter of minutes, the stadium was flooded with police, fire, and EMS personnel.

The agents that were assigned to the marina had arrived to assist. This included Haggerty and the HRT guys. The massive stadium had become a combination of make-shift medical center and crime scene. Amidst the chaos, Nick heard someone calling his name and he turned to see Fitzgerald approaching.

"Nick, please tell me that somewhere in this carnage is a dead terrorist."

"I read this wrong and a lot of innocent people got hurt." Nick had always prided himself on owning his mistakes. He never tried to pass the buck. But under these circumstances the impact of this quality was devastating. He did not know the number of dead and wounded but looking around the field he knew that it would be bad.

"Director Jenkins is furious. That is an understatement. She is calling for your badge. As of right now you and Martinez are on administrative leave." Fitzgerald softened a bit, "Sorry. Not my call. I went to bat for you, but you know how that goes."

"Are you serious? This is absolute bullshit!" It was Izzy speaking up after overhearing the ASAC.

"Martinez, everyone knows you guys were doing the best you could, but the Bureau looks like fools and we have to reassure the American public that we are taking a new approach to this manhunt. To put it bluntly, your ability to predict Khaled's movements have fallen short and more people are dead."

"So, what the hell are we supposed to do now?" Nick suddenly felt overwhelmed.

"Take some time to reset. I'm sure that it will pass and in time the Director will focus her attention elsewhere," Fitzgerald offered this consolation.

Declan interjected, "You're making a huge mistake. Nick and Izzy have the best chance of tracking this guy. If you cut them loose now, then your probabilities of getting the Translator drops to zero." He had a look of pure rage in his eyes, but his voice was calm in stark contrast. It was a scary blend.

"Listen, my hands are tied on this." Fitzgerald paused for a moment and then turned his full attention toward Declan, "Thank you for your assistance, but your services are no longer needed. The Bureau will compensate you as discussed."

"This guy is not done. The next attack will be on your shoulders." Declan walked away without allowing Fitzgerald a final word.

"I've been advised to collect all of the intel that you have developed on Khaled. You will need to submit a formal report to my office immediately. If I had any say, it wouldn't be this way." Fitzgerald was the one to walk away this time.

"Son of a bitch." Nick sat on the Eagles bench. Shoulders slumped and head down, he looked defeated. Izzy put a gentle hand on his shoulder, but he barely noticed.

"So, what's your next move?" Declan said.

Nick looked up from his momentary lapse of self-pity to see Declan and Alex standing in front of him. "Next move? There is none. We're done. They shut us down."

"In our short time together, you have not struck me as someone who gives up easily."

"This decision came from the top. Fitzgerald was just the messenger and no amount of complaining is going to change it," Nick said through gritted teeth.

"You know that our little ragtag group of misfits are the only ones capable of finding this guy." Declan, steely-eyed, continued, "We know how he thinks and where he is going next."

"We have lost the resources and support of the Bureau."

"All the good that did us trying to stop him so far," Declan said sarcastically.

Nick looked up at his new friend and realized that he was right. All of the assets at the government's disposal had not yielded Khaled's capture. Nick knew that with Declan they had an advantage that none of the intelligence groups would possess. "What are you suggesting we do?"

"You have a group of four well-trained people willing to do whatever it takes to get this asshole. Maybe without all of the politics, we will be able to work faster and actually get ahead of the Translator." Declan allowed a slight smile to break across his rigid face.

"Screw it. I'm in." Nick stood and looked at Izzy.

"I just got freed up on a paid vacation." Izzy returned his smile in support and followed with, "Let's get this bastard."

"One condition." Declan said, halting them, "Alex is with us on this now too."

"I assumed that was a given when you said the four of us," Nick said as he walked toward the stadium exit adjacent to the concession stand. The only exit that had not been destroyed by fire. "We are already behind the power curve. Let's get moving. We have a terrorist to hunt."

41

Khaled was sitting in the cheaply furnished room of the Brookside Motel. The color of the curtains had been washed out from years of sun and replaced with a dingy yellow, contributed from past occupants' non-compliance with the no-smoking policy. Khaled himself was now a contributor to the room's decay as he lit a hand-rolled cigarette. He was mesmerized by the video footage from his attack on the stadium.

The quality of the footage was excellent. It had been captured by the cameras used to record the games. Football was big in Texas and even high school games were aired on local television. Khaled watched in disbelief as Enright was seen intercepting Morales's niece and nephew seconds before the tunnel's flames unleashed their fury. He had taken another opportunity from him and the Dust Devil was finding it incredibly difficult to suppress his rage.

Khaled had already been in contact with The Seven and they relayed their great pleasure with his latest success. The next media release had already been sent and it would be heard by the American people soon.

The media loved to share the numbers, comparing it to attacks of the past. The count was ever-growing. His mission in Texas had left more injured than dead, but the real impact was the fear imparted to small-town America. No place would feel safe anymore. Images flooded every news channel depicting men and women, standing on their porches with handguns and rifles at the ready. The false bravado of terrified people.

Khaled still had a lot of work to do before he disappeared again.

"Well, the media didn't help your cause. No wonder the Director gave you a temporary boot," Alex said to Nick as the four sat around the cherry wood table in Alex's kitchen.

"I know. Jesus, the next thing the news will say is that I am the terrorist." Nick said this as he stared at his image on the television mounted on the wall in the adjacent living room, visible because of the open floor plan of the house. The news showed a picture of him sitting in the stadium's bleachers. Nick realized that this picture had to have been sent to the media by the Translator. He was sitting so close to them and they never saw him. The thought was equally as terrifying as it was frustrating.

The other image the news had focused on was of Nick making his run for the announcer's booth. It felt that the media supported the agenda set forth by The Seven, implicating that the government agencies were incompetent. The profit motive of the twenty-four-hour news companies' mandate to outdo one another had compromised a balanced and impartial approach, replacing it with sensationalized stories with unchecked facts. The general consensus of the Americans polled had listed the current President's approval rating at an unprecedented sixteen percent. People called for his resignation. The television debates from the so-called *experts* explored solutions from the safety and security of their desks.

"Well, I've become the damned poster child for a failed agency." Nick said the self-deprecating statement to himself.

"Screw the media. You know better than most that what they say is half-assed and way off the mark. Let's focus that energy on finding this bastard," Declan redirected.

"Since Izzy and I had to turn in our badge and gun to Fitzgerald until the inquiry is completed, we're limited in weaponry."

Declan and Alex looked at each other and exchanged cocky smiles. "Nick, you came to the right place." He gave the come-along gesture with his hand as he walked from the table to a closed door located down the hallway. The four stood outside the seemingly benign door. The only thing that stood out as unique was the electronic keypad above the handle.

Alex punched in his code and there was an audible click of the locking device's release. The door opened to a small eight-by-ten room. There was a sturdy table in the center and the expanse of the back wall had two very large safes. On the table, Nick observed a box of gun cleaning supplies.

"Welcome to my man cave," Alex said laughing. "I have been preparing for this day for a long time." Alex went over and unlocked both wall safes, exposing their contents to the rest of the group. Even Declan looked impressed.

"Are we planning on waging World War Three?" Izzy jested quietly, suddenly feeling slightly out of place among the three battle-tested men.

"The war has already begun. We just have to end it." Izzy looked over at Nick, surprised to hear that those words had come from his mouth.

"I'm not sure what it's going to take, but we need to be prepared if we are presented with an opportunity to take out the Translator," Declan asserted himself. "We were able to figure out his Texas plan even if we missed the target. Now he has only one place left to go. The FBI will hopefully keep a team assigned to Mason and his family, but that depends on if they trusted our intel." Declan paused looking at the two agents and rolled his eyes, demonstrating that he understood the politics of administrators. "Best-case scenario is that they beef up visible security and send Haggerty's HRT to assist. Worst-case is they leave a skeleton crew and move the rest of the agents off-site."

"If our plan is to go to Virginia and provide security to Mason then we need to have a different approach than we did here," Nick said. "We tried to move quietly here in Texas thinking that we could lure the Translator into exposing himself. We've learned that he is better than that and he will not be baited."

"So you're saying that we harden the target?" Izzy asked, following the gist of Nick's train of thought.

"Yes. We need to centralize Mason and his family into one location so that we can set up our defenses."

"I like it. Let's stand toe-to-toe with this asshole and bang it out. It's just one man and we've got some good toys to assist with that." Alex's smile reappeared as he extended his arms toward the contents of his safes, like Vanna White revealing a prize.

"I have some gear too that may be of some assistance," Declan said.

"I figured that ridiculously heavy bag you brought didn't contain a microwave," Nick said, and the two chuckled softly.

"Let's get to it. The longer we stand around here, the harder it will be to get ahead of Khaled," Alex said as he began pulling a variety of weaponry from the safes and laying them on the table.

"It may already be too late as it is." Nick said this grimly.

Declan pulled out his phone and called Mason. "Hey Moose, it's Ace. We're still in Texas but will be heading your way soon."

"How's Alex and his family?" The raspy voice of Mason crackled on the other end.

"He missed. They're good. He's going to be with me when we arrive. It'll be like a mini-reunion." Declan felt both excited and edgy, gathering his old team together for this mission. "The Translator is better than we thought. He has been three steps ahead of us this whole time. I don't think we can risk exposing your children."

"What do you want to do then?" Mason asked.

"Your house is pretty secure, right?" Declan knew the answer having been out to the place and lovingly referred to it as the compound. "Bring all of your children to you. Treat it like a lockdown until we get there."

"The FBI security team leader said that HRT was on its way here to provide protective services. I am sure that we will be fine. When do you think you will arrive?"

"We'll be leaving here in less than an hour, but it will take us two days. The Bureau cut us out. So, no fast-flying jets for us. And we can't fly commercial with the goody bag of supplies we're carrying." Declan said this knowing that two days was an eternity in a situation like this. His only solace was that he assumed that the Translator was also traveling by car. Even with that being the case, they were behind him by at least a day if not more.

"I'll take care of things on my end. Keep me posted if anything changes," crackled Mason.

"Sounds good. Steak Sauce out." Declan clicked the phone and ended the call.

"Steak Sauce," Izzy said smiling.

"What. It's just a thick and delicious marinade added to a perfectly cooked steak, enhancing the flavor of the meat." Alex answered in a smart-ass tone and then smiled, "Just something we used to call ourselves. Long story and if I told you, I'd have to kill you." Alex laughed bringing his dimples to life.

"They know," Declan advised his friend. "No secrets between us now."

42

Your government cannot protect you. Look at their incompetence in stopping the last three attacks. They will tell you that they are close to catching us, but they are not. They are lying to you. Just as the politicians are lying to you now about pulling out of Iraq. The American military can mobilize in a matter of days, yet here we are two weeks later and not one soldier has left our country. Your lives are in the hands of your government officials. Our demand is simple. Leave Iraq and the bombings stop. Stay and they never will. You, the American people, will never feel safe again.

The powerful message's impact resonated. Much of this had to do with the fact that The Seven's presentation was a departure from traditional terroristic rants made by extremists. The Seven never raised their voices. They spoke in perfect English. The seven covered faces sat abreast at a table. Numerous references had been made to the symbolic image of Christ's last supper. The members in the video were set against a backdrop that could have been mistaken for the oval office. The polished quality of the video itself was clear and professionally made, unlike the grainy videos of past groups.

The news channels fed this message to the American people day and night. They had become a silent partner in the spread of fear and panic across the United States. Raw video footage had begun to trickle in of protests and violent clashes with law enforcement. Crowds formed in protest outside the White House and various federal, state, and local law enforcement agencies, calling for action. The looting had begun. As in any state of emergency where protective resources are redirected or drained, there will be those who take advantage. The looters never took necessary household items. It was always liquor, sneakers, and clothing. But the Seven's message had motivated these smash and grab opportunists to add a new item to their shopping list... guns.

Khaled enjoyed the fruits of his labor that played out on the television set as he sat in the corner of the café, enjoying his morning espresso. He was no longer Darius Johnson of Austin, Texas. His new identity was Francis "Frank" Belfort of Evans, Georgia, and his license plates reflected this. He had lightened his complexion slightly and used green contacts to give his dark eyes a hazel appearance. The change was impressive and to any passerby, he would look as though he were the byproduct of an interracial relationship.

The nondescript Honda had several aftermarket storage containers installed that could only be accessed by pressing a specific combination of knobs and buttons on the radio and A/C affixed to the dashboard. Commonly referred to as "traps", these storage spaces enabled criminals to stash contraband. For Khaled, these containers held the tools of his trade. He was confident that no police officer would ever find them if he happened to be stopped and searched. He had no fear of these local law enforcement agents and therefore showed no signs of nervousness as he passed them along the roadways on his long journey from Texas to his next objective.

"Jesus. You have had a rough go," Jay responded to Nick's debrief of his recent encounter with Khaled and his subsequent administrative punishment.

"Yeah. It's not how I saw this thing playing out. I really thought we were going to get the drop on him in Texas. None of us can figure out how he knew to place a decoy on the boat. He's never taken that extra step before."

Nick was hoping that Jay's connection in the world of counter-espionage would shed some light on their situation.

"Maybe he had decoys set on all the other attacks, but never needed them because you guys weren't close enough to pick up on it."

"Maybe. Something just felt off. Alex's sister received the invitation for the boat trip just prior to our arrival in Texas. It was like he knew we were coming and wanted us to find that." Nick was still skeptical that there wasn't something more going on behind the scenes with the Translator.

"Do you think he has someone on the inside?" Jay said this knowing the implications.

"The thought had crossed my mind. No surveillance cameras have picked him up anywhere. There hasn't been one validated sighting of him since this thing began. And the most troubling part is that he is always a few steps ahead of us."

"Who else knew that you were heading to Texas?" Jay was buying in that there was a leak, or worse, a co-conspirator in the ranks.

"Nelson was the only one who knew the details when we left Connecticut. The Austin office knew that we were arriving but had no additional info until we landed. Even Haggerty and the HRT guys had arrived under the assumption that they had been mobilized for the terrorist, but they were not briefed until I met with him and ASAC Fitzgerald." Nick was trying to find the link as he spoke.

"The only one in question would be Nelson from your agency. It's also disconcerting that he was quick to pull you out after the stadium attack. It doesn't show good judgment but doesn't give me anything definitive either. I can look into him and let you know what I find." Jay had unmatched resources in the area of picking apart someone's hidden secrets, and Nick had used this on more than one occasion in the past.

"Thanks. I hope it's nothing and I can go back to thinking that Nelson is just an idiot and not a potential terrorist," Nick said, trying to add levity to the situation.

"How's Enright working out?" Jay asked mischievously.

"Solid guy. Like I said before, I wouldn't be alive to talk to you if he hadn't stepped in. His former teammate, Alex Morales, has joined our merry little militia."

"I still haven't found much more on their team, but I did find a little something. Apparently, the one device recovered from that failed attack was analyzed and documented by Mason Richards." Jay let this information settle with his friend.

Nick looked in through the plate glass window of the Whataburger at Declan, Alex, and Izzy, sitting at a corner booth. The group had stopped in the outskirts of Dallas at the Texas fast food staple after passing through the Metroplex and onto Interstate 30. They still had about twenty hours of driving before they arrived at Mason's house in Virginia. "Wait a minute. So, you're telling me that their former unit commander was the one who did the workup on the bomb maker?"

"Yes. Why do you sound so shocked? It makes sense because that unit obviously operated in the realm of counter-terrorism and were experts in the field," Jay said, trying to understand Nick's reaction.

"Because Declan has been talking to Richards this whole time. He forwarded him the same picture that I sent you and he told Declan that he would have to check his notes." Nick breathed and slowed his rate of speech, realizing that he must have sounded panicked. "You are telling me that an expert in a field comes across an intact device from an infamous terrorist and can't give any insight without looking for some notebook! That doesn't make sense. I would imagine that he would be able to recall some pertinent details immediately. Why would he give Declan the runaround?"

"I didn't realize that Richards had been advised about the bomb. Knowing that, I'm a little suspicious. Hard to tell what that means though. People who operate in units like Alpha One have a tendency to be extremely guarded. I'll see what I can find." Jay hung up.

Nick stood with the phone down by his side, processing this new realization. He walked slowly back toward the group, trying to make sense of it all.

"Anything from your source?" Declan asked, taking a large mouthful of his made-to-order cheeseburger slathered in jalapeños.

"What did Richards say about the bomb stuff?" Nick asked softly.

"What do you mean? Why?" Declan reflexively became protective of his former commander, not sure what Nick was getting at with his question.

"Don't get so defensive. I'm just trying to sort out some information I received." The tension between the two began to grow.

"What information? You're asking me a veiled question about my former commander. I need to hear you speak in plain language about what it is you are getting at." Declan shifted his position at the table so that his shoulders now squared to Nick's. Even in his seated position, Declan looked menacing, as if he was a tiger about to pounce.

"Easy boys. Let's figure this out. We're all on edge and we need to slow things down." Izzy's voice seemed to have an instant effect on both men. She could see some slack in their previously rigid shoulders.

"Sorry. I should've been more direct. No secrets. My source said that there had been one bomb analyzed from the Dust Devil's attacks overseas. By Richards," Nick said, offering the clearest explanation without exposing Jay.

"Hmm. I mentioned to you that Mason remembered something about a similar type of bomb that he disabled when we were overseas, but that he had to find his notebook to get the details." Declan said this with a hint of confusion in his tone, unable to make the connection that had Nick so upset.

"You and Alex are experts in secret squirrel stuff, right?" Nick continued without allowing an opportunity to answer his rhetorical question, "I have some expertise too. Most recently in regard to the human trafficking cases that I worked during my time out here. The point is, I could tell you just about every detail of one of my victims' assaults and the people responsible. I could do this without ever wasting time looking for my old case file or notebook." Nick let this sink in with the group and in particular, with Declan.

"Shit. That's something I never even thought about." Declan began rubbing his temples as though suddenly inflicted with a migraine. "Too much going on trying to out-think the bad guy that it never crossed my mind."

"Declan, are you saying that you think Mason has something to do with this?" Alex was now becoming unnerved.

"I don't know what it means, but I know this. The Translator has been outmaneuvering us this whole time. There are only a handful of people that have been aware of our plans thus far." Declan was calm in his delivery.

"So, what about Nick's boss, Nelson? He knew where they were going at all times," Alex said, frantically trying to find reason in this madness.

"What would be his rationale? He has no connection to Khaled. Plus, he put Nick and Izzy on administrative leave. Why would he do that if he wanted to keep tabs on us?" Declan sighed. The weight of what he was about to say next burdened him. "Mason was close with Khaled when we were in the village. Closer after his daughter's death."

"You are talking about Mason "Moose" Richards for God's sake! A legend among legends. Do you really need me to remind you?" Alex was intense, and his charismatic boyish charms were no longer present.

"I know who I'm talking about." A low rumble formed in Declan's voice, "And I'm not saying that he did anything, but if we don't look at this from every angle then we are bound to fail." Declan looked dead into the eyes of his life-long friend. "And we don't ever fail."

"True." Alex conceded to his friend's logic.

"Okay, well I'm going to need a cold shower after watching that little testosterone show," Izzy said with a giggle that disarmed the entire group and brought out a hearty laugh from the men.

"I guess we will have a better feel for things when we get to Virginia and meet with Mason face to face," Nick said. "Let's keep everything status quo so that we don't tip him off any further. That's if he's involved. If he's not, then we have to get ourselves there sooner rather than later to have any chance of protecting his family."

"Agreed. And let's keep our minds open, as well as our options," Declan said, placing a reassuring hand on Alex's shoulder.

The group returned to Alex's SUV with full stomachs. The rear compartment was filled with their assortment of weapons and gear. Alex offered to drive for a few more hours as they continued their race east against the Translator, and whatever The Seven had planned next.

43

Declan had slept for two hours and awoke refreshed. He had learned to sleep for twenty minutes or two hours to achieve the optimal rest state. A study had been done on fighter pilots, running continuous combat sorties. It revealed that the goal for maximum uninterrupted short interval sleeping was twenty minutes or two hours. Anything in between usually left the subject groggy and with slowed reaction times. Something Declan could not afford then or now. He looked over at Alex, who was rubbing his eyes. "Pull off bro, I got this." Alex conceded to his friend's request without a word of protest.

Declan drove on into the darkness. After several uneventful hours, the SUV passed through Little Rock, Arkansas. The group had decided that they would drive continuously, taking shifts and rotating as needed. The thought was that the time they had lost in the wake of the stadium attack would be gained when the Translator stopped to rest.

Declan heard stirring from the middle seat and Izzy's head slowly rose up. He watched her as she gathered her bearings. She saw Declan looking at her in the rearview mirror and gave a tired smile. She then leaned forward toward the center console and asked quietly, not wanting to disturb the others, "Hey there, how are you holding up?"

"I'm good. Been awake a lot longer than this and in a lot worse places than a fancy SUV," Declan whispered in response.

"Do you want some company? I don't think that I can fall back asleep."

"Sure."

Izzy was silent for a moment and then said, "Do you mind if I ask you something personal?"

"I don't see why not," Declan said, keeping his voice in a hushed whisper.

"What happened that night of the shooting?" Izzy asked this with no trace of judgment in her voice.

"I'm sure you and Nick did your research on me before you came to my house that day. Did you read my file?" Declan asked matter-of-factly.

"We did. To be honest, Nick and I were shocked at the outcome. That guy gave you no choice, but your department decided to go after you on some policy violations. It didn't make sense to us at face value."

"There's a little history between the chief and me," Declan said, cocking his eyebrow.

"Enough so, that he would bury you in a righteous shooting?" Izzy still couldn't fathom how a guy like Declan Enright had been fired.

"I guess so because it happened. And the fallout left my family drowning in debt." Declan had momentarily forgotten that he was talking to one of the agents investigating his armored truck robbery. He knew that if they survived the next few days that eventually Nick and Izzy would continue that investigation. He wondered how that would play out.

"I can't imagine what that must have been like for you and your family. So, are you going to tell me why your chief hated you or are you going to let my imagination run wild?"

"I'm sure that you already know that I used to be a Narc?" Declan saw the nod of Izzy's head in the mirror. "I was working a low-level heroin case. Nothing too crazy, but the target was dealing primarily to high school kids. Because of this, there was pressure for my unit to make a case. We didn't have much on the dealer except that it was a female. I had signed up a confidential informant that was able to buy into her. So, I set up a buy/bust operation. The dealer ended up trying to flee in her car but crashed into a tree a block away. After a very short foot chase she was apprehended, but not without a fight. The cuffs eventually went on and she had some minor scrapes and bruises from the altercation." Declan paused for effect, allowing Izzy to process the story.

"That sounds like some straightforward police work. Why am I not seeing the problem? What did your chief get bent about?"

"The dealer was his daughter." Declan smiled.

"Well holy crap. For an Irish guy, you have some shitty luck." Izzy laughed, shaking her head and then continued, "But he couldn't do anything to you for doing your job."

"No, but he tried. He convinced my supervisor to investigate my use of force when I was placing her in handcuffs. When that didn't fly, he tried to say that the buy/bust itself was not within policy. All his efforts to screw me failed."

"It seems pretty harsh to go after you. Maybe if he had done a better job raising his daughter then it wouldn't have happened in the first place." Izzy's voice rose slightly at this statement, and she heard Nick stir behind her, but his eyes remained closed.

"The media got hold of the story and ran wild with it for several days. That seemed to be the final straw in our delicate relationship. I knew that I was on borrowed time, but I never thought that it would end the way it did.

"Within hours of my shooting, someone in the media found out about my military past and labeled it an execution. That phrasing made headlines and experts came in to dissect every little piece of my actions that night. Some went so far as to say that my shot grouping showed a level of premeditation." Declan felt himself rambling and stopped to collect his thoughts.

"It was an impressive shot group, but labeling it premeditated murder is one of the most ridiculous things that I have ever heard."

"Well then wait for the kicker. The guy I shot turned out to be holding an empty gun. No bullets and no magazine. The critics said that I was skilled enough to see the weapon was empty. They had a computerized simulator show the distance and my line of sight. It showed a dotted line covering the fifteen feet to the bottom of the gun. Then they showed a close up of a similar gun stating that it would have been easy to see that there was no magazine, even in low-light conditions." Declan rolled his eyes, punctuating the preposterous nature of such an assertion.

"Who fed the media that load of crap? Don't answer. I already know too many ex-this and ex-that making their way around the network expert circuit. Ridiculous!"

"Well, it's over now. I'm just trying to pick up the pieces for my family. We're juggling a lot. This is the longest I've been away from my girls since Laney was born." Declan's mind drifted to his family.

"She is sweet. When did she get diagnosed?" Izzy's tenderness was evident.

"Around eighteen months. Laney didn't communicate. She was non-verbal and had little to no expression. It was a huge learning curve for me. Val was more up to speed on it because of her educational background, but I was lost."

"You obviously love your daughter. It was evident that day at your house."

"Thank you for that. It's so hard to look at her and see nothing in return. I've waited for three years for a real hug. It's been tough on Ripley and Abigail too. Val and I spend a lot of our time and energy with Laney. Sometimes I feel like we have left them out." Declan paused. "That's what angered me most about being fired. They took my ability to provide for my family. It drained our financial resources so quickly that we couldn't get our foothold." Declan realized that he may have said too much, but for some reason, he trusted Isabella Martinez completely.

"Maybe when all this is over Nick and I can help sort some of that out. After all, we are the FBI." Izzy said this last part sarcastically and winked. "And for what it's worth, Nick and I agreed that you were one hundred percent justified in your shooting. If anything, you should have gotten a medal."

44

Khaled drove east across America's heartland toward his next objective. He took in the rippling effect of his three previous attacks. The damp road from the early morning rain now gave way to a slow rising fog, as the sun made its first appearance of the day. As he proceeded into the valley region of the Blue Ridge Mountains, Khaled pulled off the interstate and into a Waffle House.

The rustic city of Roanoke, located in the southwest corner of Virginia, displayed the influence of The Seven. Hand-made signs and banners hung from many windows on the neighboring businesses and houses. Much of it was second amendment gibberish about arming the militia to fight. *It was working*, he thought. The country was starting to divide, and people were preparing to take action. But it's difficult to fight an enemy that you can't see, and when that happens you take arms against the enemy you can. In this case, it was the American government.

As Khaled walked into the diner he was surprised when hit with the heavy smoke that filled the air. One of the throwbacks of American eateries. The Waffle House had resisted the popular trend that started in the late nineties, banning smoking. Somehow the chain restaurant lasted some twenty years later as if locked in time.

Khaled did not mind it at all and found a spot in the smoking section. He opened his tin of hand-rolled cigarettes and awaited the service of his overworked and overweight waitress. As he scanned the sea of truckers and early risers, he noted that many of these citizens were openly carrying firearms. It appeared that the U.S. was beginning to resemble the lawlessness of a third world country. Open defiance of state laws would max out law enforcement and additionally burden legislators.

The mumbled talk in the diner was focused on stopping the terrorist attacks. Khaled could not hear all of the banter, but the gist was that they all had to be prepared for anything. The irony was that for all the tough talk, they were completely defenseless, as they sat only mere feet from the most wanted man in America.

On the television, he could hear the mumblings of the President, but with the background noise of his fellow eaters, he could not clearly hear the words. Khaled read as the delayed closed captioning at the bottom of the screen revealed the President's message.

We have reached the highest state of emergency within this country since the attacks of September 11, 2001. Until we can resolve this issue and locate the threat, I am calling for all Americans to remain home. Only essential government personnel at state and local levels should report to their assigned duties. All schools and universities are to close immediately. Any recreational centers and athletic events are canceled until further notice. I give this message with the support of your state's representatives. It is with a heavy heart that I am delivering this message. Know that we are using every asset available to resolve this quickly and bring this group to justice. Your safety is paramount, and I appreciate your support.

The once loud roar of conversations and clatter of porcelain plates ceased as the message completed. A look of shock permeated the restaurant goers. The realization that their government was unable to stop the attacks was evident. The deeper and more profound impact was that no place was safe, and no target was off limits. Khaled feigned his own shock to maintain his disguise as the waitress lumbered over to take his order. He looked at her with his non-prescription glasses. This addition to his ensemble gave a humbling appearance to his features, further reducing any possible perception of the threat he imposed.

"What can I do you for, honey?" She said this with no emphasis and with the stale performance created by the daily grind of her life.

"Two eggs over easy on rye." Khaled closed the menu and took a second look at this woman. Her crooked placard affixed above her left breast was embossed in the blue letters, Nancy, a name befitting her. Nancy's forehead had already begun to perspire from the morning's laborious tasks. "Crazy things going on in the world these days." Khaled slowly shook his head for added effect. He knew that not to mention the current state of affairs would be out of place. Especially following the President's most recent declaration.

"Don't get me started. This country is going to hell in a handbasket." She said this with a slight drawl and shuffled away to place his order.

Hell in a handbasket. That phrase would soon take on an entirely new meaning for Nancy and her restaurant's patrons.

"Has the President lost his ever-loving mind?" Chimed in Nick, sitting up after hearing the radio announcement from the President. "I mean, shit, he just gave in. He has just put the entire country on lockdown!" This was said in a tone that blended equal parts anger and bewilderment.

"Never in my life..." Alex started but seemed to drift off before completing whatever thought had caused him to open his mouth.

"There's one benefit to that message." It was Declan who now spoke out.

"And what's that?" Nick said still shell-shocked.

"It won't be suspicious that we have Mason and his family remain together at his house. They will appear to be following the White House's directive. The Translator won't be able to draw out his children or send us on a wild goose chase. He's going to have to come and get them. Hopefully, we'll be there. And ready when he does."

"That's if he's not already there now. Or worse." Nick did not finish the comment, but the message was received. Both Declan and Alex had resigned themselves to the possibility, no matter how remote, that Richards might be somehow involved.

As if on cue, Declan's phone vibrated. "Moose, what's up? Did you find anything on the bombs?" Declan looked at the others as he asked.

"Did you hear?" Mason's normally calm, raspy voice was at a higher pitch. If Declan didn't know the man, he would have said he sounded scared.

"Hear what?" Declan retorted.

"Another bombing!"

"What do you mean another bombing?" All the others stared in the direction of Declan as he said this.

"He's in Virginia! A damn Waffle House in Roanoke. He hit them during the morning rush. It was devastating." Mason's voice softened as the impact of his message was delivered to Declan.

"When? Jesus, we just passed through there a few hours ago. We are on I-66 now passing exit 18 in Linden. About an hour out." Declan signaled Alex with his hand to accelerate.

"It looks like maybe an hour or so ago. It just hit the media now. Looks like he is heading this way too. I tried to tell the agents assigned here that he was probably coming, but they were redirected to the bomb site. Only two agents remained, one internal and one on the perimeter." Mason's rasp was more prominent now, sounding more like a wheeze. "It will be better when you guys get here."

"Let the perimeter guy know that we will be arriving in a black Chevy Suburban. There are four of us. See you soon. Steak Sauce out." Declan slid the phone back into his pocket and looked around at the group. The impact of another soft target attack was disheartening and infuriating. Both emotions fluctuated in their facial expressions.

"He sounded genuinely shocked by this latest development. I know Mason and he was truly frazzled." Declan proclaimed this to the group and Alex nodded in relief.

"Either way we need to be prepared for a battle when we reach the destination," Nick said, reaching into the back compartment. He began distributing the gear bags so they could load up.

An uneasy silence fell over all of them. The only sound was the voice on the radio describing in detail the carnage witnessed at the Waffle House explosion. Nine dead and twenty-three wounded.

45

The agent was standing in plain sight near the edge of the long driveway in anticipation of the SUV's arrival. Alex slowed the Chevrolet as he approached the decorative red brick half-moon retaining wall adorning the end of the driveway. The agent looked young and held a hand up, signaling Alex to stop. He walked toward the driver's side. He exposed both badge and gun on his right hip, declaring his authority to the vehicle's occupants.

Alex nodded. "Richards is expecting us. Tell him that the Steak Sauce has arrived."

The agent, who identified himself only by his last, Munson, relayed the strange greeting over the radio. Mason confirmed that it was okay to let the visitors in.

Munson waved them forward and then resumed his statuesque position, looking out toward the street. Alex wanted to tell him that the bad guys never used the front door but figured it would be wasted on him. He was too green to be taught the finer points of security during this brief encounter. Time demanded their efforts on other preparations.

The driveway ended in a roundabout and Alex pulled to a stop in front of the red brick-faced colonial. The massive white pillars that spanned the front porch gave way to a handcrafted oak door with an ornate frame painted in classic white. Nick leaned over to Declan and said, "Remind me what your boss does for a living. I may need a job after this is over."

Declan chuckled, "Don't think that I haven't thought about it too. He does some type of governmental consulting and develops tech for special ops guys. Totally outside of my skill set. I'm a better soldier than a scientist. Mason was the rarest of breeds. He excelled at both."

The door swung wide and the broad shoulders of the man, appropriately nicknamed "Moose," filled the extra-wide frame. It became readily apparent how this man had been so aptly named. "Thank God you guys are here." He extended his hand to both Nick and Izzy as they exchanged pleasantries. Declan and Alex each received an enormous bear hug.

Nick noted the larger-than-life charisma of Richards and instantly realized why the accusation of his involvement was challenged so heavily by his former teammates. Nick regretted having made this judgment. There was no way that Mason could have had anything to do with the terrorists. As they entered the massive dwelling, Nick noted that the walls were decorated with paintings depicting every U.S. conflict dating back to the Revolution. *Everything about this man screamed patriot.*

"Where's Trish and the kids?" Alex asked of his former commander.

"I have them tucked down in the basement." Richards gave a quirky smile and continued, "It's more of a fallout shelter slash man-cave than a basement."

"What's the deal with all of you ex-special forces guys? Have all of you prepared for Armageddon?" Izzy jested sarcastically.

"Life has taught me that if you don't prepare, then someone else will. You know the old saying, *luck favors the prepared*," Richards raspy voice boomed. "And I consider myself a very lucky man." He finished this statement with a playful wink.

Mason punched a code and the heavy door released its lock. Nick looked at the thickness of the door as it opened and realized that it could probably stop a rocket. As an Army Ranger, he had the opportunity to move in the special operations circles, but he could tell these guys were at a totally different level. It was humbling to be in their presence. Three of the four remaining members of a unit that nobody knew existed were taking him into a secret hideout. It was like Batman inviting him to see the Bat Cave.

Mason began his tour of the lower lair. A soft electronic whir of a line of computers filled the air. The room looked like something that you would see at NASA or the Pentagon. It was clean and organized with one large table that had multiple workstations. Nick noted something familiar about the table but couldn't place it.

"Wow. This set up is impressive," Izzy spoke up.

"Thanks. I'm completely autonomous down here. This is incredibly important for my work."

"What work is that?" Izzy asked, noting that Richards was being extremely vague and not expecting an answer.

"Not sure you have the clearance." He said this in a way that was not condescending or rude, but clear enough to drive home the fact that the details of his work would not be discussed with anyone in the room.

"Moose, it looks like you created your own skiff," Alex said, surveying the equipment.

"Skiff?" Izzy asked.

"It's slang for Sensitive Compartmented Information Facility. We used them a lot for intelligence sharing and operation planning. A great way to communicate without fear of compromising your intel," Alex explained briefly.

"In its simplest form, that's exactly what this is. But I don't want to bore you with the nerdy details," Mason Richards boomed. His gregarious laughter that followed snapped the group from their trance-like stares.

On the far wall was another door with a keypad similar to the one upstairs. Richards gestured for them to follow. "The next room will not be as cold. I keep this one at a lower temperature because of the heat generated from the computers."

The thick door opened to a room that seemed out of place from where they had just come. It was as if they had walked through the wardrobe into Narnia. There was a roaring fire in the fireplace. The center of the room had a red felt-covered pool table. Leather couches and recliners were centered around the fireplace with a large wall-mounted television affixed above it. There was a full-sized kitchen and dining area that could comfortably seat twelve.

"Hey Moose, when can I move in?" It was Declan that spoke this time. Nick realized that this must be the first time he had seen this too.

"Any time my friend. You just have to get these kids to leave." He laughed as he pointed to his children that were sprawled out in various positions of comfort. "Hey guys, get off your lazy butts and come give Uncle Declan and Uncle Alex a hug." At this command, four of Richards children leaped up and moved in on the two former members of their dad's old unit. The twin teenage boys were in that too-cool-for-school awkward phase of their lives, giving a fist bump before immediately returning to their video game. The youngest two girls, who looked to Nick to be between five and eight, gave wonderfully tight hugs. He watched as Declan twirled the youngest around, arms tightly wrapped around his neck and her feet dangling in the air.

"My girls ask about you all the time. I can't wait to tell them that I saw you." Declan was down on one knee and holding the little one's hands, looking deep into her eyes and speaking with a soft sincerity. Nick watched this battle-hardened soldier's tenderness and found a new level of respect for the man. The girls then retreated to their play area.

"Where's Mandy?" Declan asked, not seeing Mason's oldest daughter.

Richards gave a dismissive shrug, "I couldn't convince her to come. She's as stubborn as her old man." As he spoke, Declan thought that he registered an underlying sadness in the large man's response.

Richards brought them to the kitchen where Trish, his third wife, was cutting the crust off two peanut butter and jelly sandwiches. "Trish, this is Nick and Izzy from the FBI. And these other two yahoos need no introduction." Formalities aside, the adults gathered around the table to figure out a plan.

"The security detail left behind by the FBI is weak. They look like they are twelve years old. You saw the guy outside? He is completely useless. The one inside, Acosta, is not much better. I've got him roaming around the interior. Figured I didn't need him down here." Mason continued, "So, what do we know? Any ideas on how we stop this guy?"

"We brought some toys," Alex said referring to the large military duffel bag resting by his feet. All of them were wearing bulletproof vests and were armed.

"That's all well and good, but how do you kill someone you can't see. This guy is a ghost. We need to draw him out somehow." Mason had a pensive look on his face as he spoke. "I have a top-notch security system here." He lifted up a tablet which displayed cameras covering the grounds of the property. He then tapped an icon and the cameras switched to the interior surveillance. "They are continuous and cover the majority of both the inside and outside of the house. Motion sensors are also enabled, but Bozo One and Bozo Two have been setting them off every fifteen seconds so I disabled the audible alert."

"Okay, well that's impressive," Nick said. *How could the Translator reach them?* He tried to think like the enemy but found it difficult to do.

"So, we have surveillance covered and we are armed for battle, then there really isn't much left to do, but wait," Alex said confidently.

"I still feel like we are missing something. This guy is patient. He's smart and has maintained his ability to stay one step ahead of us this whole time," Declan interjected, pausing only momentarily before he continued. "We have to draw him out into the open. I assume he's already here."

This last statement left everybody at the table silent. The reality that they may have only been an hour or so ahead of the Translator had suddenly dawned on them.

"Like bait? Who the hell wants to be bait for this guy?" Izzy said this voicing her frustration. "I mean, Jesus, you guys refer to him as a ghost. If one of us were to put ourselves out as a lure, then it would be a guaranteed death sentence."

"Maybe. Maybe not." Mason spoke, "We can assume he knows we are all here. I will even concede that he probably has the schematics to my house. I know that I would if the roles were reversed." Alex and Declan nodded in agreement. Mason added, "But what he won't have is all of my modifications."

Declan realized that Mason was right. "We can keep your family here in the bunker and the rest of us can expose ourselves in the house. He is going to have to come for us."

"I agree. We have another advantage." Nick paused for effect. "We are ready this time. No more guesswork. He can't draw us out with misdirection. If Khaled wants to get to your family, then he has to go through us."

Mason gave an unspoken look of appreciation to the four that had driven halfway across the country to put their lives in harm's way for his family. He then took his tablet and a backpack full of equipment and the group ascended the stairwell. The secure door protecting Mason's family hissed, alerting them that the locking mechanism had engaged.

46

Khaled's attack on the Waffle House had the desired effect. The once robust security detail assigned to Mason Richards's home had been pulled out to assist in response to the bombing. The two agents left behind were not skilled and appeared to be new to this type of work.

Hiding in plain sight had become a specialty of the former school teacher. He was now wearing the light gray jumpsuit of a lineman technician. He had attached a rectangular magnetic sign to the driver and passenger side doors letting any nosy neighbors know that he was there on official business for a company called Old Towne Electric. The residents of this neighborhood would recognize the reference to the city's famed historic downtown area, adding a level of validity to his presence.

He parked along the curbing at the end of the cul-de-sac. There was a wooded area that ran beneath the power lines. Just beyond was the visible cedar wood paneling of Mason Richards's fence line. Khaled walked beneath the overhead wires looking up as if inspecting their quality. A neighbor had stepped out to walk their small dog. Khaled gave a friendly wave and went back to his clipboard. The man barely took notice of him as he went about his evening duties of picking up the droppings of the family pet. To Khaled, the domesticated animal looked more like a large rat than a canine.

There was no resemblance to his last disguise in the new look he had adorned for this mission. He looked more like Kid Rock than the clean-cut Iraqi man that lay beneath the makeup and wig. His long dirty brown hair was pulled back into a ponytail beneath the white plastic hard-hat that he wore. A pair of yellow tinted wire-rimmed glasses masked the shape of his face and distorted his eye color. Khaled had shouldered a heavy bag containing his necessary tools for tonight's mission. He set the bag down at the base of the telephone pole that overlooked the rear of the target's property. Night quickly began to fall. A hint of colder weather was present in the slight breeze that accompanied it.

"Hey Acosta, I think that it would be better if we had the two of you outside covering the perimeter. We can handle the inside stuff." Nick presented this request in a subtle tone. He knew that if he ordered the young agent then the topic of Nick's administrative leave might surface.

"Sure. Looks like you and your crew are well prepared," he said with no trace of resentment. Nick had seen that the crop of new agents came in with a sense of entitlement. Maybe a lifetime of societal rewards for mediocrity had played its part in the millennials' jaded attitudes toward work, but Acosta seemed to have none. "Do you really think this guy is coming?" A trace of nervousness was evident in his voice.

"I don't think. I know. And we've concluded that he is already here. So, do me a favor and don't get killed." No humor in Nick's voice. The seriousness of the statement caused the young agent to pause and take a visibly deep breath before moving out from the kitchen to the front door. Nick could tell that Acosta had no former military experience and that his training at Hogan's Alley was probably the closest he'd ever been to a battle. Nick had a genuine concern for this young man's life, but the situation dictated hard decisions.

"I don't like waiting," Alex said as he stroked the black exterior of his MP5. The nine-millimeter assault rifle was strapped loosely around his shoulder and centered on his chest using a one-point sling system. The sling, comprised primarily of bungee cord wrapped around nylon webbing, allowed him movement in close quarters and an ease when transitioning to a sidearm.

"Hey Mason, besides the surveillance, what else do you have in the way of defenses?" Declan asked of the large man holding his tablet and examining the live feed from outside.

"Not much else. The basement fortress has always been the defense plan. At least we will have the advantage of seeing him first." Mason said this with some resignation as though realizing it still might not be enough.

"I'm going upstairs to find a vantage point where I can set up. I'll be in a room that gives the best angle of the backyard," Alex said as he stepped away from the kitchen.

"Why the backyard?" Izzy asked.

"Because that's the direction I would come from." Alex smiled.

"Use Mike's room. It overlooks the pool and most of the yard that isn't blocked by trees. At the top of the stairs take a right and it will be the second door on the left," Mason directed his former teammate. He delivered his information like a commanding officer, and Nick noted the strength in his voice. He had a presence that dominated the room.

"How many access points are we trying to cover?" Declan asked.

"Front door, a rear slider, and a poolside entrance through the attached cabana."

"If we are focusing our resources in the most logical direction of attack, then we need to cover the back two with the most manpower." Declan read the group's facial expressions of concurrence and continued, "Let's leave Munson and Acosta on the front door. Nick, you and Izzy set up in the rear living room area with the sliding door. Moose and I will cover the cabana entrance."

"I sent everybody a group text. This way we can communicate silently, and everyone can have instant updates." Nick said, contributing his piece to the plan since the Alpha One guys had taken control of the operation.

Alex texted that he was in position. He'd found a good shooting location. Unlike in movies, skilled shooters did not lean out windows when scanning for targets.

In the real world, the one Alex and Declan survived in, he had learned to be several feet back from the opening, creating a point of aim without exposing his position. The lights were off in Mike's room. Alex never turned them on when he entered in case the Translator was already watching. His MP5 was not ideal for the situation, but Alex had trained extensively with the weapon and was accurate at its effective range of one hundred twenty-five meters. He positioned himself in a comfortable seated position on the bed. His legs crossed Indian-style and each elbow rested comfortably on the interior pocket of the knees. This gave him enough height to see out into the backyard and the support to maintain the weapon at the ready for an extended period of time. Set for the impending battle, his eyes scanned the darkness of the yard below.

"Do you now see why Alex and I were so offended at the suggestion that Mason had anything to do with this terrorist shit?" Declan whispered in Nick's ear as they began moving to their positions. Mason was walking ahead small-talking Izzy.

"He's a great guy and my suspicions were dispelled the moment we walked in the door. I still can't figure out how this Translator keeps getting the jump on us," Nick responded.

"Hopefully it ends here tonight." The confidence in this statement was tempered with a hint of concern.

47

Nick looked over at Izzy as they huddled behind the large white leather couch located in the rear of the living room. He didn't know what to expect in the coming moments and wasn't sure if this position would give them any more of an advantage than standing out in the backyard. If the Translator was to use one of his devastating bombs, then all would be for naught.

There hadn't been an opportunity to process what occurred between them the other night in her hotel room. Nick knew that now was not the time but hoped that he would have a chance for that conversation. *If they survived.*

Izzy turned to him, obviously aware that he was staring at her. She reached across and gave his hand a gentle squeeze as their eyes met.

A quick popping sound like that of a champagne cork came from above them on the second floor. It was followed by a loud thud. Nick's trance was immediately broken, and he moved fast toward the stairwell. "Stay here! Cover the door!" Nick commanded. Izzy nodded her understanding as he disappeared around the corner and could be heard bounding up the stairs.

Nick entered the room labeled with the teenager's moniker, Mike. Scanning the room his eyes quickly picked up the massive heap on the floor near the foot of the bed. His subconscious took over and his brain reverted to his years of tactical training. Nick dropped to the floor and low-crawled to Alex, who was barely recognizable in his current state. The plush cream of the carpet was quickly being replaced by a thick dark red. The exit wound at the back of his head was massive and his body position had left his legs up, forcing the blood to flow more intensely. Nick knew without question that death had been instantaneous. He stayed low and rolled on his side taking in the small hole in the window pane hoping to get an idea of where the shot had originated.

Nick felt awkward about what he did next but knew that it needed to be done. He sent a text message alerting the others. *Alex dead. Long range headshot. Rear window. No visual.*

From the lower floor of the house, a loud yell erupted that sounded almost bear-like. Nick knew that Declan had just received the news of his friend's death. *And through text message nonetheless.* Nick began his slow retreat out of the room and back to Izzy.

The next message was from Mason. *Movement rear fence line. Moving toward the pool area.* Nick saw it as he took position behind the couch with Izzy. It was difficult to make out. There was a quick flicker like that of a flashlight and then it was lost in the darkness behind a tree. The two agents waited, breathing more rapidly as their heart rate increased with the sudden release of adrenaline.

"Let's take the fight to him!" Declan had never lost focus in battle before, but Alex's death had sent him into overdrive.

"We have to hold our position. Without a target, we become one. I haven't seen anyone pop back out from behind that tree. I wish we had night vision goggles," Mason said with a palpable frustration.

"What's your surveillance showing?" Declan asked. The impatience noticeable in his voice.

"Whoever is out there moved along a path that wasn't covered by my cameras," Mason said in disbelief.

"It's got to be him. He's that good. Hit your floodlights and I'm going to open up on that tree." Declan shouldered his Colt M4 Commando and took aim on the tree's lower trunk. "Sometimes the best way to draw fire is with fire."

Mason did not argue with his former teammate's logic. He sent a quick text to alert the others: *Going loud.* Mason pulled up the controls on his mobile phone and activated the exterior floodlights. The M4 erupted to life in the cadenced beat of three-round bursts of automatic gunfire. The rounds found their mark, chewing the bark off the thick oak's trunk. Nothing. No movement.

Declan expended the entirety of his thirty-round magazine. Then silence crept in. The waiting felt like minutes when only seconds had lapsed. Then a flash of light shot from behind the tree and moved toward the pool area at an inhuman speed. Its path was lined with the L-shaped center point formed by the rear of the house and the attached cabana.

Gunfire sounded from the cabana and the living room as all of the remaining team members unleashed their rounds at the impending target. The speed and erratic maneuvers of the object, now recognizable as some type of drone, hampered the accuracy of the shots.

The lights of the drone went out as it dropped from the sky, coming to a rough landing on a patio table set along the pool deck. Nick realized that he had been holding his breath and suddenly released the air held tightly in his chest with an audible exhale. He looked at Izzy and shook his head with bewilderment. "That was crazy."

Izzy opened her mouth to respond when the patio exploded into a blinding white light. The concussive wave of fire that followed brought with it glass shards and splintered wood from the sliding door.

Her eyes were slow to recover from the bright flash of the blast. As she tried to focus. The images around her appeared as though she was looking through a kaleidoscope. Tracers and white halos encircled all of the objects in the once beautiful living room. She pulled herself along the hardwood floor littered with debris. Izzy pawed her way toward Nick who was flat on his back and did not appear to be moving. Desperation and panic filled her at this sight and she increased her pace as best she could. Her right leg was not cooperating as she slid across the floor. Izzy looked back to see that her ankle was twisted in the opposite direction. Her brain registered the damage to her leg and the pain became overwhelming. A queasy feeling began to cloud her thoughts, but she pushed it back, desperate to get to Nick.

Nick's chest rose and fell in shallow respiration. Izzy had pressed her head lightly against his ribcage, feeling the movement. Her vision was not fully restored, and she had to assess his injuries by touch more than sight. As Izzy moved her hands across to Nick's far side she felt the wetness on his right arm. Frantically she searched for the source and bit her lip out of shock when she found the large piece of glass lodged just above the elbow. The blood that pulsed from the wound was a bad sign that the shard embedded had cut the brachial artery.

Izzy relied on the medical training that she received while in the Army. She had to restrict the blood flow with a tourniquet. Izzy removed her shirt and undershirt. She took the thin material of the tank top and twisted it until it was taut. Izzy wrapped the make-shift tie-off around Nick's bicep a few inches above the wound. She cinched it down using a square knot. Izzy then inserted her small flashlight into the knot and began twisting clockwise until she was unable to turn it any further. She locked the flashlight in place using a cord from a broken lamp. Izzy reached down and felt Nick's wrist to ensure that there was no pulse in his wounded arm. Satisfied, she looked at her watch and marked "T" on his forehead with the time using his blood as her ink. The effort taken to complete the task was draining under her current physical condition. Izzy sent out a message to the others and slowly she slipped into darkness atop of Nick.

48

The crunch of breaking glass seemed to be echoing from a distant place. A flickering of grayish green began to filter into Declan's eyes. It took a moment to register that he was looking at his olive drab tactical pants. The last thing he remembered was the drone. He tried to move his hand to wipe what he assumed was blood from his brow, but his arm wouldn't cooperate. It took a moment to realize that his wrists were secured by zip ties, as were his ankles. The chair was made of wicker, but the interior frame was metal and gave no indication of budging as he struggled against the restraints.

As the fog in his head began to clear, he stared at the man seated in front of him. He looked like a rocker from an eighties big hair band. Thoroughly confused, Declan waited for his head to clear. Everything felt like a bad dream.

"I apologize. My appearance is not one that you are familiar with. Allow me to reintroduce myself." He moved slowly, removing the latex nose and wig. A moment later he had wiped the foundation from his skin revealing a darker complexion. "Better?" The Translator was stoic. No inflection in his voice.

Declan said nothing. He was not willing to indulge this madman with any sort of banter. Confident that the Translator had won, he resigned himself to death. He had accepted its inevitability long ago and would not give this man any additional gratitude in hearing him plead for his life. His eye caught a glimpse of Richards, whose body was sprawled across the floor apparently dead.

"Your friend is not with us. Actually, none of them are." Khaled let this news wash over the Golden Man, Enright. "The blast was more effective than I anticipated. I had been looking forward to more of a fight, but unlike your American action movies, the reality of combat is far different. But you know that better than most. Just like the way they portray you soldiers as liberating heroes." For the first time, a flash of anger crossed Khaled's normally serene facial features.

Declan closed his eyes, using this time to silently say goodbye to Val and his girls. He allowed each of their beautiful faces to come to him. Seeing them in his mind gave him a sense of peace that was coupled with the sad resignation that he would not hold them again. He quietly hummed Laney her song one last time.

"I see that this conversation will be one-way since you seem committed to your silence. Very well. I would have assumed that you were filled with questions, but since you are not I will not waste my time." Khaled paused only for a moment before continuing, "I will tell you this. I have one more trip to make when I leave here. Your wife and three beautiful daughters will be returning from Georgia soon. You won't be there to greet them, but I will."

Declan's natural urge to strangle the man before him took hold at a subconscious level. His sinewy muscles tightened, pulling hard against the ties that restrained him. The plastic edges cut into his flesh, causing him to bleed.

"I want you to know that they will suffer the same fate that you shared with my beautiful Sonia. Your house will burn and collapse on top of them. My only regret is that you will not be there to helplessly watch as it happens. That was to be the real punishment, but your new friends at the FBI put a stop to that back in your driveway." Khaled let out a slow exhale and then smiled. "What do you think they would do to you if they ever figured out that you had robbed that armored truck? It's too bad that I didn't get to watch that situation play out, but they are dead now, so I guess it doesn't matter."

"Who gives a shit anyway if you are planning on killing me?" Declan engaged him now realizing that he must stall in the hopes of finding some way to overcome this man and save his family.

"Now you talk? Good. It felt strange to get to this point without some type of dialogue. You and I have been through so much together." Khaled smiled again.

"What the hell are you talking about?" Declan was not sure where this was going but knew the importance of buying additional time.

"What drove you to rob that bank truck?" Khaled said this in a way that sounded sincere.

"Why should I tell you anything?" Anger at the surface of every syllable.

"Well for starters, it will give you more time. Time to try to find a way out of your current predicament. Which you will soon find a futile endeavor, but one that you will no doubt explore." Khaled spoke as if he were a professor mediating a class debate.

Declan realized that the Translator was as intelligent as he was ruthless. "Okay, I'll play your game. And I have some questions for you too."

"I assumed that you would. But first answer mine." Khaled rested a silenced handgun on his lap. "We don't have all day. The blast that rendered your group useless a few minutes ago will be bringing in the local authorities and I prefer not to be here when that happens. Although, I have something set to give me a head start."

"I hit bottom after being fired from my job. I did it to support my family. That's the long and short of it."

"Why did you get fired?" Khaled asked in a tone that seemed to mock the question.

"I shot someone, and the chief didn't like it," Declan said vacantly.

"Jamal Anderson," Khaled said the name of the young man Declan shot.

"Yes."

"What if I told you a secret about Mr. Anderson?" Khaled seemed almost giddy at this. And saw the confusion on Declan's face.

"What the hell are you talking about? Are you saying that you had something to do with that? Why the hell would anybody agree to a suicide by cop?" Declan strained to grasp this strange innuendo.

"It was quite simple. I found a young drug addict who was panhandling outside a convenience store. After engaging him in a simple conversation over a cigarette he told me about his hard life. He told me about his infant child and how the boy was being raised by his grandmother after child services had taken away his parental rights. It's funny how much people will tell you when you are willing to listen. I am well connected and locating the address of where his child was being raised took no time." Khaled surveyed Declan as he absorbed this information. "Leverage. He believed that I had his grandmother and infant son. I can be very persuasive. I gave him the gun and took his cell phone. He was instructed to create a disturbance that would draw police and to wait for you. I knew where you were on that night and that you would undoubtedly respond to play the hero. I told him to talk to you and that you would try to talk him down. He was instructed to point the gun at you and your fellow officers or his child would be dead."

"You're a sick man. You went through all this for me? Why not just kill me and get it over with?" Declan seethed.

"That would have been too simple. If I wanted to kill you then it would have happened. I needed you to feel what I felt. I needed you to have everything stripped away. I wanted to be the final piece of straw that broke you." Khaled's voice was steady as he relayed his intent.

"You try to hide behind the death of your daughter. You've destroyed your precious Sonia's memory. She wouldn't recognize the man who used to be her father." Declan could tell that his words hit the mark as he watched the Translator lean forward. The muscles in his jawline rippled as he clenched.

"Never speak her name again," Khaled said through gritted teeth.

Declan was silent, taking in the fine line that he was walking with the Translator. He decided to change the topic and try to buy a little more time in hopes that the cavalry would arrive. And maybe they would not fall victim to whatever trap was set. "How did you stay ahead of us this whole time? If you are going to kill me, it can't hurt to tell."

Sirens could be heard in the distance, but the Translator seemed unfazed. He cocked his head and mockingly put his hand to his ear as if trying to hear. "I told you that I have something in place for them. It's an interesting device. Triggered only at a specific decibel. One-hundred twenty decibels to be exact. That of a fire engine." As if on cue, a loud explosion rocked the house.

"I am on borrowed time now, so I will make this brief. In response to your question and not that it matters, but I had some insider help." Khaled smirked and cocked his head toward the body of Mason Richards.

"Richards?" Declan was the last man standing of his elite former unit Alpha One and was now learning that his commander was working with a terrorist. The news was devastating. Nick was right, but it was too late.

"We were close, and he knew that the death of my Sonia had sent me off the deep end. He wanted to console me because he felt responsible."

"He felt bad for you, so he helped you kill innocent Americans? I am not buying it." Declan's skepticism was evident in his tenor.

"Money. It all comes down to money. Your former commander had earned quite a bit in special operations technologies and his company had grown exponentially during the early stages of the war. But your country has a short memory. Contracts died off and Richards quickly found himself struggling to stay afloat. He had become desperate. And desperate men make bad decisions. You of all people can attest to that."

"I don't see it. He's no terrorist," Declan announced, but it fell flat and seemed more a statement made to convince himself.

"No. He believed that he was a true patriot. He allowed me to operate in your country to boost the war effort. *Fresh blood will remind the people of what's at stake.* His words, not mine."

"He let you come after us? After our children?" Declan felt the rage of this betrayal pour out of him.

"No. He never agreed to that. That took some additional persuasion. And once in, I had to ensure that he would not back out. I sent him proof of life in exchange for each device that Richards, the Technician, created."

"Proof of life?" Declan questioned, trying to follow the Translator.

"His oldest daughter, Mandy," the Translator said, sighing softly before he continued, "The proof came in different forms. Sometimes a call or video. Other times it was in body parts. But each time, Richards came through with my demands."

"Where is she now?" Declan questioned intensely.

"Dead," Khaled said with no remorse. He then continued, "I had planned on sharing that news with Richards, but it did not work out that way."

"Well, I guess we are done here," Declan faced his death with an eerie calm.

Khaled raised the gun and pointed it at the Golden Man's head. Declan slowly inhaled, controlling his heart rate. In a moment, it would all be over. He closed his eyes, allowing darkness to take its hold.

The sound of the gunshot was devastating. The heat of the warm blood that splashed over Declan's face was shocking. It took him a moment to realize that it was not his blood. His eyes opened in a squint as they fought to keep the blood out.

Slumped in the chair in front of him was the Translator. His face no longer recognizable. Declan did his best to scan the room for the shooter. He saw the movement. Richards still sprawled on the floor was now gripping a revolver.

"Moose, you're alive?" Declan said in shock.

"Not for long. I'm sorry." With those simple words, Mason "Moose" Richards turned the gun on himself and pulled the trigger.

Declan stared at the scene before him. His mind reeled. Trying to process everything was a daunting task. One without a definitive end. This moment of deep reflection was interrupted by the loud crash of the front door and the sound of a tactical team clearing the house.

49

"You look like shit." Declan said this to Nick who was in a hospital bed recovering from his second surgery to repair the damage to his right arm.

"Thanks. You look like a bucket of roses yourself," Nick retorted softly, barely audible over the hiss of his nasal cannula.

Declan had a concussion and several broken ribs but had staved off any serious injuries from the blast. The doctor told him that he only needed to stay overnight for observation.

"I just checked on Izzy. She seems good. The break to her ankle was bad and tore a lot of ligaments," Declan said, relaying the update. "She's one tough lady. I don't know how she mustered the strength to get over to you. I hope you know that she is the reason that you are sitting here today."

"I know." Nick felt a strange need to say more but couldn't find the words or the strength to expand on that.

The room returned to the hum of the lifesaving machines that filled the space around Nick. The two men who had shared so much over the last two weeks now found little to talk about with the threat gone. Nick grabbed his small wax cup and chewed some of the ice chips that the nurse had left. He still couldn't eat solid food yet and was being nourished by IV, but the ice chips helped.

"Any news on your arm?" Declan hesitated, fearing that the answer might not be good.

"The doc said that the last surgery enabled me to keep it. Although, the recovery process won't be easy." Nick looked over to his right side where the pressurized brace wrapped his arm. It was suspended by cables, elevating it slightly during the recovery. His fingertips were the only part of this appendage that was visible. A clip was attached to his pointer finger monitoring his pulse.

"I was afraid to ask, but that is great news. You've got a long road ahead of you, but I have seen how tough you are and know that you will overcome that hurdle." Declan put his hand on Nick's uninjured shoulder and looked at him with complete sincerity as he spoke. "I'm proud to know you, Nick."

"Thank you for that. The feeling is mutual. I'm so sorry for the losses you suffered." The plurality of the statement referred to both Alex and Mason. Even though Declan had learned of Richards's involvement, the loss of his former commander had taken its toll.

Declan gave a slow nod, understanding Nick's message. "As much as it pains me that Mason is dead, I think the bigger loss was in his betrayal. You were right, and I couldn't see it. Sorry for being so blinded by my loyalty."

"There's nothing to be sorry about. As soon as I met the man, my suspicions dropped too." Nick paused recalling something. "Do you remember when he brought us to his basement and his miniature computer lab?" Nick asked rhetorically and continued, "I had a déjà vu moment when I saw the large table but couldn't place it. Nelson told me that it was Richards who sent the recordings and that the videos were made in the basement. The other members seen in The Seven's video releases had been mannequins. And since their faces were covered nobody noticed."

"It's still surreal to think that my former commander, a true patriot, would wage attacks against innocent civilians just to further his business." Declan said this slowly, shaking his head in disbelief.

"I think The Seven is real and that Mason somehow became their patsy. But it sounds like the links to any other members of their network died with Richards and the Translator. I guess that it's someone else's problem now," Nick said, wincing in pain as he made a slight adjustment in the bed.

The news had been running wild with the story since it was released to the media. The Office of the President released a statement to the American people vowing transparency in the investigation. The name and picture of Khaled Abdullah, the Translator, had been released. The viewing audiences had been reassured that he was now dead and the direct threat from the group known as The Seven had been thwarted. No specific details had been released about the circumstances surrounding Khaled's death. The information regarding Mason Richards's involvement had been redacted in the interest of national security.

Endless waves of press conferences were held to quell any fear of additional attacks. The President requested that people return to their daily lives and lifted the nationwide lockdown. The aftershocks were still being felt across the country, and conspiracy theorists were popping up everywhere to inject their distrust of the government. Declan listened with half an ear to the broadcast in the background. He knew that it would take a very long time for the country to return to its norm.

"So, you two went back to hero status in your boss's eyes?" Declan referred to Nelson's sudden change of heart regarding their involvement in the case.

"Looks that way. The Bureau spun the administrative leave, stating that it was a ploy used to lull the terrorist into a false sense of security." Nick was in awe of the political games played by people who had long ago forgotten what it was like on the ground floor. "So much for transparency." Both men laughed out loud until their pain caused them to settle.

Declan was being discharged from the hospital in a few hours. The FBI had their private jet on standby, ready to get him back to his family. Val and the girls were now safely back in Connecticut. Whitney Rodgers remained with his family until Declan could return.

"Thank you for letting me be a part of this. I owe you. More importantly, my family owes you. If there's ever anything that I can do for you or Izzy, never hesitate to ask." Declan stood slowly under the discomfort in his ribcage.

"There is one thing," Nick said quietly as his eyes flickered, fighting the exhaustion rapidly setting in.

Declan leaned on the railing of Nick's bed for momentary support. "Anything. Name it."

"The bank," Nick said in a whisper.

Declan said nothing, but he worried that his face had subconsciously betrayed him. He was caught off guard by Nick's statement. He controlled his breathing and looked directly into the eyes of his new friend, wondering where this conversation was going.

"Nelson asked for an update when we talked. He was going to assign it to another agent since I am incapacitated, but I explained the dead ends on all the potential leads. He agreed to keep me on it, suspending the case. It will not be reopened. After a reasonable amount of time, I will close it permanently. I guess I have more pull than I did before. I put my newly deemed hero status to work." Nick shifted slightly toward Declan causing the metallic frame to creak. "Take care of your family my friend."

Those last words hung in the air, like the humidity of an afternoon summer rain, and Declan realized their deeper meaning. He nodded, showing both understanding and respect for what this agent, this friend, had done for him. Declan turned and walked into the pale light of the hospital corridor. Nick allowed sleep to take him.

Declan stepped out of the jet and walked down the steep staircase to the tarmac. He moved gingerly, favoring his injured ribs that had not responded well to the bounce of his recent landing. Declan's eyes scanned the expanse of the runway until he saw what he was looking for.

Val stood by a large SUV that had been donated by the FBI to replace the one damaged by the fire. They had been more than generous in compensating Declan for his service, paying him enough to cover two years of his former salary in contractor fees. That, coupled with his "earnings" from the bank job, would enable his family some long-overdue stability.

His girls ran to him as if they had not seen him in years. Their long hair bounced on their dainty shoulders as they closed the distance rapidly. Laney did not run. She stood behind Val awkwardly and walked in her shadow, as his wife made her way to him.

The little arms around his neck and the barrage of kisses that followed immediately lifted him away from the terribleness of the past few weeks. Laney peeked out from behind Val as the two received each other in a warm embrace. And then the most amazing sound filled Declan's ears.

"D-a-d-d-y." Laney's voice percolated in the air and a tear fell from Declan's face. For the first time in a long time, that tear was filled with joy.

50

"If I hear the word 'hero' one more time from the mouth of some political fat cat, using us as an image booster, I think I'm going to lose my mind," Nick said to Izzy through his teeth. They stood in the podium's backdrop where Director Jenkins was in the process of delivering her pride-filled speech, carrying with it all the accolades that they had heard several times before in the weeks since their showdown in Virginia. Nick's arm was still in a brace, but the surgery had held, and the artery was now in the healing phase. Izzy was on crutches, refusing to be wheelchair bound. Her lower leg was in a cast after having been reset with the help of some pins and screws. Nick looked at her, admiring her beauty and resilience.

Declan gave a subtle nudge on his opposite side, leaned in, and whispered, "You're staring at her again. You might as well just kiss her right here for the world to see."

Nick looked at his friend and gave a sheepish smile as he felt the warmth permeate his cheeks. The two started to giggle like little school children after pulling off a prank. The more they tried to contain themselves, the more difficult it became. The pressure was amplified by the stage and audience that was spread out across the south lawn of the White House. Izzy flashed her eyes back toward her two male counterparts with the corrective glare of a mother to her children. The giddiness subsided.

She smiled and whispered in the mock tone of a parent, "Now boys, don't make me scold you in front of all these nice people." Izzy redirected her attention as the Director concluded her portion of the speech and introduced the President of the United States.

President Carson Travis took the podium, and although the three had previously sat with him in private, to see him standing there now was impressive. The confidence and poise that he demonstrated gave his modest frame a commanding presence. It was his gift in the political arena and had endeared him to the American people, even when they disagreed with his policies.

This ceremony today was the first time that the White House had acknowledged the efforts and sacrifices made by Nick and his friends. The President began by describing the terrible acts committed against innocent civilians and the tireless efforts of so many. The three had signed non-disclosure agreements that redacted many of the details. Several of the facts were altered in the interest of the people. It had been a long-standing practice that the government held back pertinent information, fearing that the average American could not handle the truth. The FBI did not want the black eye for administratively suspending its agents ultimately responsible for stopping the threat. That piece had already been spun to look as though it was done as an intentional ploy to draw out Khaled. Mason's involvement had been completely erased. It was believed that if his role had been exposed that the information would do irreversible damage to the military. More importantly, it had the potential to expose the missions of Alpha One. All involved had signed the agreement, understanding the heavy consequences if violated.

The President had made his opening remarks. He now had begun a vague description of the brave actions taken by Nick, Izzy, and Declan, who stood directly behind him. Declan heard the words but felt slightly adrift, still reeling from the betrayal of his friend.

The FBI Director, impressed by Enright's valor, had offered him the opportunity to take on a full-time role as a consultant within the Bureau's counter-terrorism unit. He initially resisted the idea, primarily due to the challenge of relocating Laney. But Director Jenkins assured him that his base of operations would be in Connecticut. Although there would be some travel associated with the assignment, Declan and Val agreed that it would be a great opportunity. The fog of his family's financial stress had finally lifted, and he felt a sense of peace.

President Travis paused momentarily and stepped off to the side of the podium, turning toward the three award recipients and then continued, "It is with great honor and unmeasurable thanks that I present these three, stalwart keepers of the peace, with awards of the highest caliber. I bestow upon FBI Special Agents, Nicholas Lawrence and Isabella Martinez, the Public Safety Officer Medal of Valor. This award is the highest honor that can be given to a law enforcement agent, and is a reminder of your bravery and sacrifice shown when faced with the extreme danger of a relentless enemy."

Cheers, like a massive wave crashing upon the shore, rose up from the grounds of the south lawn. The President again paused for effect and when the roar subsided he continued, "Declan Enright, The Presidential Medal of Freedom recognizes the selfless actions that you took in pushing back against the wolf as he beckoned at our doorstep."

Again, the crowd erupted, but out of the thousands of onlookers, Declan only focused on the four faces that mattered to him. A gentle smile crossed his face as he saw Val and his girls standing in the front row.

After shaking the President's hand, he turned and stooped slightly forward, allowing the ornate medal to be fastened around his neck. The President placed a firm hand on Declan's shoulder, sending a shockwave of pain to his ribs that were still on the mend. Declan then stood erect, showing no outward sign of the throbbing in his ribcage. The white star of the medal centered on his upper chest. The background filled with applause. He gave a wink to his family as Val returned this gesture, blowing him a kiss.

Declan stood there looking out at his family and thought how close he had come to losing everything. The Translator had that happen to him, destroying the fabric of who he had been. Declan pondered if the roles were reversed. What would he do if he'd experienced the tragic loss of any of his daughters? He had no answer for that question.

The three award recipients stood shoulder to shoulder and faced the crowd. They were now forever connected by their shared combat experience. A bond that could never be broken. His former team was completely decimated, but as he looked to his left at his new friends, the pain of this realization was eased slightly.

"I can't believe that you're leaving." Izzy didn't try to hide the heavy sadness in her voice.

"You know that the only reason I came here was to support my mother after my dad passed, but my role has changed. She now requires the full-time care of a live-in facility. The arrangements for her have been made. She will be in an excellent nursing home out there. It specializes in those suffering from dementia. I feel that I will still be honoring my father's dying request and that will give me some peace of mind." Nick had said this flatly, trying not to expose his feelings. Before Izzy could argue, Nick quickly added, "I also left some unfinished business out in Texas. It's complicated. Something I've never talked to you about. I will someday. When the debt is settled."

Nick and Izzy had somehow avoided talking about what happened that night in the hotel room. Recovering from their injuries and suffering through long, tedious hours of debriefings had occupied most of their time. Then, they had to prepare for the award ceremony with the President, something not taken lightly. Now that it was all over, and the dust had settled, the two were forced to address the elephant in the room.

"You have unfinished business out West, but what about here?" Izzy was obviously questioning his feelings about her.

"You could come with me. The Director has given us our pick of assignments. You'd be a huge asset out there."

"My family ties are here. You know that. I can't just up and leave them." It was clear in both voice and body language that Izzy was becoming frustrated.

"You could create some new family ties," Nick muttered.

Izzy stared at the man standing before her. The person that she had come to respect above all others. She heard his words and was completely caught off guard by them. "I can't take that leap yet." She saw the pain in

Nick's eyes and immediately continued, "Why don't we give it a little time and see what happens after you get settled in Austin."

"Sure. Sounds like a plan." Nick tried to sound optimistic and upbeat.

The two embraced awkwardly, taking care to avoid each other's injuries. Izzy's soft hair fell across his shoulder, carrying with it the familiar scent of coconut. With a gentle hand under her chin, Nick slowly turned Izzy's head up to take one last look into those beautiful dark eyes. Unable to resist, he pulled her closer and passionately pressed his lips against hers. The kiss felt so natural and comfortable. Nick worried he would lose the courage to leave and pulled away faster than he wanted to. Although this last moment together wasn't long, Nick knew that he would never forget it. He hoped Izzy felt the same way.

Neither said a word as they separated.

PURSUIT OF JUSTICE

For a young victim of human trafficking, FBI Agent Nick Lawrence is the only hope.

"A gripping and action-filled storyline make this sequel a standout page-turner."
—Booklife Prize Critic's Report

Nick Lawrence rejoins his old unit, the FBI's Violent Crimes Against Children task force.

The career move puts him in Austin, Texas—and onto the case of a young girl on the run.

She's been thrust into a foreign land against her will. Armed only with a set of skills bestowed by her father, she embarks on a perilous journey to keep a promise—as she is hunted by a ruthless human trafficking ring.

Nick teams up with local law enforcement, intent on saving the girl and dismantling the criminal organization trying to reach her first. But as a greater conspiracy unfolds, Nick finds himself in a deadly game of cat and mouse.

The opposition is more powerful than he could have imagined—and they're intent on silencing him, and the girl, forever.

Get your copy today at
severnriverbooks.com/series/nick-lawrence

)

ACKNOWLEDGMENTS

Michaela, this book would not have been published without you pushing me to write it. Thank you for making me realize that this was a story worth telling. You have an incredible strength of character that is beyond your years.

Greg, thank you for pushing me forward when I hit those moments of doubt. You were amazingly supportive and crucial to this book's creation, whether you know it or not.

Steve G., thank you for being an amazing sounding board for my ideas. Your passion to pursue writing inspired me to make the leap. Rangers lead the way!

Steve P., thank you for letting me vent at those critical moments. Beyond that, thank you for your support and friendship in this and everything else.

Dave, thank you for letting me bounce pieces of the story off you, even if those sessions took place in the captivity of a government vehicle.

Kevin, thanks for reconnecting with me after all these years. I am glad that you were able to be a litmus test for the realism of the military aspect of the characters.

Eric, thank you for being able to advise me on the qualities of Laney's character, as well as the portrayal of the relationship with her father. You're an amazing friend and dad.

Denis, thank you for providing me with the critical feedback that assisted in humanizing Declan's coping mechanism.

Bruce, thank you for taking the time out of your relentless writing schedule to provide me mentorship. Your willingness to assist an unknown author speaks volumes of your character. I will pay that lesson forward.

To my crew: Joe, Tina, Frank, Mike, Dave, and Dave: Thank you for putting up with me over this journey, especially the last few months. I appreciate all of your support and friendship. Take a well-deserved break... because book two is out in July!

To my family, thank you for always being there for me throughout. I don't think that this book would have been a reality without your support. I love you all.

Brielle, I kept your note of encouragement in my notebook during this whole writing process. Maybe we can work on getting that dog now?

Emmalene, I love that you started working on your own books. I can't wait to write more with you.

Korinna, I know that I drove you crazy during this process. I am glad that I was able to pull you away from our girls long enough to get your input. Thank you for all that you do, keeping our crazy train running. I love you.

ABOUT THE AUTHOR

Brian Shea has spent most of his adult life in service to his country and local community. He honorably served as an officer in the U.S. Navy. In his civilian life, he reached the rank of Detective and accrued over eleven years of law enforcement experience between Texas and Connecticut. Somewhere in the mix he spent five years as a fifth-grade school teacher. Brian's myriad of life experience is woven into the tapestry of each character's design. He resides in New England and is blessed with an amazing wife and three beautiful daughters.

**Sign up for the reader list at
severnriverbooks.com/authors/brian-shea**

Printed in the United States
by Baker & Taylor Publisher Services